ID0952219

THUNDERBIRD

ALSO BY CHUCK WENDIG

CHUCK WENDIG

THUNDERBIRD

MIRIAM BLACK: FOUR

SAGA PRESS

LONDON SYDNEY **NEW YORK** TORONTO NEW DELHI

SAGA PRESS
AN IMPRINT OF SIMON & SCHUSTER, INC.

1230 AVENUE OF THE AMERICAS, NEW YORK, NEW YORK 10020

+ Text copyright © 2017 by Chuck Wendig + Jacket illustration copyright © 2017 by Adam S. Doyle + All rights reserved, including the right to reproduce this book or portions thereof in any form whatsoever. For information address Saga Press Subsidiary Rights Department, 1230 Avenue of the Americas, New York, NY 10020 + SAGA PRESS and colophon are trademarks of Simon & Schuster, Inc. + For information about special discounts for bulk purchases, please contact Simon & Schuster Special Sales at 1-866-506-1949 or business@simonandschuster.com. + The Simon & Schuster Speakers Bureau can bring authors to your live event. For more information or to book an event, contact the Simon & Schuster Speakers Bureau at 1-866-248-3049 or visit our website at www.simonspeakers.com. + The text for this book was set in New Caledonia LT. + Manufactured in the United States of America + First Edition + 10 9 8 7 6 5 4 3 2 1 + CIP data for this book is available from the Library of Congress. + ISBN 978-1-4814-4871-0 + ISBN 978-1-4814-4873-4 (eBook)

TO ALL THOSE WHO LOVED
MIRIAM ENOUGH TO HELP
RAISE HER FROM THE DEAD

THUNDERBIRD

PART ONE

NONA DECIMA MORTA

ONE

THE QUITTER

Miriam runs.

Her feet pound asphalt. Ahead, Old Highway 60 cuts a knife line through red rock and broken earth, the highway shot through with hairline fractures. Big clouds scattered across the sky like the stuffing from a gutted teddy bear. The side of the highway is lined with gnarly green scrub brush, plants like hands reaching for the road, hands looking to rend and tear. Beyond, it's just the wide-open nowhere of Arizona: electric fences that don't contain anything, craggy rocks and distant peaks like so many broken teeth.

Run, she thinks. Sweat is coming off her hair, into her eyes. *Fucking hair dye. Fucking spray gel hair bullshit. Fucking suntan lotion.* She blinks back sweat carrying all those chemicals, sweat that burns her eyes. *Don't pay attention to that. Just run.* Eyes forward. Clarity of thought and vision. Or something.

Then her foot catches something—a rock, a lip of cratered asphalt, she doesn't know, and it doesn't matter, because suddenly she pitches forward. Hands out. Palms catching the macadam, bracing herself so her head doesn't snap forward and crack in half like a tossed brick. A hard pain jars up her arms, through her elbows like a flicker of lightning. Her hands sting and throb.

She gets up on her knees and then starts coughing.

The coughing jag isn't brief. She plants her hands on her knees and hacks hard, and between hacks she wheezes, and between wheezes she just hacks harder. It's a dry cough of broken sticks and dead leaves until it's not—then it's wet, rheumy, and angry, like her lungs have gone liquid and have decided to disperse themselves up and out of her mouth.

That mouth that wants a cigarette right now. Lips that would plant around the filter and suck smoke deep. Her whole *body* wants a cigarette, and the nic fit tears over her and through her like a plague of starving locusts. She shudders and bleats and laughs and cries and, once again, coughs.

Her palms pulse with her hummingbird heartbeat. The skin abraded.

Footsteps behind her.

Heavy. Boots hitting hard.

Sweat pours off her now—spattering on the road.

"It's hot," she gasps. "It's fucking hot. It's *Hell*-hot. It's wearing-the-Devil's-humid-scrotum-as-a-hat hot."

"They say it's a dry heat."

Louis clomps up alongside her like a Clydesdale.

She looks up at him. The sun hangs behind him, so he's just a shape, a shadow, a black monolith speaking to her. *Oh, Louis,* she thinks, and then he turns just so and her eyes adjust. And she can see the black electrical tape crisscrossing his eyes. She can see his pale face, his wormy lips, a tongue that traipses over broken teeth. And when he moves, she hears the rustle of feathers, the clacking of beaks.

Not-Louis. The Trespasser. Her companion that only she can see—a hallucination, a ghost, a fellow traveler to wherever it is she's going.

"You know what else is a dry heat?" she asks. "Fire."

"It's only April."

"It's, like, almost ninety degrees. I should've come in December."

The Trespasser stands over her. Like an executioner ready to drop the head-chopper axe down on the kneeling sinner.

"Why are we out here, Miriam?"

She rocks back on her knees, cranes her head back, eyes closed. She paws at the water bottle hanging at her hip. With her teeth she uncaps it (and even there she thinks: *my teeth want a cigarette too, want to bite into the nicotine like it's a cancerous Slim Jim god I want it so bad I'd kick a baby seal just to get one taste*), then drinks deeply, drinks sloppily. Water over her lips, down her chin.

Up in the sky, vultures spin on an invisible axis.

"*We* are not out here," she says, wiping her wet mouth with the back of her hand. "I am out here alone. You are—well, we still don't know what you are, do we? Let's go with *demon*. Invisible, asshole demon. You're not here. You're *here*." She taps her temple, then drinks more water.

"If I'm up there, then I'm with you, and we are still *we*," he says. A loose, muddy chuckle in the well of his chest. "Why are you jogging, Miriam?"

"It's not jogging. It's jogging when rich, limp-noodle assholes do it. When I do it, it's called *running*, motherfucker." She sniffs. Coughs again. "I do it because I need to get better. Get stronger. Faster. All that."

"What are you running from?"

You, she thinks. But instead she says, "It's funny; anyone who sees me running asks me that. *Hur hur, is something chasing you?* Yeah. Death. Death is chasing me, and chasing everyone else, too. That's what I'm running from. My own clock spinning down. The sweep of the Reaper's scythe."

"Not like you to run from death."

"Things have changed."

Another damp, diseased chuckle. "Oh, we know. You're trying to get away from us. From you. From the gift you have been given."

"It's no gift," she says, finally starting to stand. The sun is punishing. It feels like a fist trying to punch her back down to the ground. "But you know that. And you don't care." She thinks, but does not say: *As soon as I find the woman I'm looking for, you're outta here, pal. No more trespassing for you.* Miriam has a name: Mary Stitch. AKA, Mary Scissors. A woman who can, if the story is true, help Miriam get shut of this so-called "gift." She wants it gone. She *needs* it gone before it swallows her whole.

"You're not done yet," the Trespasser says. As she stands, she sees Not-Louis's eyes have become black, glossy circles—crow eyes, rimmed with puckered gray skin and the start of oily feathers that thread underneath the skin like stitches. "Not by a country mile, little girl."

She sucks in a bit of sweat from above her lip and spits back at him. The Trespasser doesn't even flinch. Instead, he just points.

Miriam follows the crooked finger.

There, way down the highway, she sees the glint of light off a vehicle. *Her* vehicle—it's where she parked it. A rust-red, rat-trap pickup truck. A *literal* rat trap, actually—when she bought it, rats had made a nest in the engine, chewed up the belts and wires pretty good.

But then:

Another car.

This one, coming from the opposite direction. Hard to make out what it is—the sun catches on it like in a pool of liquid magma. Despite that, Miriam can see the back of the car fart out a noxious black cloud. She can hear the bang of the engine, and she can see something roll across the road—a hubcap?—that hits the tire of her Ford truck and drops. The car stops across from her truck.

Then all is still.

"What is that?" she asks. "Who is that?"

She turns to the Trespasser but he's gone.

And yet his voice reaches her:

"Go and see."

Shit.

TWO

NOT DONE YET

Miriam runs. Again. Because, apparently, she is a glutton for punishment. She tells herself that the quarter-mile or so between her and the two vehicles is *psssh, pffft*, no problem at all, but three steps in and her feet feel like they're encased in cement and her calves feel like sausages about to split and spill their meat. Still, she runs. She tells herself it's because she has to.

Ahead, the truck and the car roam into clearer view. Past the flinty, flashing sun. There, on her side of the road, the pickup: Ford F-250 from 1980. Rust has taken over most of the cherry red paint. Across the highway: a Subaru station wagon. An Outback. Also old—maybe ten years, maybe more.

She hears the engine *tink*ing and clicking. A smell hits her—bitter, acrid, sweet. A charred fan belt, cooked antifreeze.

A hundred yards away now. The driver-side door to the Subaru pops open. A black woman steps out. She's rough and ready—a stone whetted to a sharpened edge like a caveman's axe. A survivor. Like Miriam.

As Miriam slows to a jog and then to a walk, the woman points.

"Stay back!"

The woman's hand moves behind her, to the waistband of her jeans—she turns just so, and Miriam sees something back there. A gun. Tucked. The driver doesn't pull it. Not yet.

Miriam holds up her hands, slows her walk. "Hey. Yo. Relax. That's my truck right there. No harm, no foul. Just gonna scooch on past, get in the truck, and go." Fifty yards now separate them. Maybe less.

The woman's eyes flash from Miriam to the truck and back again.

Inside the Subaru station wagon: movement.

And that's when Miriam gets it. Because she sees a small face, round and wide-eyed, peer over the dashboard. A boy. Young, maybe ten years old. Blue T-shirt with some red on it—the Superman logo, she realizes. Just the top of it. She's a mother protecting her kid. Right?

Miriam thinks to ask if everything's okay but her gut clenches: *Just let it go. Don't get involved.* This is a trap. The Trespasser put her here—she doesn't even know if it works like that but she doesn't care. She just wants out, away, *hasty la visty*, crazy lady. And maybe the crazy lady wants away from her, too—Miriam must look like hell. Sweaty pits, chapped lips, pink-and-black hair matted to her forehead. But then her dumb mouth starts forming words and those words escape like canaries from open cages and she says, "Do you need help?"

"You got a cell phone?"

"I . . . do. You want me to call somebody?"

The woman leans forward like she's about to pounce. "I want you to give it here. I want that phone."

Miriam arches an eyebrow. "Yeah, no."

"I want the phone and the keys to the truck."

"I will make a call for you and I will drive you somewhere."

"Oh, I know where you'll drive me. You ain't taking my boy back." And then the gun comes out—a little thumb-dicked .38 revolver. Snubby, priggish nose pointed right at Miriam. The woman clicks back the hammer. "Keys. Phone. Throw them over."

"If I throw the phone, I'll break it."

That seems to stun the woman, like she's too panicked to think clearly and this tiny little hangnail has snagged the whole damn sweater, threatening to pull it all apart

"Fine," the woman barks, irritated. *"Fine.* Just . . . just come over, and you can hand them to me. No nonsense. Don't mess with me or I'll put this in you." She thrusts the gun forward, as if to demonstrate. The woman doesn't look like a killer, but she *does* look desperate—pushed to the edge. Miriam knows that people at the edge will do anything. Any dog trapped in any corner will bite.

Miriam creeps forward. Her body throbs. Even in the heat, she represses a chill. No idea what's happening here. What's driven this woman to this? She tries not to care. But the carapace she's carefully crafted is cracked—makes Miriam weak. Her hand ducks into her pocket, pulls out the little burner phone and the pickup's key ring. She jingles them like she's trying to distract a cat.

Thirty yards.

Twenty.

"C'mon, c'mon," the woman says, impatient.

Miriam knows she's not going to give over the keys or the phone.

That's all she knows, though. What happens next, she's not sure.

Ten yards now, and Miriam slows her walk, tries to buy herself some time. "You don't have to do this. We can be pals." *You take my truck and my phone and I might have to feed you to the coyotes, lady.* "I don't know who you think I am or why I'd want to take your son—"

The woman waves the gun. "You people need to leave us *alone."*

Five yards. She starts to hand over the keys and the phone—

Two minutes ago, Miriam's whole body ached, but now, every cell is awake and alive and without any pain at all, juicing on the natural narcotic of hard-charging adrenaline. With her free hand the woman reaches across—

Miriam flings the keys. Not enough to hurt—or, at least, to do damage—but enough where a jingly-jangly projectile launched at the woman's face will offer up the interference Miriam needs. Her gut check is right: this lady isn't combat-ready. While desperate, she's not trained to deal with distraction. The gun goes wide, the woman makes a sound—"Nuhhh!"—and Miriam grabs the gun wrist and slams it back—

THREE

SNIPE HUNT

There the two of them stand. Wrestling back and forth with the revolver. The key ring hits the ground with a cymbal crash. The strange lady's cell phone takes a tumble too—spinning corner to corner until it hits the asphalt, cracking the outer case. Gracie throws a punch, tries to piston it into the woman's side, but the crazy white bitch bends her body—the fist misses, and the woman catches it, twists it, pins Gracie's hand like she pins the other one. But Gracie isn't done. She won't be taken again. She won't let her son be taken again. Everyone is an enemy and she has to get free so she drives a hard knee up into the lady's middle. Her finger does this involuntary squeeze and—the gun in her hand bucks, firing up at the sky, up at the gods, *bang*—gunsmoke plume and brimstone stink. Inside the car, Isaiah is screaming, pounding on the dashboard, face a mess of tears—

And then there's another gunshot—

The strange lady staggers to the side, blood suddenly soaking through her white V-neck T-shirt, competing with the sweat under each armpit—and then she coughs up blood and drops. Gracie screams, looks at the gun in her own hand, wondering how she did this, trying to figure out how her pointing the gun at the sky somehow fired a bullet that killed the woman wrestling with her—

And then another gunshot rolls across the sky like thunder and Gracie's head snaps to the side and all the thoughts she had and all the fears and all the love goes ejecting out her temple along with her blood and her brains and all the things that made her who she was.

FOUR

TAG, YOU'RE IT

It all starts to play out just like the vision. So much so and in such proximity, time-wise, that it feels impossible to Miriam—less like one of her visions and more like a funky case of *déjà vu*, except this particularly funky case ends in her death and the death of the woman in front of her.

That happens in about thirty seconds.

Panic throttles her. Everything seems to slow. The woman—a woman Miriam now knows is named Gracie, thanks to the vision of death that comes any time Miriam touches her skin to the skin of another—throws the punch and Miriam, as if just playing back a recording of what was always going to happen, ducks it, catches the wrist, and slams it against the Subaru.

Inside, the child starts to cry.

She doesn't know how to stop this.

This thing of hers—this *power*, this *unrequested burden*—has rules.

One of them is: she can only stop death by causing death.

Want to stop a murder? Then the killer must first be killed. The books have to be balanced. The ledger made square. And now an absurd and horrible thought runs through her like a rampant infection:

Maybe I kill the woman first.

Kill Gracie, interrupt the cycle, get out of the way.

She thinks this even as she tries to pull away, tries to hit the ground, but Gracie's knee does what it was predestined to do, and it drives up into Miriam's middle—*oof*—and blasts the air out of her.

Everything goes spinny, like she's a little kid on an office chair whirling wildly about. The revolver starts to drift downward and she points it upward, and Gracie's finger does that involuntary twitch and *bang*. Goes off. To the sky. To the clouds, the gods, the vultures—

The vultures.

Fear assails her. She doesn't want to do this. The last time she did it, she entered the mind of a hungry seabird called the gannet—not just one bird but many, a ravenous flock of the scissor-beaked motherfuckers—and saved her mother's life by tearing apart a man named Ashley, a man who hunted her and opposed her at every turn. She still has nightmares about it.

But now she has no choice. Even as she tries to resist it, she knows that reflex, knows that all the cells inside her body are screaming to survive, a chorus of *save us, save us, do what you must* and then her eyes close and there's this vacuum sound—*shoop*—and it's like being on a super-fast elevator rocketing to the top of a skyscraper. And next thing she knows, she's not Miriam anymore. She's not even on the ground—she's in the sky, turning on an invisible axis, soaring on vectors of heat pushed up from the Arizona desert.

FIVE

THE WIDENING GYRE

Behold the black vulture.

A big bird, the black vulture: the one in which Miriam finds herself is bigger than most, with a wingspan of five feet—like a reaper cloak cast wide—and weight coming up just shy of ten pounds. Others like it wheel about the sky, and Miriam finds her mind in those, too. Fragmented like a punched mirror—pieces of her scattered. Turning, turning.

It is believed to be a carrion bird, the black vulture. And that is true, to a point: humans are poor janitors of the world they inherited. A car strikes a deer: nobody comes along to clean its smashed skull and spackled guts off the road. Or an armadillo or a marmot. Or even just garbage tossed out a window—garbage that maybe stays where it landed, or maybe gets picked up and put in a bigger pile: a garbage dump miles away. Vultures are glad to be the janitors that humans will not be. Eating what is left. Gorging. They will even do this for human remains: the Old World vultures eat the corpses left in the sky burials of Tibet, or on the Towers of Silence in Zoroastrian practice, thus releasing the soul from the body. (The vultures care little about souls and care very much about eating.)

In fact, the black vulture's head is featherless for just such eating. Its wrinkled, scrotum-like scalp can plunge all the more easily into a carcass with nothing to halt its entry or its exit—the bird sticks its entire head inside the animal, beak and eyes and everything, feasting on all the best bits hidden from view.

But it is a mistake to think of the black vulture as only a carrion bird.

The vulture is a bird of prey.

Cattlemen know it. They know that when a calf is pushed from its mother's body, all knobby-kneed and snot-slick, a wake of vultures (for vultures are very social birds) will descend on the newborn calf.

They will kill it. They will peck out its eyes. They will rip off its nose or tear out its tongue. They will stab at it with their hooked beaks, tearing it, ripping it, until it goes into shock and they may feast with comfort.

They can do this with many small or newborn creatures.

Vultures will eat the dead. But they also like to kill.

Unlike turkey buzzards, the black vulture relies on sight to spot prey, and were this a wooded area, they might not be able to spot the man in desert fatigues below—but they do, because they have good eyes. He moves. The sun flashes in the flat of the scope, the bolt of the rifle.

Distantly, Miriam thinks: *ten seconds.*

It's like a rope, invisible around the vulture's neck. Yanking it downward. And when this one dives, so do the rest of them. Wings back in a sharp V—long neck and featherless head craned forward, talons thrust down.

Wind whipping.

One vulture, then three, then seven.

Seven birds and nine seconds.

Tick-tock.

The man—broad-shouldered, pot-bellied, a scruff of beard on his face so patchy it might as well be half another man's beard glued to his cheeks, aviator sunglasses capturing light—he must hear the ripple of feathers.

He looks up. Mouth open in shock. The rifle clatters to the flat rock on which he lies, and he staggers backward, reaching for a pistol at his hip—

Another distant thought from Miriam, a grim reminder that once again, this thing she does has *rules* and one of the rules is that fate is elastic—it likes to snap back to its shape even when it bends and stretches, and just because the man dropped his gun that does not mean he will not again pick it up and again complete the circuit that fate has made. He can still kill Miriam. He can still kill Gracie.

Maybe even the boy.

And so, he must die.

He takes a step backward, raises the pistol—

The vulture has a peculiar defense mechanism. Miriam did not know this but now she does (she suddenly knows way more about vultures than she ever anticipated, thanks to inhabiting one): the vulture has a septic mouth, a toxic gullet, a belly full of half-digested mess that was already rotten before it entered the vulture's body and has only stewed in the decomposition inside the cistern of the bird's horror-show stomach—

And it can regurgitate those contents at will.

Translation: the black vulture uses its vomit as a weapon.

Here, *seven* vultures do just that thing. Beaks open. Throats bulging. Hot, disgorged vulture barf—a scalding, acidic, sour gut slurry—launches forth, striking the man in the face. The pistol barks a shot. The bullet goes wide.

The first vulture, the leader of the wake, hits him like a train to the chest. Talons ripping into the buttons of his fatigues. He topples backward. His head strikes a rock. Skull breaking. A hooked beak plunges into the soft meat of his nose. More birds land upon him. Talons tearing fabric. Beaks poking in through the rent clothing, seeking skin.

His body begins to shake as it is disassembled. His foot kicks out, knocks his rifle off the rock. The pistol in his hand slides away with a clatter. Trauma rocks through his body. Death descending upon him in a rippling flurry of rot-stink wings.

SIX

BACK IN BLACK

Eyes shut. Her jaw works. Her tongue flattens against the roof of her mouth and she can taste the septic puke taste, and she can taste the hot coppery jets of blood and the fatty strips of human meat and then her eyes are popping open like the doors of a cuckoo clock before she rolls over onto her hands and knees.

She, of course, pukes.

What comes out of her is mostly just water. And the remnants of a granola bar. But she half-expects to see a human finger or a pair of aviator sunglasses clatter against the road.

Miriam feels for the water bottle. Not much left, but it's something. She takes a gulp, swirls it around. Cheek bulge, swish swish spit.

Looking up, she sees the Subaru sitting there. And her truck: gone. No—not gone, but certainly going. There it is, way in the distance now. Half-mile off and heading the other direction. The engine rattling as it always does.

Or did, because she doesn't have it anymore.

"Goddamn fucking fuck," she hisses. She takes the last mouthful of water, and this, she drinks. Stands and groans. Of course the woman took the keys (and her phone, by the looks of it, broken as it is) and stole her truck. *At least the loon didn't shoot me in the face before she stole my pickup.*

Of course, the sun might do her in before long anyway.

She heads over to the Subaru. Door's unlocked. She finds a mostly empty bottled water in the cup holder. It's warm and meager, but it's something.

Inside of the car isn't much to look at. Dirty, dusty, the dashboard cracked. She feels around for the keys. Nothing.

Think, Miriam. Think.

She should be worrying about survival—about where to go next—but all she can think about is the taste in her mouth. And the man out there in the desert, a *sniper*, who tried to kill . . .

Well, who the hell was he trying to kill?

The woman, right? Not Miriam. But here a little splinter of doubt works its way under her mental fingernail: *What if he was trying to kill me, not her?*

Who wanted the woman? And her son?

What the fuck is going on here?

She snaps her fingers. Okay. Two choices here—one, walk. She knows there's a rinky-dink gas station, what, about two miles thataway. But, she also knows that out there in the wide-open rocky nowhere, a man lies dead. A man who was going to kill her with a rifle. That man might have a phone.

That's the plan, then.

Miriam heads into the desert.

THE LIVING GRAVEYARD

Her mother looks soft and weak. Like she's melting away, her definitions slowly lost. *Persistent vegetative state*, they're saying. Which is why Evelyn Black is here. In this place with the other living dead. Zombies lined up, two or three to a room. Here it's not humans that talk to one another, but what sounds like machine banter: beeping, hissing, clicking. Like robot caretakers talking about their day tending the barely living.

When Miriam last saw her mother, the woman was still . . . somewhat there. Mostly gone, but she'd make these appearances, like her mind was rocketing toward the surface, a dolphin breaking free of the sea's constraints, and once in the open air she'd laugh and gabble and babble and then: *sploosh*, back down to the deep dark nowhere. Conscious, but only just that.

Now that's gone. Evelyn has retreated entirely. Must've gotten tired breaching the surface of her own awareness so many times. Somewhere, while Miriam was gone, the woman sank. *Glub, glub, glub.* A flurry of bubbles.

The river is rising.

That. An old thought. A mean memory like a bully who caught her behind the playground, fists out and ready to throw a quick punch.

Miriam shudders.

"I went to Colorado," she tells Evelyn. "I found . . . well, I found a way forward. Took me a while, but . . ." She puffs out her cheeks, exhales. Suddenly frustrated, she says: "Can you even hear me? Are you even in there? Do you even give a shit that I'm here? *Can* you even give a shit?"

Beep. Hiss. Click.

Her mother like a wax doll that's only a little bit melted.

"I'm going back out on the road," Miriam says. "Arizona this time. Everything's sorted with you here, so . . ." Evelyn had money stored up. Enough to cover this. And, Miriam thinks, enough to give her a little traveling money, too. The lawyers made everything easy. It's not like her mother's in the ground, not yet. Miriam gets to play custodian of the dead, the accountant to a ghost. Nobody contested shit. The only trick is going to be what to do with Uncle Jack. For now, she has money. Some she can take with her. But as soon as she runs out, she's going to have to pay him a visit. And she's going to have to sell her mother's house right out from under him. Poor scuzzball.

Miriam sighs. Starts to stand.

Her mother's hand darts out, catches Miriam's wrist. Vise grip.

The room darkens. The window—once framed by the light of the pale late-winter sun—is swallowed by spreading shadow.

Her mother's head lurches up—the neck long, too long, bones crunching, spine crackling like a whole sheet of bubble wrap given a vicious twist.

"You weak-kneed cunt," her mother says, the woman's voice a gravelly, shattered thing. "Leaving me. Always leaving. Running away. Little quitting bitch. You can't just turn it off, Miriam dear. You are who you are. It is what it is." Her mother's hand closes tighter on Miriam's wrist—Miriam tries to pull away, but it's like her wrist is pinned under a boulder. Then Evelyn's mouth cranes open, the jaw popping like a broom handle splitting, and a scorpion the yellow of infected mucus skitters out onto the balcony of her gray tongue, and her voice rises again, louder this time and drier, like she's gargling a throatful of dust: "A storm is coming, daughter of mine, and you can't outrun it—"

"Everything all right in here?"

A nurse's voice. Big guy, ginger hair, even more gingery beard. Miriam looks down: her mother is again on the bed. Supine. Staring up at nothing. Mouth a flat line, open just so, as if experiencing a moment of tiny surprise.

"Yeah," Miriam says, her voice dry. "Fine. Everything's fine."

SEVEN

CARRION BAG

It's barely a body anymore. It sits there on the rock, just a few feet off the ground: a lobster-red sack, wet and exposed, stuffed into the tatters of gore-soaked fatigues. The vultures still gather upon the body like a clutch of deliberating judges, and Miriam thinks to shoo them, but she doesn't have to.

They don't take flight. They merely hop and flutter aside, turning around like sentinels, gathering in a ring and watching her. *Making room for me*, she thinks. Room for one of their own.

Black eyes staring. Beaks clacking. One of them still has a string of meat hanging in its mouth—it cranes its head back and *snap snap snap* eats it right up like a late-night stoner gobbling up the last crumbs in the Doritos bag.

Even in the heat she can't repress the shudder that runs through her.

She looks back over her shoulder. The Subaru sits some three hundred yards back. Her head throbs. Everything feels woozy, boozy.

At her feet: a rifle. She doesn't know shit about guns, but it's more a hunting rifle than anything military-looking. Wood stock, scope. She bends down, takes a gander and sees the words REMINGTON 700 etched in the barrel.

Not far from that, the pistol. Black, boxy, small. The rifle is too much, but the pistol? "Hey, free gun," she tells the vultures, who stand and stare as she scoops up the gun and tucks it in her back pocket. "You guys want it?"

They don't.

Now: the corpse.

The heat from the rock rises, carries his smell with it. It's not a rotten odor—this is fresh death, a hot Krispy Kreme donut stuffed with blood and voided bowels. Coppery, greasy in the nose, so thick she can almost taste it. Then the real stink hits her—the rancid rancor of vulture vomit just about kills her.

Her gorge rises. She bites it back. Breathes through her mouth.

Miriam steps over to the carcass. Then thinks better and goes and gets the rifle—the rifle that becomes her tool. She pokes and prods with the barrel. (Careful, of course, not to go blowing the body apart unnecessarily. Not that the guy could get any deader, but she doesn't feel like covering herself in his *spray*.) First she uses it to tap the side of his pants pocket—it thuds against something hard. Maybe a wallet, maybe something else.

She holds her nose, leans back while reaching forward. Turns out it's both: she pries from his wet pocket a wallet *and* a cell phone. Wallet is beat-up brown leather. Phone is a basic jobby: just a candy bar brick. Kind you might get free with a phone plan—not far from her own burner, which Crazy Gracie stole.

Miriam scoots back, then pops the wallet.

Arizona license. Steven McArdle. Got forty bucks in there and a MasterCard, both of which she pilfers. "Don't mind if I do, you murdering dickwhistle." A sudden nostalgic glow washes over her, like remembering Christmas from your childhood or calling upon some memory from college, except here it's robbing a dead body of its wares that feels like old times. Her finding folks who were going to die, then conveniently maneuvering herself to be present at their ineluctable ends to snatch the cash and cards from their wallets. The golden haze of nostalgia suddenly feels like a radioactive glow cloud. Still, money's money.

The phone, she turns on. And it's got a security PIN.

Gah! She's about to use both feet to kick the body off the flat rock—but then she sees something sticking out of his back pocket, too. Like a handkerchief. Yellow as a goldfinch. She reaches forward, thumb and forefinger like a pair of pincers working an autopsy.

It's like a handkerchief, but it's not. Rectangular. Like a small flag.

Actually, by the looks of it, it really *is* a small flag. A crudely stitched image decorates the fabric: a dead tree like a skeleton's hand, its branches decorated with simple five-point stars. And coming from above: forked lightning that has not yet struck the tree.

Below the tree, three words:

THE COMING STORM.

Not sure what the hell that means. She takes it, rolls it up, tucks it in the pocket of her own shorts (running shorts, ugh). Then she thinks: *this guy might be military. Or some kind of military fetishist.* She remembers the Mockingbird killers—the Caldecott family with their rapist patriarch, Carl Keener. The killers had their own love of tattoos: the swooping swallow. She moves to the other side of the body, sees that the vultures have already done her work for her—beaks tearing a flap of fabric away from the arm, the meat beneath it still intact.

There, the tattoo of a scorpion.

. . . and a scorpion the yellow of infected mucus skitters out onto the balcony of Evelyn Black's gray tongue, and her voice rises again, louder this time and drier, like she's gargling a throatful of dust: "A storm is coming, daughter of mine, and you can't outrun it. . . ."

Miriam pats the rest of him down. Keys? None. Which means either he walked here, or someone dropped him off. None of that makes much sense. How did he know the woman would be out here? How did Steven McArdle know that this was his spot to set up shop as a sniper? Her mind twists around it, but the logic evades her grasp. Too many things unseen. Too many parts missing.

She scrambles down off the rock. Everything feels cold now. Even in the heat of the Arizona sun, Miriam is shaking like the last leaf on an autumn tree.

The phone rings.

It vibrates as it does, humming down through her hip bone— she tries to dance away from it like it's a hornet in her pocket. Realizing what it is, she reaches in, pries it from the pocket, then looks at the caller ID:

Unavailable.

She draws a deep breath, thinks *fuck it*, then answers the call.

A man's voice on the other end. Deep. Slow. Bit of a twang to it.

"Is it done?"

She stays silent.

Again the man speaks: "Damnit, Stevie—are we good? Did we get the boy back or what?" And then it's like he figures it out, because he says, "Who is this?"

"Your mom," Miriam says.

The man ends the call.

She sniffs and frowns. "That's no way to talk to your mother, jerk."

EIGHT

GETAWAY STICKS

Miriam walks. Her specialty, it seems. It goes like this for a couple miles—one foot after the next, plodding along down the ribbon of highway headed west out of the San Carlos Apache reservation. Every step becomes a sure misery, and she can feel the sun cooking her like a hot dog in a microwave—every thud of sneaker against asphalt robs something from her.

Ahead, though, what she worries might be an oasis though she damn well knows it's not: a gas station. A beat-ass Chevron station, the sign hanging by one loose bolt, swinging in the faint wind. The pumps look like sad old men huddling together under a crooked roof to get out of the sun. Out back sits a tow truck, pitted and dented. It's the only vehicle here that she can see.

She heads inside. The floor is cracked and buckled. Red dust and loose rocks kick about. A few shelves here and there. A freezer in the back. No air conditioning running—just metal fans blowing, streamers tied to the cages.

Behind the counter, a young guy stands, skin the color of an old penny. Lean and lanky, like a Slim Jim. Long dark hair pulled back in a ponytail, nose like a broken eagle's beak, mouth a grim line.

She plods in through the door, the bell doing its *ding-a-ling* thing. He gives her a quick look, then looks back down at whatever magazine he's reading—but then, time for a double take. His head lifts again and this time he surveys her with a curious mix of worry and amusement.

"You okay?" he asks.

"Peachy," she says, and she hears her voice is so thick with sarcasm, it's practically dripping all over the floor.

"You look like a piece of meat that's been left in the oven too long."

She leans up against the counter, less to get close to it and more because she's legit afraid she might fall. "That's sweet. I bet you say that to all the girls." Her whole face throbs like a stubbed toe. She drums her fingers. "I need water. Like, I need water now. Like, give me water, or I'll kill you with my mind."

He grunts, scowls, then points. "They're in the little case to your right."

Miriam looks down, and sure enough: a hip-high refrigerator, humming. It's so far. Okay, sure, it's like . . . three feet, but right now that feels like miles. She asks, "Can you get it for me?" But he just gives her a look like she's a whackaloon fresh from the cracker factory, so she sighs, makes a long *ugh* sound, then stoops to get a bottle of water. She hangs there at the fridge for a moment, the door open, the cold air washing over her.

"I would straight up fuck a snowman right now," she says. "Just to cool down." She wrenches the cap off the water with her teeth, then spits the cap onto the floor. She guzzles water. Throat full. It almost shocks her. She *urps*, tries not to puke. Pushing past it, she keeps drinking until the bottle is empty.

"You need to close the fridge—"

"Like, it wouldn't be for love. It'd just be cheap, tawdry snowman sex—I'd basically be, like, a snow hooker." She tilts the empty bottle, lets the last drops hit her tongue. "He could stick his carrot nose wherever he wanted. I'd give him the greatest snowjob of his life." Her knee nudges the fridge shut, but not before she reaches in and fetches a second water bottle. "Get it? Snowjob?"

"What is wrong with you?"

"What is wrong with *you*?" she asks. She realizes it's not the best comeback, but at this point? It's all she's got.

He just shakes his head, goes to ring her up. "That it?"

"Yeah."

But then she sees.

"Wait," she says.

Behind him, racks upon racks of cigarettes.

And boy howdy, they're fucking cheap. She feels like a kid in a candy store. Or a teenager looking at his first porno mag. Which treat to choose? Her whole body sings an eager song, and every molecule inside her body joins the chorus of *want need smoke nicotine tar cancer sweet cancer oh, god, put it in me*—and suddenly she has this weird image of her *post coitus* with a snowman in a ratty motel bed, and they're both smoking, and he's melting, and she's breathing out frosty breath and puffs of cancer and the *desire* for it lives in her salivary glands. A dog drooling at the sound of a match striking.

He follows her gaze. "What do you want? Brand? Pack or carton?"

"They're so . . . cheap."

"You're on a reservation. No tax."

"Oh, man. Can I be an Indian?"

"Not how it works." He shrugs. "And I think we're called First People now. Just let me know what you want."

"I want . . ." Her mouth forms the start of many answers: Marlboro, Camel, American Spirit, so many choices it paralyzes her. And then the words that come out of her mouth are: "I'm quitting." The two words spoken slowly, sluggishly, like she's having a stroke in the middle of saying them. *Iiiiii'm quiiiiittiiiiing.* Her eyes squeeze shut and she buries her face in her hands. Behind her hands, she spits out: "I'm-quitting-smoking-and-so-I-will-not-buy-cigarettes *goddamnit shit fuck fuck shit*."

"Okay. Whatever."

She bares her teeth like a rabid badger. "Don't *whatever* me, fucker. I am caught in the throes of a *permanent* nic-fit and even one whiff of horseshit from anybody right now and I will tear your head off your neck and stick cigarettes in all of your face-holes and smoke them through you *all at once*."

He stares. "You have to go. Just take the water."

"I need a ride."

"So, go get a ride."

"Call me a cab."

He frowns. "No cab gonna get you out here."

"Then you need to drive me."

"I need to— Look around. It look like anybody else is here?"

"No. And no customers, either. That tow truck work?"

He sighs. "Yeah."

"I'll pay."

"How much?"

She brought no money of her own. But the dead man had cash. "Forty bucks do you?"

"Where you headed?"

"About twenty minutes east. Miami." There she thinks: *what irony*. From Miami, Florida, to Miami, Arizona. One a glitzy neon-smeared monstrosity sitting on the water. The other a landlocked nowhere copper town.

"Gimme fifty bucks and I'll do it."

"I don't have fifty. I have forty."

He shrugs. "Oh, well."

Miriam represses a growl.

Then she thinks, *well, the dead man had more than cash.*

"You take credit?" she asks.

NINE

BLOOM SOON

The truck rumbles as it rolls down the road, the whole thing rattling like an old airplane breaking apart as it lands. Occasionally, the truck shudders and bangs, the tow hook on the back swinging and creaking.

Out there, in the scrub, massive cacti stand tall—like guards standing vigil over a dead world.

"They'll bloom soon."

"Huh?" she asks.

The driver tilts his head. "The cactus. The saguaro." *Sah-WAH-ro*, the way he says it. "Soon they'll bloom. Big, pretty-ass flowers on top. Then red fruit. You can eat the fruit, I guess, but the birds usually get to them first."

Miriam turns toward him. Looks him up and down. "What do you know about birds?"

"They shit on my truck." He points to a pasty white splotch at the top corner of his windshield—the patch seeded with some kind of small dark seeds.

"No, I mean . . ." She turns all the way into it now, committed to the conversation. "What do you know about, like, people who can *become* birds? Or . . . you know, they can sort of telepathically enter the minds of birds."

He laughs, then looks. His smile falls away like a bone dropped by a confused dog. "You're serious."

"Yeah. What of it?"

"It's a crazy-ass question, is what."

"Well, I just figured—"

"Figured what? That I'm a fuckin' Indian and know magical shit?"

"No! No." She pauses. Then clears her throat. "So, to clarify, that means you *don't* know magical shit?"

"Oh, oh, hold on, lemme pull over and go find some Brother Peyote, and he and I can go on a journey to ask Great Spirit about all the mysteries of the universe, including weird white-ass bitches who want to know how they become birds and whatever." He makes a *pssh* sound and waves her off.

"That's cultural appropriation, dude."

"What?"

"Calling me and my kind *bitches*. That's *our* word."

"Don't blow this back on me. You probably think my name is, like, Geronimo Running Squirrel or something."

"Chief Two-Bears Wampumdick?"

"That's my cousin."

She snorts, laughing. "Okay. Good one."

"Yeah." He looks angry, but then he laughs, too. "Girl. You a trip. My name's Wade Chee. I'm not a drunk. I don't own a casino. I don't know fuck-all about birds or magic or any of that. Whenever I want to answer life's great mysteries, I ask my iPhone. End of story."

"My name's Miriam." She sticks out her hand. This feels familiar. In a truck. With a stranger. Hand out, fingers eager for that sweet psychic tickle, that taste of death she knows she wants but that she *needs* to escape—it's almost tangible, this desire to suddenly have his hand in hers and to see how and when he's going to die. But he just laughs it off.

"Your hands look a little fucked up. I'm good."

She turns her palm toward her—abraded from falling on the highway. "Oh. Yeah." *Touch me. Let me see.*

"This is you," he says, gesturing by way of tilting his chin. Ahead: AMERICA'S BIG-VALU MOTEL. The sign itself a big fake American flag, the stars and stripes burned out in dead neon. Below it a smaller sign: TV! POOL! KITCHENETTE!

"This is me."

"That credit card you gave me. Wasn't in your name."

"Did you just figure that out? Think my name was really Steven?"

He shrugs. "He your husband?"

"No. I stole the card."

"You're honest."

"I can also see how people are going to die when I touch them. And I can, once in a while when the chips are really fucking down, telepathically enter the mind of a bird and make it do things."

"You're high."

She shrugs. "I really, really wish."

He puts out his hand. "Okay, okay. Tell me."

"Really?" His hand is long—a narrow palm with knobby, bony fingers. The nails chewed. The skin cracked. She takes his hand and feels the desert dryness—

He feels cold but the fever eats him up like a fire gobbling ice, everything melting down, waves of cold washing over boiling water, and the flu he had has gone, given way to pneumonia, and old Wade, now sixty-three, rolls over to the side of his bed and starts coughing again—a gargling, howling cough, his lungs bucking like a train going too fast down narrow-gauge mountain tracks, and then it all just stops—his lungs catch, his heart stops, everything feels like a pimple pinched between thumb and forefinger and—

She pulls her hand away. His raspy fingertips hiss against hers.

"How old are you, Wade?" she asks.

"Thirty."

"You got another thirty-three years on this earth. Then a flu-and-pneumonia combo knocks your ass into the grave."

He shrugs, like it doesn't matter, or like he doesn't believe. "Okay."

"Okay."

"It's been interesting, at least." He laughs again.

"See you, Wade."

And then she's out. The tow truck rattles off. The motel awaits—a mud-colored rectangle, like a bunch of shoeboxes shoved together. Pair of dead fat-bellied palm trees out front. A rusted swing set off to the side. No swings, just the frames.

Dead ahead is room six. Her room.

She doesn't have the key anymore—Gracie took the key ring on which it hung. But that's okay. Because Miriam has someone on the inside.

Deep breath. Long sigh. A body wracked by want—for a cigarette, for seven cigarettes, for a touch of death, for a person to be on the other side of the door that isn't. She goes to room six. She knocks.

Gabby answers.

FLORIDA

Then.

Miriam, by the sea. With a phone. It's time. She calls Louis.

He does not answer, but she leaves him a message. "It's me. I love you. I need you. And you're going to help me get rid of my curse. Call me back. Did I mention I love you? I love you. I love, love, love you."

She sits. And smokes. And waits for him to call her back.

And just as the sun dips below the horizon and is gone, he does.

"Miriam," he says. His voice sounds small and faraway.

"Louis! Louis. I love you. I need you. I think I found a way forward—I know! I know." As she speaks, she paces, her cigarette hand doing all these wild drunken butterfly movements in the air, the ember swirling, ash falling like snow. "I get it. This is all . . . this is all *crazy*, and I know I'm the one who left you, and I told you not to follow, but things have changed, and I see a way out—"

"Miriam, I'm getting married."

Wind whips. A salt spray from the sea peppers her face.

"Wh . . . what?" She feels like a rag wringing itself out. All of who she is and all of what she hoped for spattering out onto the floor beneath her. "I don't get it."

"I met somebody. Her name's Samantha. We're engaged."

TEN

THE CICATRIX IN ROOM SIX

"You look like Hell," Gabby says, and Miriam's first thought is perhaps not as repulsive as her brain gets, but in the moment, it's pretty rotten—she thinks, looking at Gabby's scarred-up face, following the slashes and intersections of puffy pink scar tissue carved into the young woman by Ashley Gaynes, *You're one to talk*. And it's right there that Miriam knows that if she does indeed look like Hell, it's because that's where she is one day headed.

If I'm not already here, her brain adds cheerfully.

Miriam gives a shrug and a half-smile (one pickled in the guilt of her own mental treachery) and slides past Gabby. Patting the young woman on the shoulder as she goes, which is, like, a super-condescending move, but it happens. Too late to take it back now. Maybe someone has that psychic ability, but it ain't Miriam. It's just, the thing is—

The thing is, Gabby feels fragile.

Miriam knows that in about three years, Gabby will go into her bathroom, eat a water bison's weight in pills, and then go lie down and die.

She will do this because her face is ruined.

It's not ruined. Not really. The pieces are fucked up, maybe, but just because you break a pretty vase doesn't mean it isn't still beautiful. (Hell, Miriam of all people appreciates broken things more than others.) Even now, no makeup, just yoga pants and a

37

pink pajama tank top, she's still a sight to behold: blond hair in careless peaks, black-rim specs, tattoos on her arm of shipwrecks and mad krakens. The scars don't change that. But Gabby won't hear a word of it. She thinks the cracks in her facade have made her unlovable.

And Miriam isn't helping on that front. Gabby wants them to be together. And Miriam resists.

Because of Louis.

And because she's a radioactive milkshake you don't want to drink.

And because getting close to Gabby means probably breaking Gabby further—as she's already done—and hooking up just means Gabby is exposed. And that's what Gabby *doesn't* need. That girl's heart needs to be buried deep. Wreathed in gristle and mounded beneath calluses. That little Care Bear needs to harden right the fuck up. Maybe then, with some steel in her spine, Gabby will decide—on that dreadful day three years hence—to leave the caps on the pill bottles. To say yes to life. To deny death.

It won't happen.

It'll never happen.

What fate wants, fate gets. Can't untie that rope.

Gabby's a dead woman. Time just hasn't caught up to her yet.

"I gotta shower," Miriam says.

"Wait, don't you want to talk?"

"Yes. No. Not right now. Shower first. Then . . ." She sighs. Beholds the desert motel around them: it's clownishly ugly. Gold paisley walls. Red bedspread. Darker red carpet. Couple of chairs the color of turquoise jewelry. It's like a clown ate a bunch of motley, multicolored handkerchiefs, then took a shit everywhere. She's not some kinda fashion Nazi or anything, but this room offends her on a *fundamental* level. "We still have the . . . thing tonight, the meeting, and I feel gross."

Gabby's saying something else, something about the meeting,

but Miriam can't hear her—she's too lost in her own thoughts. All of what happened is now rushing up—a gauntlet of fists sucker-punching her. Gracie. The little boy. The sniper—now dead, his taste still in Miriam's mouth like licking pennies. The phone call, the desert sun, Wade's lungs thick with pneumonia—

The shower, she keeps cold. If she could make it dump ice on her, she would. It shocks her, steals her breath. Perfect.

Her mind turns the morning's events over again and again. Like a stone in her mouth, rolled from tongue to teeth to pocket of cheek and back again.

Someone was trying to kill the woman, steal the child.

Miriam was incidental to that. A perpendicular line intersecting a problem that isn't hers. *It's not my problem. I have my own.* And yet she can feel the Trespasser behind her in the shower, breath on her neck—

You're not done yet.

She spins around. Nobody there.

The curtain slides back, rings rattling on the bar.

Gabby steps in—

She sucks in a sharp breath as the cold water hits her body. She ducks her head under it. Water cascades down over her hair and she runs her fingers through it. Then she's back up and says to Miriam, "Hey."

"Yeah. Hey. What, ahh, is this?"

"This?"

"This. You in the shower with me. *This.*"

"Figured we could save water." Gabby steps closer. Only an inch between them now. "Do a solid for the environment."

"I don't care about the environment," Miriam says. She feels an eagerness in her legs, her hips—she wants to step forward. *So, step forward already.* Instead, she does what she does best: keeps talking. "Frankly, the sooner we enter that period of *global heat death* and we can drown this rat in boiling seawater—"

Gabby takes another step. Skin on skin now. She's just a bit taller, so it's like her breast fits just over Miriam's—like they're a puzzle that actually fits. The water travels between them where it can. In liminal spaces fast collapsing.

"Shut up and kiss me," Gabby says. It comes out as a plea—a desperate entreaty with a ragged edge, hungry and coyote-mad.

Their mouths find each other—lips hovering just over lips, breath shared. Gabby's fingers find the side of Miriam's hips, an electric spark—

You're not done yet . . .

A sound in Miriam's ear like an airliner taking off just inches from her head. A deafening roar. The crack of a hunting rifle. A crying child in a Subaru.

She pulls away. Yanks back the shower curtain and hops out—almost losing her shit in the process, her hand stabbing out and catching the sink so she doesn't fall. Cursing under her breath, she steps in front of the mirror, face buried in her hands. She hears the curtain rings rattle and slide.

Miriam peeks between fingers.

Gabby stands there, looking lost, hurt, shocked.

Someone stands behind her. In the shower.

Louis. *Not*-Louis. The Trespasser. Clothes soaking through from the shower spray. He smiles. His teeth are broken rocks. A scorpion dances on the end of a dead tongue. His one eye is milky and split—a pale grape cut in half and shoved in the socket. He holds a fillet knife in his hand, presses it against his lips as if to say *shhhh*, and then brings it around in front of Gabby's throat—

Miriam cries out: "Watch out!"

Gabby startles. Looks left, right, confused.

The Trespasser is gone. Or was never there to begin with.

"Shit," Miriam says. "Shit!"

"What the hell?" Gabby asks. "What is wrong with you?"

Miriam growls: "Better off asking me what's *not* wrong with me. It'd take less time." Then she storms out of the bathroom, feeling angry at—she's not even sure who. Herself? Sure, yes. Gabby? Yep, her too. Trespasser? Louis? Stevie McArdle? Gracie the truck thief? Everyone and anyone. Her anger is big enough for the whole damn world, it seems—a bonfire at a fireworks factory.

In the other room, she kicks open her suitcase, starts flinging out clothing—she finds a white T-shirt, jeans, a pair of granny-panties. Gabby stands behind her, framed in the bathroom door.

"You're fucked," Gabby says.

"Uh, *durr*," Miriam says. She starts to get dressed.

"Why am I here?"

Miriam thinks:

Because you need me.

Because without me, you kill yourself.

I want to save your life.

Not that Gabby knows any of that. Sure, Gabby is up to speed, mostly, on the story of Miriam's life—its shape, if not all of its contents. Miriam told her how she met this other psychic, a woman named Sugar who knew how to find things. And how Sugar's own mother—a woman named Dora—was a psychic too, and in her diary explained that she met this girl, this Mary Stitch girl, who knew how to escape one's own curse. (Dora, of course, did not share *that* bit in her diary.) How for the last year, Miriam's been following this too-sparse trail of fucking bread-crumbs, looking for someone who may not be real, may not be alive, may not be able to help. Gabby's along for that ride. But she doesn't know the rest. She doesn't know where her road ends—unless Miriam can find a way to get Gabby to take a fork in the road and go another way.

"Well, Gabs, that's a question we all must ask now and again."

"Quit with the sarcastic self-defense mechanism. I mean it. Answer the question." Her voice gets grimmer, sterner. "Why did you bring me? We fucked once, you took your little vacation to Lesbian Island, and then you left me behind—just more wreckage in your unbelievably screwy life. You could've just let me sweep myself up. Put myself back together. But you rescued me. Or that's what I thought you were doing. It was something else. It was the opposite, wasn't it?" Here, now, her voice on the edge—wavering now like she's losing control, like the anger's going to explode into sadness. "Are you punishing me?"

"Jesus, no. No!" She wants to tell her what happens. She wants to tell Gabby how she dies. On the off chance it'll save her. Gabby knows what Miriam can do. She knows the power and Miriam's proven it. Maybe telling her would give her power over it. But Miriam knows how these things go. It'll only *confirm* it. Gabby will realize, *This is the kind of person I am, the kind who can't hack it.* And that will be that.

"Then, what?"

Miriam stands at the mirror. Her hair is a fucking mess. It's in that stage between *too short* and *not short enough*, where all it wants to do is stick up and out like it's trying to grab hold of something, anything, and catch a ride off her skull.

Gabby asks it again: "Then what is it, Miriam? What are we doing here?"

Miriam wheels.

"I need a friend," she says. "Okay? I have . . . like, *no* friends. And I'm tired of being alone. And I thought after everything, maybe you didn't want to be alone either, and so I made the mistake of dragging you into my human tire-fire of a life. But now I can see: bad idea. You're right. I'm punishing you. Being with me is a punishment. I get that."

"Miriam—"

"No, I don't say that as if I'm some kind of martyr—I mean it honestly. I am a thumbtack you step on and it gets stuck in your foot. Every step a misery. I get it. You should go. I'd say borrow the truck but that got stolen—"

"Wait, what?"

Miriam feels the mercury in her thermometer rising fast enough to break the glass. "Yeah, no, things are super-great right now. Been wandering the American West for the last year trying to find something and someone that probably doesn't exist. I finally decide to love a guy and he gets married. My mother is a fucking cucumber. I'm quitting smoking and I want a cigarette so bad, I'd drive a busload of orphans into the tiger pit at the zoo, and I'm trying to get healthy, which is completely dipshitted, because as it turns out, getting healthy feels worse than being unhealthy somehow, and sure, yeah, I hallucinate a ghost or demon or my own superego and sometimes that trespassing motherfucker points me toward these fun little adventures, like this morning—where a woman stole my truck and my phone at gunpoint but only *after* some guy with a rifle in the desert tried to shoot the both of us!" And the roller coaster of her rising pitch and angry words suddenly hits a patch of broken track and stops dead. She takes a deep breath and thinks but does not say: *Then I became vultures, killed the guy, and ate him.*

She implodes like an origami swan in a squeezing grip.

Begins to sob.

It's ugly-crying time. She can barely breathe. There are snot bubbles.

Gabby, still naked and wet and cold, comes up behind her and holds her. Stroking her hair. Shushing her. Miriam, through a spit-slick mouth says (words gummy with tears and snot): "I'm supposed to be making *you* feel better. You're not supposed to be consoling me!"

"We can get back to that later," she says, kissing the top of Miriam's head. "For now, let's just go with this."

COLORADO

The old man's got a head like a potato. Waxy, yellow, misshapen. An old spud, at that—deep wrinkles, skin so loose it feels like it might slough off at any moment, and a scattering of nodules and old-man barnacles growing from his face like the tubers pushing out from a potato's eyes.

He sits there at an old, cobwebby piano. A player piano. He makes these sounds as his tongue licks his lips or sticks tacky to the roof of his mouth. The sound of someone peeling an old bandage off a not-quite-healed wound. His elbow bumps the piano keys. A discordant chord plays.

"You're ahh, ahh, asking about the, uhh, ahh—"

"The house. The cabin. Up by the reservoir."

"The fourth cabin."

"The *third* cabin."

He makes a sound in the back of his throat like a refrigerator running—a low, almost mechanical whine. "Right, right, right. You want to rent one."

"I do not want to rent one," she asserts. "Like I said on the phone"—and here she's really very proud of herself because she doesn't say what she mentally inserts, *you old shriveled testicle*— "I want to ask about someone who rented it."

"I can't give out that kind of information." He shifts again—another bang of the piano keys, another wonky eruption of not-quite music.

"This would've been a while ago. Just shy of thirty years, actually."

"Ohhh, I don't know that I can remember that far."

"Let's try to conjure some old ghosts just the same, shall we? A woman came here. A pretty thing. Hair like strawberry wine. Freckly faced. Her name was Beth-Anne, but she went by a nickname—"

"Sweetie," he says. His voice quiet. His gaze distant, like he's remembering. She can see it in his eyes—like a mirror that takes a while to serve up its reflection. "Florida girl. She was, ahh, pregnant. Early. Just a . . . a . . . a bump." And here he offers a small smile and touches his own stomach, mimes his hand sliding over a pregnant belly. And then his face falls. He's really starting to remember now. "You should probably leave now."

"Do you remember why she came here?"

"You have to go."

Miriam gets up. Starts to wander toward the kitchen. "I'm going to get something to drink. You want anything?"

The old man scowls, his face scrunching up like a wad of aluminum foil. "Now, wait just a minute—"

But Miriam is already up. She's in the kitchen, a galley kitchen. If she thrust her elbows out, she'd bump into the cabinets— cabinets lined with ugly beadboard paneling. Avocado oven, banana-yellow fridge. Rust at the bottom of both. Black mold around all the fixtures—lights, outlets, cabinet handles. A smell of bacon grease and a deep dark damp permeate.

The old man—Weldon Stitch is his name, lived here in Collbran his whole life—totters into the kitchen, blocking her way out. "This is very rude. You're very rude. You don't just go into a man's kitchen and, and, and—"

She shushes him, then stoops and opens up the drawer at the base of the oven. A bottle rolls forward. Single malt. A good bottle: Aberlour, fifteen-year. She plucks it, sloshes it about, spins the cap and lets it fly off. It lands in the sink.

"That's *mine*," he says.

"And now it's mine."

Then it hits him. "How'd you know—"

"Where to find it? I've been in this house before, Mister Stitch."

"You're a thief. A thief!"

"Used to be. Of a sort." She swigs from the bottle. It's an easy, affable whisky. Not like the shit she's used to drinking. "This is good, by the way. It's smooth, like a baby's ass. Speaking of that—you don't remember me, do you?"

Again, his eyes searching her face. He doesn't have it . . .

Until he does. *Ding*.

"Danny's."

"The hardware store and bait shop. That's right."

"You bumped into me."

She grins. "I did at that. I saw something then. Do you know what I saw, Mister Stitch? I saw a scene. Five years, three months from now. The police raid this very house. Not local cops—not the guys you know. Staties. You're how old now? Seventy? Still, soon as they're at your door, you prove you're not some doddering old dong, and you go out the back window, quick as a shot." She claps her hands together. "You're fast, and by the time they break into your house, they don't realize you're heading toward the shed in the back. You forget the key, so you don't have time—you grab a brick from a nearby pile, who knows why you have bricks sitting around except that you're a messy old hoarder, and *bam*, you break off the padlock. Then you duck inside the shed and you reach past all the shoeboxes and stacks of magazines and floppy disks—really? Floppy disks? You reach up and grab—you know what I'm saying. You grab the can of lighter fluid. And the book of matches. Both of which are sitting there for just this occasion. You start squirting the fluid everywhere. Your hands are weak, though, and while fast, you're not particularly dexterous, and you get it everywhere. So, when the time comes to strike a match and set your horrible little shed on fire—*whoosh*. You go up in flames too. You try to get out but already the fire blocks your path. And you burn. And you die. You die *screaming*, flailing around like an old bear who just tore open one helluva beehive."

The old man just stands there, quaking.

And then, like in the vision, he moves fast.

His hand darts. Grabs a kitchen knife from the block nearby. *Shing*.

Thing is, he's fast *for an old man*.

She's fast for a hard-living piece of road trash. And before he can bring the knife against her, she clubs him in the head with the bottle of Scotch.

Tunk. He drops. The bottle gurgles, splashes. Loses half of its very fine liquid. Miriam scowls. Knife clatters. She kicks the blade away, under the oven.

At her feet, Weldon Stitch mumbles and blubs. His hands paw at the floor and he tries to get up. But his head is fucked up now: an apple gone rotten.

His chin drops back to the floor and he moans.

"Death is clarifying," Miriam says, taking another pull from the Aberlour. The bottle makes a *fwoomp* sound as it sucks away from her lips. "You learn a lot about how a person lived by how they die. Not always. Sometimes, it's just some random, goofy happenstance. I touched a guy once and found out that he'd one day die when a washing machine comes off the back of a tractor trailer, slides right onto his hood, shears through the windshield and roof of his car, and takes his head off clean at the neck. Random. But! Even there? That was the guy. That's who he was! He spent most of his life in the car on sales calls. He died how he lived like so many do. Coke habit, fatty food, cigarettes, skydiving, whatever. I saw your death and I was like, gosh and golly, what is in that shed? So, I went out there—first

I found the key in here, on that pegboard by the front door that looks like a trout—and it's no surprise to you what I found, you fucking monster."

"Leave me alone. I'm a good man."

"Say most terrible men." She clucks her tongue and crouches down over him like a gargoyle at the corner of a cathedral. "This isn't how I figured it would go, but here we are, Stitch. You're still alive, and here's the deal: I'm going to let you live if you give me some info."

"I don't have anything you want."

"You know where your sister is. Mary Stitch. She was your first, wasn't she? You're a bit older than her. Twelve years or something like that."

"I never touched her." But she hears in his voice the tremors—the deception inside him is tectonic. It makes him shake when he lies. "She's my half-sister. Different mother."

"You tell me where she is, I let you live. You can destroy all the evidence out in that shed. You can go on your merry way."

"I don't know where she is," he mumbles. "I swear it."

Miriam *thunks* the bottom of the bottle right next to his head. The floor shakes. "I'll promise I'll pulp your skull like a pomegranate, Stitch."

"Okay. Okay! She—okay. Last I heard, she was in Santa Fe."

"Santa Fe."

"Uh-huh. She was part of some . . . some biker thing there. Shacked up with a fella. I don't know his name; she—she—she wouldn't tell me."

The smell of shit and piss hits her nose. Stitch has lost control.

"That it?" she asks. "Anything else? I find out anything else, I'm going to come back here, Weldon. And I'll set fire to you myself."

"An RV park. She was staying in an RV park. Los Surenos or Suenos or something. Mexican-sounding."

She pats Weldon on the back of his head.

"You did good, pig," she says.

Then she slams the bottle down on the back of his head. There's a crunch. Blood doesn't spray, but it slowly spreads beneath him like jam from a shattered jar. His body shakes like he's on one of those vibrating motel beds, and then one leg kicks out—sending his slipper spiraling away—before everything goes still. Miriam tries to drink from the Aberlour, but the base of the bottle sticks in the back of his head. She lets it go and it stands there, mocking her.

Shit.

After that, she goes out to that shed, grabs a couple of the shoeboxes there—each heavier than she'd like, dense with the horror that got the sick old fuck off—and throws a couple of them on top of him. She closes her eyes so she doesn't have to see what's on there.

Then she gets a phonebook. It's near the phone that hangs on the wall near the kitchen. A rotary phone, of all things.

She finds the number for the local FBI office.

She dials it.

A woman answers.

Miriam gives her Weldon Stitch's address.

Then she says, "You'll find a dead guy here. Kid-toucher. You should come and clean him up. Send this along to an 'Agent Grosky,' will you?"

ELEVEN

TAXICAB CONFESSIONS

Night in Arizona.

The taxicab—a minivan with a cherub-cheeked, avuncular driver named Juan—shoots down Route 60 toward Phoenix. The city lighting up the desert dark like magma carving channels through the glass and concrete canyons.

"You think this meeting is a good idea?" Gabby asks. "Is it safe?"

Miriam shrugs. "No idea. It's a swanky little boutique hotel in Phoenix—"

"Scottsdale," the cab driver says, interrupting. "You said Scottsdale?"

"Whatever," Miriam says, frowning. "Isn't it all part of the city?"

He gives her a look that says, *No, no it's not.* She holds up her hands in mock surrender, then rolls her eyes.

"This is your life, isn't it?" Gabby asks.

"Huh?"

"Just . . . traveling around, kicking up clouds of dust."

"More or less. But I'm tired of that. I'm tired of my life. That's why we're doing this. That's why we're going to meet this asshole, see if he knows where Mary Stitch is. She's here. I just know it." Or so she's been told. Of course, she's been told this before, and Mary Stitch—a.k.a. Mary Scissors, or sometimes, Mary Ciseaux—had already been gone. She doesn't stay long in one place. But Miriam can feel it in her gut like pinching fingers—she's close. Real close now. Just gotta keep going. *Kill the curse.*

They pass a billboard outside. Pistol on it. Big Glocky-looking gun. Bullet shooting out with the name of some gun store on it. Gabby scoffs.

Miriam raises an eyebrow. "What?"

"What what?"

"You scoffed."

"I didn't scoff."

"You audibly, visibly scoffed. It sounded like the combination of a scuff and a cough which is, I think, the very definition of *scoffed.*"

"The gun thing is all."

"What? The billboard?"

"Gun violence in America is at an all-time high."

Miriam blinks. "I guess." She thinks about the pistol she stole from the dead man in the desert. And how it sits in the bag of money she has sitting at her feet—a fact she decides not to mention to Gabby just now. Gabby knows about the money but not about the gun. The money is five hundred bucks in small bills. It's the price Gabby helped negotiate for the information they seek. It's also the last of their cash. But it's a price Miriam has to pay.

"This area freaks me out," Gabby says.

"What? Why?"

"It's super-conservative."

"Is it?"

Gabby makes a face. "Don't you follow politics?"

"Do I look like I follow politics? I don't have time for politics or TV shows or movies or any of that."

"You *totally* have time for all that," Gabby says, laughing an incredulous laugh. "You don't have a full-time job. You don't have a job at all."

Miriam scowls. "And you do? By the way, being me *is* a full-time job, Little Miss Judgeytits."

"My tits would never judge you."

"I bet."

"And me helping you is a full-time job too."

"Uh-huh."

Gabby reaches over, touches her arm. "Seriously, I hope we find what you're looking for tonight. I'm sorry. I know it's hard. Especially lately."

Miriam told Gabby about the events in the desert—the boy, the woman Gracie, the sniper. (Though she continues to withhold the part about *hey, I can become birds and sometimes eat people* because that seems about four or five bridges too far.) Gabby, to her credit, listened, nodded, shushed her. And even now it continues. The soothing, the loving gestures. Gabby's fingers tracing reassuring lines up Miriam's arm. The occasional squeeze of her wrist, hand, or shoulder. The reminder that there's someone else out there. Someone else who maybe actually cares about her.

"Thanks." That word, croaked out, like a frog under the toe of a stepping boot. She's not used to someone being nice to her. It's weird. It makes her uncomfortable. Which, Miriam thinks, says a whole lot. None of it good.

TWELVE

SCUZZ AND THE SKIZZ

The hotel is so boutique hipster bullshit, it makes Miriam want to soak her chest in rage-barf. Pink floppy chairs contrastingly shoved in brushed steel frames. Blue neon framing the room. Big words bulging from the walls hung as art: DIVA, LUXE, WOW. A dull, thudding bass—lazy trip-hop like someone on Molly made it with their iPhone. Pretentious black-and-white photos on the wall of things that have nothing to do with anything: a chess piece, a homeless man, an oboe, a laughing supermodel cutting red peppers in a kitchen. Miriam passes each and finds her face twisting up tighter and tighter, like a screw spun so far into the wood, it splits the board.

The elevator dings. She and Gabby enter.

The wall behind them is a giant photo of what looks like a bearded lumberjack pressing a finger to his lips, as if to say, *Shhhh, I'm a douche.* His handsome face looks soft, not hard. Another model. "That's not a real lumberjack," Miriam says, growling.

Gabby shrugs. "So?"

"These things are important to me," Miriam says.

Gabby asks, "Authenticity in elevator art?"

"Yeah." She blinks. "Okay, I probably shouldn't care about that."

"Probably not."

"I care too much. That's my problem."

Gabby smiles. "I think that's pretty low on your list of problems." **53**

The elevator dings again.

Doors open.

Long hallway. Blue walls, lemon yellow accents. More pretentious photography. This hotel is trying so hard, it's going to strain something. Pop a nut, give itself a hernia. Hell, the design already suggests a place in the throes of anesthetic aneurysm.

"Room 522," she says.

They head to the door. The three digits in the room number are each a different font, like it's a ransom note.

Miriam knocks three times. Loud.

Inside, music thuds. An erratic bass line. A musical arrhythmia. She knocks again. The volume drops.

The door opens a couple inches. A narrow sliver of white-dude face stares out. Faint hair on his upper lip like a dusting of Oreo cookie crumbs: a crustache. His lip curls in an amused sneer.

"Sup," he says.

"*Sup*," Miriam mimics.

"You need something? You don't look like you're from Triple Visions."

"I don't know what that is. We spoke on the phone last week."

"Huh?"

"I'm looking for Mary Scissors."

She gestures with the tote bag.

The realization dawns on his face slowly. "Aww, ha ha ha, yeah, yeah, sure. Come on in, ladies."

The door closes, the locks disengage. The room is like the lobby downstairs. Nothing matches. Looks like God got high and painted everything in fluorescent highlighter.

"I'm Buzz, yo," the white boy says. Miriam offers her fist to bump, but he either doesn't notice or doesn't care. She wants to see how he dies, wants to get that taste of it—she tells herself it's because it's good to know, that it's important to see because of what she might learn. But part of it, too, is that she wants it.

Hell, not just part of it. Most of it. *All* of it, maybe.

"Yeah, I know your name," Miriam says. She tries to shake the desire scratching at her door like a monster inside a child's closet. "Like I said, we spoke on the phone."

"Sorry, sorry, yeah." He bumps the desk chair over with his knee, the casters rattling on the floor. He sits, kicks back, gestures to the bed. "Take a load off, ladies. R*elax*."

Miriam and Gabby share a look.

They sit after silent agreement.

"I don't want this to take long," Miriam says. "I brought the money. I want to know where Mary Scissors is. Easy deal to make."

"Chill, chill. Can't we get to know each other?"

"We're not going to fuck you," Gabby says.

Miriam, impressed, thumbs toward Gabby. "What she said."

"Nah, nah, nah, I ain't trying to play you like that, ladies." He licks his crustache, like he's thinking about it anyway. "You gals lezzies?"

"She's straight," Gabby says, and the bitterness there is so plain, Miriam can actually taste it on the back of her tongue.

"Uh, excuse me, I'm bisexual," Miriam says, "Thanks."

"Bisexual isn't a thing," Gabby says. "It's like trying to be a vegetarian while saying you also sometimes eat meat."

"Some vegetarians eat eggs, and that metaphor totally sucks anyway because people can eat both meat and vegetables—it's called being an omnivore and I'm basically a sexual omnivore and I don't think we should be having this discussion in front of—"

She's about to say "Buzz," but when she looks over at him, he's pulling out what she first thinks is a fountain pen—it's long, black, with a silver end and what she soon realizes is a mouthpiece of sorts. Like a tiny musical instrument. He wets his lips and sucks on it. When he does, the end glows blue.

"What are you doing?" she asks.

"Smokin', yo."

"Smoking what? Some sort of Tron cigarette?" Then, to Gabby: "See, I watch movies. I know Tron."

"The new one, or the old one?"

"There was a new one?"

Buzz chuckles. "It's an e-cig."

"An e-cig." Miriam blinks.

"Yeah, yeah. Electronic cigarette."

"That's not a real thing. You're just making that up."

"You never vaped?"

"'Vaped?' Now I know you're just dicking around with me. If this is what smoking is coming to, I'm glad I'm quitting."

He exhales a cloud of what looks like fog. "It's cool. They got flavors."

"Well. You look like a fucking asshole. And the only flavor I need for my smokes is *tongue cancer*."

He frowns. She pushed too far.

"How do I know you're not cops?" he asks.

"Because we're not?" Gabby says.

"If you think we're cops, then you're even dumber than I thought. Listen, Dirt-Lip. Let's move this dog and pony show along, okay?"

All jocularity has been bled from his face. He sucks on the e-cig again, blows another vapor plume. He says, "You wanna know where Skizz is, you're gonna have to prove you ain't po-po."

"Skizz?"

"Mary Scissors. We call her Skizz, like in Skizzers."

"Fine." Miriam sniffs. "What do you want us to do?"

He laughs, pulls out a little black satchel. The e-cig hangs out of his mouth as he unzips it. It's like a little shaving kit, except instead of shaving gear, it's three hypodermic needles, two spoons, a tiny packet of white cloths, a lighter, and a baggie of white powder.

"I want you to shoot up," he says. "Buy the ticket, take the ride."

"I'm quitting smoking, not starting heroin," Miriam says. "Besides, I'm pretty sure undercover cops totally do drugs."

"You want your info, this is how. I wanna know you're on the up and up."

He wants to get us hooked so we buy his shit, she thinks.

"You work for the cartels?" she asks. Would make sense. Arizona is right up against Mexico. They have power here—presence.

"Hell, no. They make stepped-on, shitty stuff. This is synthetic. Cheap, clean, beautiful." He hands over the satchel. "Fire it up."

"Fuck yourself. No." She starts to stand. And then sits back down.

Gabby gives her a look. "You're not seriously going to—"

Miriam looks at the bag.

Remembers the gun in it.

No. That won't work. No guns here. Not now. Not yet.

But she needs the info he has. *Needs* it. This thing she has is worse than any addiction. Touching people, seeing their deaths—it's a curse, yeah, and it's all well and good to keep calling it that. But the hunger for it twists in her marrow like a chewing maggot. She's addicted to death. It's become a part of her—woven into her fabric, half the squares sewn to her crazy-ass quilt. She hates that.

It's gotta go.

"I need to know where this woman is," she says. "So, fine, lets all get goofy." She starts taking things out of the satchel. The items within are a mystery to her. Suddenly frustrated, she barks: "I don't know what to do with this shit."

"I'll help," Gabby says, taking the kit.

Now it's Miriam's turn to offer the quizzical look.

Gabby says, "I used to use. High school. It was a thing. I got over it." She pauses. "Some of my friends didn't." She starts to tap the powder into the spoon. Flicks the lighter. In seconds, it's like melting snow—the granules of white join each other, their margins breaking down. Then it's gone, replaced with a bubbling liquid. "You don't wanna do this."

"I know I don't. Just cook."

The scuzzy fuck vapes and watches and chuckles. Like he gets off on it.

Gabby dips the needle tip in the bubbling broth.

Then sucks it up into the syringe.

"Miriam," she says, handing it over. "Be careful."

Miriam winks.

The needle tip drips—a glistening bead like morning dew.

Then she grabs Buzz by the wrist—

Two years from now, four months, seven days, Buzz is in a souped-up Honda hatchback driving down the highway at night, dipping his chin and biting his lip to the bass booming so loud out of his car's stereo, it's a surprise the whole thing doesn't vibrate apart, and he looks over and sees a white Caddy sliding up alongside him with a bunch of vatos ridin' dirty, and he lifts his head and nods at them, and the one in the passenger side—face so gaunt and so long, he's like a deer skull with skin stapled to it—nods back, and then the back window rolls down and Buzz realizes a half-second too late that they're holding guns, submachine guns, and then bullets start chewing into the Honda and chewing into Buzz, too. He screams, hot lead opening his middle, glass peppering his cheeks. He cuts the wheel, steers into the highway divider, and then the car is flipping like a can kicked down the road, everything spinning, and he's not wearing his seatbelt, and so next thing Buzz knows, he's on the ground, bleeding, surrounded by glass, his car ten feet ahead of him on its side. He laughs, and the laugh makes him belch up blood, and then he hears an engine revving. When he turns his head, he sees the Caddy coming. In reverse. Buzz screams. The tires mash his head like a banana under a little kid's Big Wheel. And that's the end of scuzzy Buzz—

—and then Miriam jams the needle in his arm, thumbing the plunger.

The dealer's eyes go wide as the spoon that cooked the horse, and he clubs an easily ducked fist toward Miriam. Then his mouth goes slack and his eyes go unfocused.

"Buh," he says.

Drool wets his drooping lip.

Miriam stands. Snaps her fingers at Gabby. "C'mon. Help me get Scuzzy Buzz into the bathroom."

"What are we doing?"

"Improvising."

CROW BAR

In the hills outside Atalaya Mountain—down a long canyon road looped and curved like guts spilled and twisted, amongst the pinyon pines and the sagebrush—sits an old biker bar. Crow Bar. From the outside, you'd think a madman lives here—it's an old double-wide trailer whose outer walls are covered with a random assortment of forgotten shit. Hubcaps nailed to the walls. Broken mirrors and bits of once-colorful pottery bleached by the sun and speckled with red dust. A shattered birdbath. Pickaxes. Iron skillets. Like inside is a black hole sucking all manner of junk and desert detritus toward it.

Inside ain't much different. Long bar framed in tire rubber. Stools, none that match, many metal, many rusted. No tables— no *room* for tables. More garbage hanging from the ceiling: bike chains, an ammo belt from a WWII machine gun, Mardi Gras beads.

But inside doesn't matter.

Because Jerry Carnacky—a guy they call Jerry Carnage—isn't going to be in there for long. He's sitting. He's drinking. This is a safe place. A *you don't fuck with me, I don't fuck with you* bar. Made all the safer because those fucks from the Ladrones Viciosos are dead and gone. Not all of them dead, okay, but all of them gone. Scattered like broken teeth.

But that win is a loss, too. Mary did this for them—Mary,

with her gifts. Mary, with her big bush and mournful eyes.
Mary, sweet Mary. She was gonna be Jerry's hot old motorcycle
mama. She's like them raw, rough broads out of those *Easyriders*
magazines that Li'l Jer used to steal out of Pop's toolbox in the
garage. All those natural women. No fake tits. No baby pussies.
Real goddamn motherfucking women. They had soul, but they
looked like they'd pop you in the mouth, too, if you said the
wrong thing. Tough bitches. Jerry likes tough bitches.

Mary could've been in those pages.

Mary Scissors. He hated that name. Apt as it was.

She's not with him anymore. He said, "You're mine; you
can't go." She said her job was done and she was never his. And
Jerry, hoo boy, Jerry threw himself an epic shitfit. Like a monkey
cranked tight on meth. Okay, now, he never hit her. Not really.
He'd never do that. Sure, he threw a lamp. Kicked a hole in
his own wall. Broke a goddamn coffee table clean in half when
he stomped on it. Every broken thing just making him want to
break more things. When he ran out of steam, she just asked
him if he was done, and he said he was, and then she gave him a
small kiss on his salt-and-pepper cheek and walked out into the
setting sun and was gone.

He misses her.

He'd cry, but he can't muster the tears. Last time he
cried was when his dog—an old long-bodied hound named
Dickripper—got hit by a car on the highway.

A man's allowed to cry over his dog. That's just a rule.

So, no, he's not crying, but he is drowning his sorrows in
some tequila from just south of the border—it's cheap shit, but
it isn't swill, and it tastes like the sunset into which his sweet
Mary walked.

Time comes and brings the sound of a bike roaring outside, engine guttering and going quiet. Then he hears the door
behind him open—it can't open without making a sound, given

the fact it brushes a set of old wind chimes made from a set of little wrenches. Jerry looks up, sees the bartender—a scraggly-bearded strip of beef jerky named Delmar—scowl like someone just unzipped and started pissing on the floor. "You can't bring that in—" the bartender starts to say.

Those words, swallowed up by the hungry boom of a shotgun. Damn near cuts Delmar in two. Bottles pop. Liquor spills. Jerry jumps off his stool, but he's half in the bag, and he falls into another stool while reaching for the Bowie knife hanging at his hip—

The butt of the shotgun cracks him in the mouth. He swallows teeth. Chases them with blood. Next thing he knows, he's being dragged outside, and he looks up and sees that it's Johnny Tratez, meth cook for the now-defunct Ladrones Viciosos, doing the dragging. Tratez must be sampling his own goods, because his whole face is drawn wide, stretched out, skin so tight it looks like it might rip—the man's mouth is a cavern of screaming rage, his eyes bleary and unblinking. Even his nostrils are flaring big enough you could fit a couple of 20-gauge shells up in there. He flings Jerry out the front door, into the broken stone parking lot, not far from the old withered hitching posts where bikers lash their rides.

Then a boot to the face.

Jerry is on his hands and knees. Drool and blood spattering against the ground, the dust swallowing it up, a tithing to the hungry earth.

He coughs.

He paws at his hip for the knife.

Then: the wasp buzz whine of an engine revving up. Not a bike engine. Something else. Jerry lifts his head, blinks and tries to get his eyes to focus—

"My *hermanos* are dead because of you!" Tratez roars. He's just a blur, his hands up in the air, holding something. Waving it around. *"Chinga tu madre.* Now I cut you up like you cut us up. *Te meto la verga por el osico para que te calles el pinche puto osico hijo de perra!"*

The blur resolves.

Tratez has a chainsaw. Not a big one. A little jibber-jabber. Not for chopping down trees but good enough to cut up a thick branch or maybe a cactus.

The meth cook raises the chainsaw in the air like he's from that movie and runs at Jerry, full speed.

A truck slams into him.

An old pickup. A Ford.

Tratez's whole body flies like he's on a rope and someone just yanked him in the other direction. He slams into a set of bikes. But Tratez is on meth or something worse. Tweakers are like rabid dogs—takes a couple shots to put 'em down. And oh, Johnny doesn't disappoint: he hops back up on a leg that is plainly broken (white bone shining through rent skin) and pogo-sticks his way back toward the truck, the chainsaw waving, buzzing, growling in the air—

The Ford's door swings wide. A young woman steps out.

She twirls a Louisville slugger, a cigarette plugged between her lips.

Tratez hops toward her.

She takes time to line up her shot. She points, like the Babe. Then swings hard with the bat. The bat clips into the side of the chainsaw. The whirring blades bite into Tratez's face, and the man screams. His one leg goes out from under him, and he drops like a kicked-over coatrack.

The chainsaw growls and eats halfway into the cook's face.

Vzzz, vzzzzz, grind, spray.

Then it stops.

So does Tratez.

The woman—hair black and blue like an electric bruise, her

face flecked with red—sniffs and, around the cigarette, says, "Hi, Jerry. Need a ride?"

"Guh." Jerry spits blood. "Yeah."

"Good. But you should know: this ride isn't charity. You're gonna have to sing for your supper." She gives one last look at the body on the ground, her gaze lingering. She shudders. Then, back to Jerry: "Well? Hop on in."

THIRTEEN

TRUTH SERUM

Buzz hangs by the shower nozzle. Hands stretched wide. Wrists bound together with his own shoelaces, and his belt used to dangle him from the fixture. His feet touch the tub—he's short, but not that short—but they have his feet bound up too. Those with the cord ripped out of the hotel's alarm clock, which, despite all the barfy design flair of this boutique atrocity, was the most pedestrian little black alarm clock Miriam had ever seen.

She looks him over. Wonders if that's how she looked once. When the killers Harriet and Frankie hung her from a shower nozzle in the Jersey Pine Barrens—putting Miriam on display for their boss, the one she called Hairless Fucker: Ingersoll.

The memory rides through her like a river of rats.

"Wh . . . what are you doing," Buzz says, his words pushed through sluggy, froth-bubbled lips. The heroin is doing its job. His eyelids flutter. The drug like an invisible thumb punching his pleasure buttons. "Whhh . . . whhh."

Gabby stands behind Miriam. Framed by the doorway.

"Miriam," she says in a low voice. "What *are* we doing?"

"Getting information," she says, then turns back to Buzz. "Hey. Buzz. You're a drug dealer, right? I've met quite a few of you, now. I meet *all kinds* of interesting people. I meet the standard run of wanderers and weirdos: truck drivers, janitors, folks who clean up roadkill, buskers, whatever. But I've also met serial killers. And psychics. No, no, *real* psychics. And I've met FBI agents—real and pretend—and cops, and just last year, I met an ex-Army interrogator. Worked for the CIA for a time. Old guy. He told me this interesting little tidbit—and when I hear interesting tidbits, I'm like a hamster with a piece of sweet carrot. I tuck that tidbit into my bulging hamster cheeks and save it for later."

"Buh . . . buhhh. Bitch."

"*Two* bitches," Miriam corrects. "Two badass bitches, each as crazy as one starving coyote. Now, to continue my story? So, he told me that the CIA was obsessed with the idea of a *truth serum*. Right? A magic drug you administer and then the captor goes 'blah blah blah' and spills what he knows. They tried using heroin withdrawal in this way. Right? Get an enemy combatant hooked on heroin—riding the ol' H Train—and then he starts to go through withdrawal, which is apparently like having your soul torn out through your mouth and asshole simultaneously. So bad, you'll do anything for a hit, including tell the truth."

"I don't . . . I don't use this stuff. . . . You can't . . ."

She smacks him. It echoes sharp in the bathroom.

His eyes blink.

"Stay with me, Buzz, because I don't have time for the whole *nightmarish plunge into withdrawal* thing. I've got ten minutes at best, and if I don't get what I want, I'm going to—well, kill you, probably."

Gabby can't seem to contain the small gasp that comes out of her. Miriam shoots her a reassuring look accompanied by a short shake of the head, as if to say *no, not really, I'm just pretending*.

But in the back of her mind, she knows she's not pretending.

She'll kill this guy.

And that's fucked up. He's a douche, not a murderer. In fact: *she's* the murderer. Grosky called her a serial killer and, ha ha ha, what, no, of course she's not. Except—what if she is? Easy to justify her killings, of course: she kills bad people. Other killers. Molesters. Rapists. The men who are monsters.

This guy's crustache and e-cig are offensive.

But not kill-worthy.

Right?

(She tells herself it's just the cigarettes. Or, rather, their lack. She's a lot more murdery without nicotine, it seems.)

No time to worry about this now, Miriam. It is what it is. You are who you are. Two precepts she hopes direly to change.

She clears her throat, plasters the sinister smile back on her face, and says, "Now, what this Army guy I talked to figured out was that their hook-and-withdraw tactic was actually too complicated. Because you know what people like to do on heroin, provided it's good stuff and not shit? They tell the truth. They tell the truth because they just want to experience the high—they want to roll around in sunshine, drool, giggle, and sleep. But the interrogator keeps asking them questions, keeps—"

And here she leans in and smacks him again. His eyes blink and he makes a sound like "Muhhh."

"—*harassing* them, and they'll spill their guts just so they can be left alone and enjoy the high. So. Now I'm going to ask you. Where is Mary Scissors? Tell me now and I leave you alone to hang here and enjoy the ride."

"Skizz," he murmurs.

"Yeah. Yes. *Skizz.*"

"I'm not gonna . . . Puh—puhlease just go—" His eyelids flutter like moth wings after a child has rubbed all the powder off.

Smack.

"Wake *up*, you crusty, vaping turd. Mary! Scissors! Now!"

"She's . . . gone."

"Gone?" No, no, no, no.

"She left us. Left our crew. Gave us what we needed, then . . ."

His eyes close.

Her hand forms a fist and she drives it into his middle. His eyes bulge. Desperation is a drill boring into her brain stem.

"Then *what*?" she screams.

"She bailed on us." Every word he speaks punctures a bubble of saliva that forms over his lips. He tries to whistle, but he just blows spit. "Hightailed it."

Her guts sink. Her shoulders sag. This isn't possible. She was so close. She could *taste it*. A bleakness settles into her then. She's chasing a phantom.

A year ago, she was given her way out: the name of a woman who could help her "cure" her condition. Who could *kill* this horrible thing that grows inside of her, swelling in the place of the child she once lost.

I need it gone. Lest the curse consume her. And then become her. Because that's what it feels like, some days. Like her psychic power is in the driver's seat and she's belted into the backseat, screaming as the car careens forth.

But suddenly, the dream of excising her curse is fast turning to vapor. The woman who was supposed to help her, Mary Scissors, is gone. And she's really just a name, anyway, isn't she? A specter she's chasing down the highway. Miriam's never met this woman. She could've been bugfuck shitballs. Mad as a starving rabbit. What's the point? What's the point of any of this?

Tears mar her vision. She blinks them away but they keep returning.

She hasn't felt this way since she wrote her own diary.

Dear Diary . . .

She slams down a mental wall. No reason to revisit those memories.

She sniffs. Clears her throat. Gives a stiff nod. "Right, then. I guess we're done here."

Buzz says, "But."

Miriam blinks. "But what?"

"She's gotta . . . still be in town. Or nearby."

Hope flares. A match struck in the deep dark. Light and heat pushing back shadow.

"Why?"

"Pro . . . probation officer. Manda . . . manda . . . tuhhh." He breathes loud, whistles through his nose. His eyes shut.

"Manda? Amanda? Mandy? Wake the fuck up!" Miriam's about to yell, kick, scream, slap, but it's like he anticipates what's coming, even through his opiate haze.

Buzz says, "*Mandatory*. Meets once a month. Pima County Superior Court. In Tucson. Drug tests and alla th . . . thaaaat."

Holy shit.

Mary Scissors is still in town. Or close enough: Tucson is only an hour away. Which means—

Miriam still has a chance.

A chance to find Mary Scissors. A chance to change her own destiny.

She faces Gabby. Feels the smile tug at her cheeks—a smile big enough she feels like she might turn into Ms. Pac-Man, her head splitting in half, hungry for pills and ghosts. Gabby asks, "Is that it? Is that what you need?"

"It is."

Gabby grins. Her scars stretching.

Miriam turns, pats Buzz on the cheek. "We're done here. Thanks, Scuzzy Buzz. We bought you the ticket, so enjoy the ride."

Buzz gurgles and passes out. Miriam grabs the bag of money, hooks her arm around Gabby's, and they get the hell out of there.

FOURTEEN

TWO STARS, CRASHING TOGETHER

They fuck in the cab ride back to the motel.

BLACK HOLE

The two of them lie there, all glistening sweat and panting breaths. Headlights from the motel parking lot shining on their bodies. Gabby's leg is draped over Miriam's. Miriam's arm is flopped across Gabby's chest.

The last hour replays.

Tongue-wrestling in the back of an Arizona cab, hands down each other's pants, fingers searching. Back at the motel, crashing through the door, shedding clothes like a magician flinging handkerchiefs all over the stage. The pressure of four fingers in the small of her back. The comfort of a face between her legs. A tongue there, hungry and insistent. Her spine arching—every synapse about to blow like an overloaded fuse box. Her mouth finding the scars across Gabby's face. Kissing a line along them. Hands cupping her ass. Twist of pain sweet pain as thumb and forefinger twist her nipples—tune in Tokyo, tune in Tokyo. Heat and light. Sheets tangled. Laughing and moaning and grunting and laughing some more. Teeth and tongues and little kisses and big kisses and—

"I thought you said you didn't want this," Gabby says.

"I say a lot of things."

"But weren't we supposed to just be friends?"

"We are friends. This is friendly." She feels Gabby watching her. She turns, meets Gabby's gaze. Here in the half-dark, her

71

scars are almost invisible. "You're harshing my buzz here, lady."

"Ugh. Buzz. I don't want to think about him."

Miriam laughs. "What an asshole."

A little voice inside her echoes Gabby's question: Why? Weren't they supposed to be friends? Miriam pushes the protest to the back of her mind but it keeps popping back up: *You did it because you felt good and wanted to feel better.*

"You were amazing tonight," Gabby says.

"I was?"

"You were."

She *hnnhs*. "Maybe I was. So were you. You got some bona fide badass in you."

"You really might find this woman. Mary."

"I might, at that."

"And you really think she can . . . help?"

That word, *help*. Gabby won't say help with what, because Gabby doesn't like talking about Miriam's curse. Maybe because she doesn't really believe it. Maybe because she *does*, and it's too scary to contemplate—a world far bigger and more fucked up than imagined, Horatio.

"I don't know. I hope so."

Gabby leans in, kisses her shoulder. "I hope so too."

Miriam lurches forward, sitting straight up. A craving sprints up her spine. Her skin crawls like she's covered in ants. The nic-fit has presence, as physical as a python winding its way around her neck. Her mouth can taste the cigarette she wants to plug between her lips right damn now.

She winces. A mad laugh keens through her gritted teeth. It isn't a happy sound. Gabby sits up with her. "You okay?"

"I want to smoke."

"You're quitting."

Miriam thrusts up a finger. "No no no. Don't tell an addict they're quitting. It's like telling a cranky person they're cranky.

It just makes it worse. Like, seriously, I know we just had a very lovely time, but don't think I won't bite you."

"You can bite me." Gabby runs a hand down Miriam's spine. Her hand reaches the lift of Miriam's hip, then slides around between her legs. Miriam shivers. Hot and cold, her body wet, her mouth dry. "I can make you feel good. I can even give you something to put in your mouth . . ."

A crisp gasp comes from Miriam. Then she pulls away and steps off the bed in a tangle of sheets. "That sounds awesome. It *really* does. But I need to smoke. I need to smoke the way a fish needs water. I'm sure I have an emergency cigarette around here somewhere." She flings open the nightstand drawer. Looks under the alarm clock. Goes to the ugly chair in the corner and pops up the cushion.

She has no memory of hiding a cigarette anywhere. But, she's been drunk a few times, and—maybe she did it then? Maybe *Past Miriam* was planning on doing *Future Miriam* a really nice favor, and maybe she left a little present—

"Come back to bed," Gabby says.

But Miriam, she tears through the room like a pissed-off housecat: pawing through things, flipping stuff off flat surfaces, *fuck this, fuck that, fuck this thing over here, where's my fix.* A magazine flops. A lamp rattles. A remote control spins to the ground and quickly she snatches it up and bangs it hard against the heel of her hand—

The battery compartment pops off.

Inside: no batteries.

Instead: one cigarette broken in two halves. Little specks of nicotine sandwiched between them. She plucks them out with pinching fingers. Sniffs them. *Ahhh.* Holds them up like precious little gifts, then swings them through the air like a symphony conductor with his baton. She hums "Ode to Joy."

"Miriam—" Gabby says.

"Oh, god." A grim revelation tears the scales from Miriam's eyes. "I don't have fire. I don't have fire!" A caveman's anxiety seizes her. "Quick, find some shit in this room that we can rub together to make flame." She snaps her fingers, her whole body thrumming. "No, no, I know, you wanna say, *We can rub our bodies together to make flame*, and that's super-cute and I promise soon as I smoke this *one* last coffin nail I'll get right back to quitting and then *we* can get right back to doing awesome things with our many digits and orifices, but for now—"

A phone rings.

Gabby arches an eyebrow. "Is that my phone? That's not my phone."

"My phone is gone." That woman stole it.

Miriam kicks over a pillow that had fallen to the floor.

Underneath: the dead man's phone. The one that belonged to the sniper. Steven McArdle.

Don't answer it, don't answer it, don't answer it.

Miriam answers it.

She sits across from him at a Fort Lauderdale coffee shop, and she tries not to show how much sitting this close to him hurts her. She refuses to give even a glimpse of how the space between her guts and her heart aches: a sucking wound. How she feels like a little kid who wants to cry so hard, she can't catch a breath. A little kid who lost a favorite doll. A doll without its stuffing. An everything without its everything, which means she's left with nothing.

Louis can't see any of that. Instead, she keeps this dumb, fakey-fakey smile staple-gunned to her face. A big-ass sleep-aborter mug of coffee sits cradled between her hands, and she tries hard not to show how, right now, the thing she wishes for is not to drink it all but rather to crush it between her palms.

"I'm surprised you wanted to meet," she says.

Outside, it's blue skies and palm trees. A skateboarder whizzes past. A surfer walks by, board in hand pointing the other direction. Seagulls swoop and shriek. Louis's eyes follow them. Like he doesn't want to look at her.

"I thought it'd be good," he answers. "Closure and all that."

"Closure," she says. "I am a big fan of closure. I close things all the time. I close doors and windows and jam jars and circuits and captions. I even closed my mouth once."

"Just once?"

"Just once. Never again."

He laughs. A soft, gentle sound. He's gone a little gray around the temples. Black hair peppered with iron filings. And he's scruffy, too—a beard coming in. She remarked on it when they first sat down, and he said Samantha—"Sam"—liked beards a lot, so, ta-da, growing a beard.

"You're still Miriam," he says.

"In the flesh." *Don't kill him. Don't kill yourself. Don't burn this place down. Deep breath.* She draws that deep breath in through her nose. The coffee smell fills her. Soothes her (a little). "But I'm trying to change that."

"You? Change?"

"Mm-hmm. Yep. Me Miriam. Me change." She pulls out a pack of Lucky Strike cigarettes. "See these? Last cigarettes I am ever going to smoke."

"Going cold turkey?"

She whistles. "The coldest of turkeys. This turkey will be frozen solid with liquid nitrogen and whacked with a sledgehammer."

"That's a pretty big change."

She nods. "It is. And I'm running now."

"Running from what?"

"Har, har. Like, running-running. For exercise."

His mouth forms an "O." "Who are you and what have you done with Miriam Black?"

"Miriam Black is trying to find a future for herself. A future in which she hopefully will not speak of herself in the third person."

"Why now?"

She sighs. Does she get into this? Easier just to say some twee, sarcastic shit and drop that mic like a hot potato. But she's trying to do differently. Trying to do *better*. And she figures if there's ever any chance of getting Louis back . . .

Finally, she says: "Because it's possible. Because now there's this . . . itty-bitty twinkling light out there. And I'm reaching for it, man. Like a kid grabbing at a firefly." She thrusts out her chin, feels the iron filings in her spine line up, magnetized. "I told you, I'm going to get rid of this curse."

Even now, her whole body clenches at the thought. She needs it to be gone, but part of her (and not a small part of her, either) wants it to stay. Just looking around, she knows how three people in this place are going to die. The doe-eyed girl behind the counter: skin cancer in fifty-two years. The scraggly old hippie who handed Miriam her drink: he's on a moped when a pickup truck wipes him out, and what's left is a crashed, smashed remix of blood and meat and blue pastel metal. The old woman with the too-red lipstick by the front, the one Miriam bumped elbows with on accident ("on accident," wink wink): lung cancer, already settled into her crinkled-up tissue-paper body, dead in two years.

These visions are a part of her. She's a knitted scarf shot through with yarn made from dead hair and red veins. They've been a part of her for a long while—but now, she's worried that it's going bigger than that.

That they're becoming her, or she's becoming them.

Something bigger, weirder, worse.

Like, soon: this is all she'll be. Just a rock in place to break the river. Her only goal and desire to bat away the reaper's scythe. Fate's foe.

Fuck that.

She wants more for herself. Or less. Or just something *different*.

They talk for a while longer. But it's awkward, erratic, like the two of them are walking around on stilts and trying to look normal. And when they leave, there's this shallow, shitty little hug, this faint embrace as if between two people who will never see each other again, and when he's gone, Miriam sits for a while still and finishes her coffee. Then she goes into the bathroom and sobs into the sink and elbows a dent in the paper towel dispenser.

SIXTEEN

LIGHTNING CALLS, THUNDER ANSWERS

Miriam doesn't say anything.

The man on the other end speaks.

"Miriam?" the man asks. Same man she spoke to out there in the desert. As she stood there over the body of Steven McArdle. Same drawn-out drawl, slow as cold molasses. *How does he know my name?* She waits, says nothing. "Miriam, if you're there, I want you to listen."

"You have the wrong number," she says. She thinks: *Just hang up.*

"You have my friend's phone."

"Your friend tried to kill me—"

"And I can appreciate that. I don't want to hurt you. But there are some things I need, Miriam. I'd like that phone back, for starters. Pistol, too, though these are not essential. What I want is Isaiah."

"I don't know any Isaiah." Not a lie.

"I want the boy back."

"The boy." He must mean the little kid in the Superman shirt. From the Subaru. Miriam feels her pulse quicken. "Well, you can't have him."

"His mother is dangerous. He's better with us. We want him back."

Us? "Well, people in Hell want Popsicles, dude. I am sorry that I cannot accommodate. Now, I don't know who the fuck you are—"

"I'd come and find you, Miriam, so we could have this chat in person. But your friend here won't tell me where you are. We got your name out of him in a moment of great pain, but everything else—he's really bearing down. He does you great honor. You must really be special."

"My friend? I don't know who you're—"

A bellow of pain comes out of the phone. At first she doesn't recognize it, can't decipher an identity in the gargled scream, until that scream dissolves into two words: "Miriam! Run!"

It's Wade. From the gas station. The tow truck driver.

Gabby watches as Miriam's voice goes a mile a minute: "*You* listen to *me*; Wade isn't my friend. He doesn't know me, I don't know him. He can't help you, so just leave him the fuck alone—"

"He knows where you are. Got a receipt here for a tow. Means he took you somewhere, dropped you off. And yet he won't tell us. That's no matter how much we"—here a sound like a sack of flour dropped on a hard floor, followed by a yelp and bleat from Wade—"try to persuade him."

"Let him go. Just let him go."

"Tell me where you and Isaiah are. And we let him go."

The words spill out of her like dice out of a gambler's cup. "Whoa, whoa, wait, I don't really have the boy. Okay? His mom took him. Ran off. Left me there. You're digging up dead ground here, so just—"

"One more chance, Miriam. Where are you? *Where is the boy?*" A murmur of voices in the background. One of them a woman. Then Wade screams again. "Last chance. Last chance to do the right thing, Miriam."

Her lips form the words. The words that would give away the motel name. The room number. Everything. But she looks over at Gabby—her face crisscrossed with scars, her eyes wide and fearful. She thinks about how *close* she is. She can about reach out and touch a lock of Mary Scissors' hair now—

Wade is helping her out. She doesn't deserve it. He doesn't know her. They're not friends. He's just a guy, she's just a girl. He's the mark, she's the con.

She could help him out now. Could save him the way he's trying to save her. But she tells herself: He doesn't die. They can't kill him. She's seen his death and this isn't it. Miriam never asked this guy to stand up for her.

So, instead, what she says into the phone is:

"Your right thing isn't my right thing."

The man on the other end groans low in his throat. He sighs. "I'm sorry to hear that, Miriam. But you should know: there's a storm coming. I fear you're about to get swept up like trash in a bad wind. I'm sorry about your friend here."

She starts to scream for him to wait. Miriam begins babbling, telling him again that she can't help him, but maybe if they sat down, they could figure it out—

But she's yelling into a dead phone.

Nobody's there. The man hung up.

Miriam screams.

PART TWO

THE SCORPION
AND THE FROG

SEVENTEEN

NIE MÓJ CYRK, NIE MOJE MAŁPY

A gulf separates them now. Last night, Gabby insisted on knowing what was going on, and Miriam wouldn't tell her. All Miriam would say was how that guy she mentioned yesterday, the ex-Army guy, the interrogator, he told her this Polish phrase, this *idiom*, that goes:

Not my circus, not my monkeys.

Meaning, not my problem. Not my business.

And that's what she said to Gabby. *It's not my circus, not my monkeys. And it's not yours, either.* Of course Gabby persisted, in part because she actually foolishly cares and in part because the thread is off the sweater and who wouldn't want to pull it? But Miriam pushed back, and pushed back harder than she meant:

"Just go the fuck to sleep. Okay?"

Lights out. Bed. And now, Miriam is sleeping for shit. She feels dried up—the air here thin and hungry, like it's sucking all the life out of her. She tosses. She turns. Gabby sleeps rolled over, back to her.

All night, Miriam lies there, eyes open. Imagining what they did to Wade—that dumb fucker who went to bat for a woman he barely knew, a woman who gave him hell, a woman who didn't deserve the kindness he granted her in the face of some kind of torture.

The best comfort she manages is to remember that she knows things.

She knows how Wade dies.

And it happens when he's sixty-three.

When it happens, he doesn't look scarred up, like Gabby. Looked like he still had all his fingers, all his face parts.

It's the coldest of comfort, and it makes her feel no less shitty.

But she repeats to herself in the faintest whisper there in the dark: "Not my circus, not my monkeys. Not my circus, not my monkeys."

Whatever *that* is—the coming storm, the man on the phone, the boy in the Superman shirt with the crazy-ass gun-toting mother—it's not her problem. The world is full of awfulness. Lines of blood and bones and ash crisscrossing each other. She doesn't have to be at every intersection. A bird pecking at the dead.

I can be free.

She tries to close her eyes.

Then she hears a scuttling sound. A *scritch-a-scratch*. She thinks: *It's nothing*. Just the motel room air conditioner being an asshole. A little bang, a little rattle, a little skitter-scrape. But then something lands on her face—

Something with little legs.

She sits up suddenly, crying out. Whatever's on her face falls off and lands in her open hands—

A dark, small shape.

She knows what it is. Her eyes adjust—the meager light from the front windows of the motel room showing the tiny legs, the flat and almost headless body, the curve of its tail.

The scorpion hurries off. Disappearing under the covers.

Miriam feels dizzy.

Somewhere in the distance: sirens screaming.

She looks up.

The ceiling squirms.

Scorpions. Hundreds of them. *Thousands.* Hanging upside-down, crawling on the ceiling, the fan, in the corners of the room. Little legs going *ticky ticky ticky.* Whisper-click, scuttle-flick. Lights from a truck outside highlight their glistening backs, yellow and opaque, an infected color—

And a body hangs there with them. A human shape. Writhing under the carpet of crawling arachnids. They part. Louis leers down. Eyeless. Mouth opens. Scorpions rain from inside his mouth, from within the hollow puckers—

They drop against her, and she brushes them off, and she grits her teeth and thinks, *This is a dream, it's not real, don't freak out—*

Louis says, his words choked around swarming scorpions:

"The poison's in you, Miriam. You can't purge it now."

A stinger sticks in the back of her hand—

She lurches off the bed, feet tangling in the sheets—

Face first into the carpet. Stars behind her eyes. Her legs kick free of the sheets and she gets her feet under her—

Sunlight streams in through the window.

Gabby sits at the edge of the bed, flicking through channels on the TV. She looks over and says with no love, "Wondering when you'd wake your ass up."

Miriam tries to talk but her voice is like two pieces of porous stone grinding together—sparks and a dry brushfire burning in the well of her chest. She coughs. Rubs her eyes with the heels of her hands. "Time izzit?"

"Almost eleven."

"Oh."

She looks down on the floor, sees the two halves of the unsmoked cigarette from last night mashed into the carpet. Nits of tobacco speckling her one knee.

Gabby ignores her.

The channels go flip, flip, flip. Strobe-light images: A woman with a knife chopping herbs. A smiling celebrity on some smiling celebrity talk show. Someone painting a wall. A dead hooker and TV detectives standing over her. A cartoon goat chasing a cartoon donkey. A gas station fire. A game show—

Miriam says, "Wait. Go back."

There. The gas station fire.

Her heart stops.

All parts of her feel like they're floating away—muscle from bone, skin from muscle, skin cells from skin cells, all her molecules sheared from one another as she is dispersed like a cloud of particulate matter in a hard wind.

It's the Chevron. Out at the edge of the reservation.

On the news they're saying they have a body, a body they believe to be that of the attendant—and son of the owners—Wade Chee. Burned alive in the blaze. They're hauling him out—covered up on a gurney, one charred hand dangling out.

"No no no no," Miriam says, lurching toward the television and fixing her gaze upon it. "This isn't possible. There are rules. *There are rules.*"

One of those rules is she's never wrong.

Death is death. When she sees it, it's a fixed point in space—a thumbtack in the map that only *she* can move.

"Miriam, what are you—"

"Someone else moved the thumbtack."

"What?"

"Someone else is changing the rules. That guy dies—or was supposed to die—*decades* from now. Not last night. Not like this. Which means . . ." She searches for it. Which means what, exactly? It's not Wade. Or someone else is like her: someone else can break the bones of how this thing works. Or, the worst possibility of them all: Miriam's been wrong this whole time. The rules she thought were the rules never were. Just a delusion. A comforting lie.

She starts to hyperventilate. All parts of her are suffused suddenly with desperate desire. Cigarette. Louis. A drink. The white dashes on the highway flicking past as she runs far, far away. Her mother. God, really? Her mother? And yet there it is: she wants to see her mother again, wants to share a glass of that too sweet crème de menthe, wants to share a cigarette—and oh, hey, now it's all gone full circle again and the nic-fit storms through her like a spooked horse.

Teeth bite lip. What fingernails she has dig into her palms.

You killed him.

You killed Wade Chee.

A gentle hand finds her arm. Gabby. "Miriam. You okay?"

"I'm about five hundred miles past okay."

"What happened? Who is this man?"

Miriam says: "He's the one who drove me here. From the desert. That's it. He's nobody. He doesn't know me and I don't know him." She grits her teeth, makes an animal sound. "I'm like poison, Gabs. You gotta get away from me. Or you'll end up worse than you were before."

She's suddenly on the edge of the confessional. Teetering, tottering, like she's ready to tell Gabby: *You die soon, too, Gabs. You eat a bunch of pills because life grinds your pencil all the way down to the eraser and because you think you're ugly and nobody loves you and I wish I could stop it but—*

She bites that back.

Too many self-fulfilling prophecies.

But there, a tiny glimmer of hope: If I can be wrong about Wade Chee, maybe I can be wrong about Gabby.

Whatever. Fuck it all.

She needs to be done with this. The curse, closed off, sealed away and bricked off like that guy in the Poe story. *The Cask of C'mon-I'm-Fucking-Done-With-This-Shit-tillado.*

Miriam stands upright, like a prairie dog at the hole sensing danger. She starts throwing on clothes. Her hair mussed, every-thing rumpled, situation normal, all fucked up. "I'm going to the courthouse."

"Right now? Why?"

"*Because*," Miriam seethes, "because, because, because! Because I need this over with. I want to be done with all of it. And whatever happened with that guy at the gas station—it's all part of it. All part of the curse. I want it gone and I want it gone now. No time like the present."

Gabby hesitates. "I'll call a cab. We'll both go."

"No." That word, spoken too harshly, too sharply—the word sharpened like a prison shiv. Miriam tries to soften it: "Gabby, no. You gotta get away from me."

"Bullshit. If you're going, I'm coming."

"This is dangerous."

"So?"

"So?" Miriam barks a dead laugh. "Jesus, Gabs, it means you could get hurt. And I can't hack the idea of you getting hurt any more than you already have." The words *Have you seen your face? That's my fault* almost come launching full-tilt boogie out of her mouth, but she quickly recalls them before her vocal cords can make the sound.

"I'm coming. We'll go to Tucson together. You go to the court-house. I'll . . . get us another room somewhere. We have the money. We didn't have to pay that scuzzy prick. If they don't take cash, I'll use my card."

Miriam's about to protest and say that they could use the stolen card from the dead man in the desert. But that created the trail that led the bad man to burn down Wade Chee's gas station—with Wade in it. Reluctantly, Miriam nods. "But you don't have to do this. I told you, none of this was on you."

"I'm in this. I've kept the trip together so far, haven't I?"

Miriam has to admit: she has. Gabby put together the budget.

Bought the maps and plotted their routes. She's gotten their rooms. Made the whole plan.

"Okay," Miriam says. "Fine." Four words in the English language pain her greatly to say because to say them feels like a kind of weakness, but right now, all four seem somehow appropriate: "Thank you. And . . . I'm sorry."

Gabby kisses her temple. "Now the big question: How do we get to Tucson? Only about an hour away. We could take the bus."

Miriam has no intention of taking the bus.

Fuck the bus. The bus is where humanity is at its grossest. People picking their toenails and eating soup and puking Canadian whiskey on themselves. Buses smell like piss and BO and Doritos. Every bus—even school buses, if Miriam remembers correctly—are full of the squawking, stinking damned. Buses are terrible and Miriam will not abide a bus ride in this heat. Or in the cold. Or anywhere at any time, not with a goat, not with a stoat, not near a boat. No boxes, foxes, bucks, or fucks. Never, ever, ever again.

Fuck. The. Bus.

Miriam says, "You really want to be on this adventure with me?"

"I do."

"Like, really for real really?"

"Really for real. Really."

"Then let's go make some trouble."

EIGHTEEN

RING OF KEYS

The motel office is plywood paneling. A plastic fern stands in the corner, strung up with wisps of cobweb. Berber carpet is stained with who-knows-what, and Miriam is thankful the buzzing lights above her head are fluorescent and not UV. Behind the industrial metal desk sits a grade-A goober, the motel clerk. He's here all the time. Sleeps at the desk.

Like he's doing now.

He doesn't snore so much as he hisses. Like wind through tall grass.

Got an overbite so big, he might swallow his own jaw if he's not careful.

Miriam says, "We need a new key."

He keeps snoring. Gabby gives Miriam a look and a shrug.

Miriam kicks the desk.

The goober startles awake.

"I need a new key."

His tongue smacks against the roof of his mouth. He itches his cheek, where a band of adult acne has bubbled up like lava from broken earth. "Huh?"

"New. Key. Room. Six."

"Where'd yours go?"

She flips through a mental catalog of snarky, jerky answers. Something about proctology on a gorilla's ass, but she just doesn't have it in her. All she says is "I lost it, okay?"

"That's a problem because we're gonna have to change the locks."

"Why?"

"Because that means anyone can break in now."

"Anyone can always do that. Since you use actual keys instead of keycards, all anybody has to do is go out and make a copy, and then they have that key forever. Which means that person could, say, copy the old key or the new key or any key at all and then years later come back, waltz right in, and serial kill whoever is sleeping in that bed."

The goober—who, by the name placard on the desk, she sees is named Kyle—just sighs. He's done. She can see him deflate like a bouncy castle punctured by some kid's braces. "Fine, fine, I'll get you another one. Hold on."

He gets up, stretches like a cat coming off a windowsill, then plods his gangly-dangle limbs into a room in the back. She hears rattling and banging. The jingle of metal. She gives Gabby the nod.

Gabby wanders into the back with him. And she really turns it on. Miriam hears her say: "Oh! Hey! Wow. Nice office back here. You must have a lot of authority. You're basically, like, the owner, right?" And of course he leans into it, talking up how important he is and basically he's the owner, *basically*.

Meanwhile, Miriam goes around to his desk.

Starts opening drawers, quiet as she can muster.

Nothing. Shit.

But then she pulls the middle drawer. Pens, paper clips, a rusty letter opener that looks like it hasn't opened a letter since Nixon was in office, a scattering of thumbtacks, and then? Bingo. A ring of keys.

Car keys.

She hoped they'd be in here. Guy like him can't keep a big set of keys like this in the pocket of his cargo shorts. She scoops them up, pops them in her own pocket, closes the drawers.

She heads half out the door then calls: "Gabs! I found the keys! Tell the nice man I found them and we're good."

Gabby comes out and Kyle trails behind like a lost puppy. *Sorry, dingleberry, but the ride's over,* Miriam thinks. She throws up her hands and makes a funny face. "Sorry! Didn't check my back pocket. I'm so silly."

"You ladies wanna hang out later?" Kyle asks.

"Sure," Gabby says, surprising Miriam. She bats her eyelashes and playfully rests her fingernail on her pouty lower lip. "We should certainly repay the kindness of such a handsome man. See you here at eight?"

"I'll be here," he says, licking his lips.

The two of them hurry out, laughing as they go.

NINETEEN

OF COURSE IT'S A WIZARD VAN

Of course it's a wizard van.

The parking lot isn't exactly crammed full of cars. The motel is mostly empty because it's a motel outpost in the middle of Arizona's dry and dust-swept vagina. So, when she pokes through the few vehicles out there—a pickup, another pickup, a Chevy Aveo, a chopper—and she comes upon the lavender van with the mural of a golden-bearded wizard shooting lightning out of his crystal-tipped staff (lightning that then electrocutes a series of rainbow dragons: red, blue, yellow, green, orange), well, she thinks she has a winner.

Gabby says, "Are we really doing this?"

"We are really doing this."

"This is bad."

"This is *very* bad. And that's good."

"I can't. We shouldn't. We could go back in, just give him money—he'd probably relish the idea of selling it. We have cash—"

Miriam unlocks the door. "Too late." She throws her bag inside.

"We haven't stolen it yet. We can just get a taxi."

Miriam nods as if, yeah, sure, we can do that, but then she hops in the driver's seat anyway and pops the passenger side. "Let's take this ugly turdboat for a drive. Kyle won't know."

"Miriam—"

"The longer you stand there, the likelier it is he'll come out and see us stealing his van."

That does it. Gabby flings her bag onto the floor and jumps in.

The van smells like weed and spilled beer. The dashboard is cracked plastic. The steering wheel is swaddled in camo-pattern duct tape.

The engine rumble-grumbles to life. The CD player spins up and starts playing, of all the songs, Ace of Base's "I Saw the Sign."

Together, they drive to Tucson.

TWENTY

THE LAWS OF GODS AND MEN

Gabby, thankfully, has her shit together. Miriam's plan is mostly just *drive south and eventually we'll run smack dab into Tucson*, but turns out that plan is actually very bad. Gabby has maps on her phone. She plots a course, finds a motel, and off they go to a Motel 6 about ten minutes from the courthouse.

They get a room, 208. The two of them crash there for the night. In the morning, Miriam drives over to the Superior Court building. The ten-minute drive turns into a forty-five minute trip because of course she gets lost—she arrives by the grace of swallowing her pride and asking a couple rando tourists for directions.

The courthouse looms. It's a massive square structure. Maybe ten stories tall. All white, punctuated by bands of black glass.

Now a new problem: she has no idea what to do.

It's not like Mary Scissors is going to be here, just hanging out. (Just to be sure, Miriam gives a good look up and down the parking lot in the rare instance that the universe has chosen to be kind to her. It has chosen no such thing. Not that she'd recognize her easily—the last photos she's seen of the woman were at her brother's house, and they were easily two decades old.) So, what then? *All right,* she thinks, *the woman is on probation for something.*

Which means there's a probation officer inside. And maybe

meeting the probation officer will tell her something. Anything. Any little clue that will lead her to Mary Scissors.

The day is warm. The air, dry. Sky so blue it looks like it was painted on.

Let's do this.

Inside the courthouse: metal detectors up front. Panic suddenly shocks her heart like a pair of defib paddles—*I have the gun.* The gun is in the van.

But she does have a knife. A small lockback knife.

But by the time she's realizing it, they're already ushering her through. And of course the metal detector goes off. And an old white dude and an old Hispanic dude come up on each side of her, sleepily telling her to empty her pockets—white guy named Hugo, the Latino gent named Jorge—and she winces and does as they demand. The knife clatters into the plastic tray. Gulp.

The cuffs clap around her wrists fast, or so she expects. But it doesn't happen. Instead, Hugo and Jorge just nod to each other, tell her to take her stuff back, go on in, have a nice day, miss.

She's almost tempted to stab one, just as a reminder why you shouldn't let people with knives into important government buildings, but that might just be the persistent nic-fit that's haunting her body like a furniture-flinging poltergeist.

Instead, she asks them, "Probation?"

Jorge says, "This floor. Down at the end, through the hall."

Hugo adds, "It says *probate* on it."

Miriam nods. Heads that way. Passes by a crowd of normals— lawyer types in black suits and dour faces, like each of them is attending a funeral for American justice. A judge in his robes. A couple chatty ladies in pastels. A lost-looking boy by a water fountain, noisily slurping.

Feet echoing on white stone.

They stare at her as she passes. They're probably used to every degenerate and deviant who walks through here, and they probably stare at them the same way they stare at her. Still. Her hair, an electroshock mess. Her white tee torn at the edges. Jeans so frayed that if she were to sneeze, they'll probably explode into a pile of threads and leave her standing there in her panties. They watch her.

Whatever. Go on and stare, fuckballs.

Into the probation offices. Glass door. Inside, a whole different world. Like a regular office. Gray cubicles. Beige tile. Drop ceiling and buzzing lights.

A woman sits at a desk at the front. Big hair, so big it looks like it's trying to eat her pink-cheeked, peach-lipped face. "Can I help you?"

"Ahhhhh." Miriam hears the sound drawn out of her mouth as she's lost for any meaningful lie. Suddenly, she feels off her game, a bird batted off its perch by the events of the last couple days. *Lie, you lying liar. You're good at this. Your two specialties are telling hard truths and spinning crafty lies.* "Ahhh, well. I'm . . . looking for someone."

So clever.

The woman gives an expectant stare.

"Who . . . were you looking for, hon?"

"A probation officer."

"Well, you've come to the right place." A bored smile. Placating.

What's the whole point of probation? Miriam thinks. *Checking up on ex-cons, yeah? Making sure they aren't on drugs, have a bed they sleep in every night, have a job they go to and—there,* that's it, that's the key.

"I'm an employer," Miriam says, settling into the groove. "One of your . . . probates? Probees? She's a waitress at this roller derby juke joint place I just opened up on the south side of town. We show movies and serve beer and then also there's gladiatorial combat with roller skates—it's like Medieval Times, but not at all like Medieval Times. I need to have a confab with her parole officer?"

"Oh. That sounds interesting. What's the last name, hon?"

"Scissors." Wince. "*Stitch*."

"That'd be Lela Quintero. Just head down the hall—" She points, and it's not a hallway but rather a channel carved between cubicles. "Turn right at the end by the copy machine and her office is right there. Near the water cooler." Miriam nods, thanks her, starts to walk away, but the woman says: "Hey, what's your place called again? That sure sounds interesting—I have a cousin who is kind of, what's the word, *alternative*, and he might like that place—"

"We don't have a name."

"You don't—well, how can you not have a name?"

"We're just a symbol. Like Prince had. It's a roller skate inside fire and—you know, it's very exclusive." She waggles her fingers, then walks on.

Miriam can feel the woman's eyes burning holes in her back.

Down the hall. A big jowly fucker with a knobby yam nose is standing there by the copier, and Miriam has to shimmy past him. "No, no, don't move or anything," she growls at him, and he just grunts. She half expects to see how he dies but it's her skin against his sweat-stained lemon-yellow shirt, and she is spared seeing him dying on a toilet or having his heart explode or whatever other indignity awaits him during his final hours.

A quick, clumsy pirouette and there's a nameplate outside the cubicle.

L. Quintero.

Another metal desk. Nobody behind it.

Good. Miriam works fast. She scoots over to the other side of the desk, opens the top file drawer—no, not in this one. The one below it is pay dirt. She flips through the second half of the alphabet, to the S folder—

There. Mary Stitch. She starts to tug the sheet up. Sees her name, her birthdate—11/7/1962. She starts to slide it out—

"Hey!"

She reflexively lets go, and the paper slides back into its folder.

There, standing at the cubicle entrance, is a woman with dark, inelegant curls. She stares out from underneath a pair of dark, tented brows. Her mouth is a scowl. Her eyes are a scowl. Everything about her is a scowl.

"Hi," Miriam says. Bright and shiny and faking it all.

"Get away from there. That's not your business."

"Oh, I was just trying to find out information on one of your . . . people? Mary Stitch? If I could just get her sheet so I can contact her—"

The woman sighs, then points to a non-spinny, non-rolly chair in the corner. "Sit. What's this about?"

Miriam winces, then wanders around the side of the desk, feeling like the opportunity is so close, and yet so far. Slipping farther away with every step. But maybe she can make hay out of this yet. She plasters that fake smile on her face as she hovers near the chair. "Yeah, it's just—I'm her employer, and she has *not* been showing up for work. So."

"Down at the Cluck Bucket," the woman says as she passes Miriam and takes a seat behind her desk.

"Y . . . yes."

"The one on 9th."

"The Cluck Bucket on 9th, yeah, yep. I'm the manager. Well. *Assistant* manager, but between you and me, the real manager, Dan, is a little—" And here she mimics him snorting coke. "He's *busy*, if you know what I mean."

Wink, wink.

"Mary doesn't work at the Cluck Bucket," Quintero says.

"Huh?"

"I just made it up. The Cluck Bucket. It's not a real place. You wanna tell me what this is really about?"

"Whoa, holy shit, you are hyper-aggro, lady." Miriam conjures an incredulous laugh. "Super-distrusting. That is . . . that's no way to be."

The parole officer plants her hands on the edge of the desk and leans forward like a puma poised to leap. Her face darkens—it's like watching all the streetlights down the block go black one by one. "You think people don't come up in here all the time, lying to me to get information on parolees? We keep tabs on all types: gang-bangers, thieves, snitches, dealers, hookers. Every week, someone comes creeping in here, some pimp wants to know where his bitch went, some thug wants to know where that informing-ass traitor-ass motherfucker is working, and so you come up in here looking like a prossie—"

"Hey, I am no prostitute, not that I judge prostitutes—"

"—who gives five-dollar handies to truck drivers—"

"Whoa. That seems cheap. Too cheap, if I'm being honest."

"And you think I'm gonna give you the goods on Mary? Not a chance. Only chance I'm gonna give you is to get up out of that chair and get out of here right now before I call the police and they can see what you're really about."

Miriam freezes. A cold wave skims the back of her neck. She can't lose this chance. This is all she has. "Please," she says. "I need to speak with Mary. Even if you just . . . tell me when she comes here, or, or, or maybe you could pass her a message for me, just a note—"

"Get out."

"A Post-it note! A few words. A phone number. Something."

The woman reaches across the desk and grabs Miriam's wrist—

TWENTY-ONE

THE FIRST DOMINO

Rare drops of rain streaking the window behind her desk. It's twenty-one days from now, and Lela Quintero is standing there in her office, hair pulled over her face like a curtain threatening to close, and she's stabbing one finger down on some papers sitting there in an open manila folder. Her other finger is thrusting hard against a woman's breastbone—a woman named Mary Stitch, a woman whose face is sallow and lean, whose gray hair is poorly tamed by a ponytail, and Lela is saying, *This is it; this is the last straw—*

Then somewhere, gunshots.

Pop, pop, pop. And Mary, her eyes go closed, and she clasps her hands together as if in prayer, hands flat that then go to fists as if the prayer becomes all the more desperate, less an entreaty to a merciful God and more an angry accusation to an uncaring one.

People screaming now, heads popping up over cubicle walls like prairie dogs hearing a train-whistle.

Lela says to Mary, "Sit down; stay here."

But Mary, she just stays standing. Rocking back and forth, heel to toe, heel to toe, mumbling something.

Pop, pop, pop.

"I'm sorry," Mary says.

But Lela doesn't hear her, and she turns to say "What?"

Mary now takes her two fists and presses them hard against

her eyes, so hard the tendons in her wrists stand out like the strings of a plucked guitar—

Then a terrible sound from above.

Boom.

Boom.

BOOM.

Like a giant boulder crashing down, louder and louder from the floors above—everything is shaking, the lights are flickering, *bzzt, bzzt,* the screaming is there but is swallowed by that terrible sound—

And then it's fire and smoke and debris—an explosion rocks the corner of the building and everything that Lela is and believes is erased, torn asunder by chunks of white brick, by spinning metal shrapnel from the cubicle frames, melted plastic and scalding toner from the copier, all of it a wave of claws and teeth—

TWENTY-TWO

INTO THE STORM

Miriam wrenches her hand away, nearly falls over the chair. The smell of smoke still sticks in her nose. She can feel the heat of fire on her cheeks.

Lela just sits there. Staring. "You're an addict. You're tweaking."

You have no idea.

Miriam swallows hard. "I have to go."

"Go. Get the hell out of here, junkie."

Her arms pulled in tight, she is the needle that threads her way back through the cubicles. The woman at the desk says good-bye but her voice is distant, echoing, and Miriam's guts roil. She hurries back out of the office and into the main lobby. There. Bathroom. Now.

She throws herself into it, knees open a stall, dry-heaves for ten minutes.

Every heave, she tries to steady herself. Tries to put out of mind the feeling of detonation. The booming. The shuddering. The air clapping against her. The rain of stones a half-second later. The boiling air, the consumptive flame.

But closing the door on those thoughts just opens the door for worse ones: Wade Chee screaming over the phone, the taste of a dead man in the desert greasy on her hungry tongue and between her rending beak, her mother in a hospital bed, the rising waters of a storm-churned river, a plague mask, a falling axe, a saw cutting through ankle bone, a knife stuck deep in a truck driver's eye—

A knocking on the stall door.

A man's voice: "Hey, uhhh, you okay in there?"

She stands up. Wipes spit from her mouth. Bile from her chin. Miriam opens the stall door, sees a narrow man standing there—he's slight, almost delicate, but trying to look tough with his sharp-cut lawyer suit and his Stetson cowboy hat. His eyes go wide and he stammers, "You're in the men's room."

The starveling monkey shrieking at the back of her mind, the one that pulls all the levers and smashes all the buttons, tells her what to do and she lurches forward and grabs his hand—

He's naked and frail and knock-kneed, standing up in a porcelain tub thirty years from now, all parts of him trembling like a shaved, nervous dog, trembling so hard he's almost blurry, and his wilted dick points down and his little button nipples point up and he's dripping wet—water clinging to a birdlike frame peppered with gray snarls of body hair, and he's calling out, "Are you coming to get me out? Darren? Darren! Are you there? Bah." And then he takes one step out of the tub and there's a sound like *swwwwwrk!* and his right leg goes way too far left and he falls hard, the side of his head hitting the faucet, neck snapping like a thundercrack—

—and even here she can feel the faint Parkinson's tremble in his hand. Parkinson's, a cruel disease, one that doesn't often kill outright but is a demonic prankster, setting up traps that *will* kill you.

But she can't help him, and the monkey inside still howls. It bares its teeth and shrieks for death, to know death, to *be* death, and so Miriam shoulders past him, pushes to the bathroom door, and goes to the elevator.

Her finger hovers over the buttons.

It chooses the third floor. Chooser of the slain. Chooser of elevator buttons.

Third floor. Court offices. White walls, tan carpet, bad paintings of desert flowers. She's led by the chin now, as if the Reaper has the curl of its scythe hooked in her cheek like a fishhook and is dragging her along. This is a ride she doesn't want, but she's on it now, and all parts of her feel callously, fiendishly alive—bright and colorful and horrible, a woman electrocuted after sucking on the broken socket in a string of Christmas lights, buzz buzz blinky blinky.

A woman in a mauve pants suit. Passing by. Head down, staring at a cell phone. Here. Now. Miriam thrusts out an elbow. Knocks the phone out of the woman's hands. Miriam bends down at the same time to "help her pick it up," just brushes her cheek with the woman's ear—

Again the woman has her head down, but this time her nose is buried in a thick file full of pages, something about divorce, something about splitting up assets, and then she hears it from somewhere downstairs—the faint popping of gunfire—and she gives a look toward an old judge tottering past, his belly straining against his black robes. He says, "That what I think it is?" And she's about to say something but those words are cut off from coming from above, *boom, boom, boom*, and then detonation—this one coming from the back, the ground shaking and breaking apart, brick and pipe and smoke and swallowing her whole—

"Sorry, I am just so clumsy today," the woman says.

"It's me," Miriam says, stammering. "My fault. Sorry." She stumbles left, nearly tripping on herself. Head forward, the woman gone, forgotten now—there, a door ahead. Glass, frosted. Register of Wills, Clerk of Orphans' Court—she has no idea what that last part means or why you'd let a bunch of orphans have a court all to themselves, but the law is absurd, so who cares.

Inside, she sees an old Hispanic woman by a whiteboard,

black pen squeaking across it, writing down court dates in a big calendar—

Miriam doesn't even pretend. She flings caution into a woodchipper and grabs the woman's hand—

The woman hurries down the hall, toward the doorway marked Register of Wills, Clerk of Orphans' Court. She hears the gunfire, feels the vibration in the floor as the explosions detonate above—dust, buzzing lights, breaking ceiling, an explosion, the door launches off its hinges, glass everywhere in a belch of smoke. A filing cabinet creaks and falls onto her, breaking her little bird bones—

"Hey!" the woman protests.

Miriam mumbles, "Sorry, thought you were someone else."

She sees a long-cheeked man, tongue sitting on his bottom lip like he's a frog hoping to catch flies. He's just hanging out by the coffee maker staring off into nothing. She darts past and pats him on the cheek—

He's standing in the corner that detonates, primping up a plastic plant like it needs the attention, and the explosion launches forth from that very spot—a monster leaping from its cave, a trapdoor spider of smoke and flame reaching out and dragging him down and tearing him to swift pieces—

The man says nothing. She just mutters an apology.

More. More. More. She needs *more*.

She tells herself she needs it because that's how she finds out what's happening, but this hissing whisper from the back of her mind asks: *Is that really true? Do you need it, or are you just enjoying the show, you sick little fucko?*

Miriam flits from death to death, from doom to doom, like a crow picking a little from this carcass, a little from that one—a choosy maggot, a fickle coyote. She reaches out and touches a lawyer. A judge. A clerk. A secretary. All death. All of them here when it happens. Erased by the explosion. Miriam can feel what it's like to be torn apart by it: some vaporized in an instant, others rent more incompletely by stone and glass, others dead by the shockwaves and aftereffects—

Now people are talking. Pointing. Who is this woman running a circuit around their office? Bumping, touching, grabbing. She hears murmurs: *Call the police.* And she wants to laugh: *You idiots have no idea, I'm not the danger, I'm the one trying to figure out who murders you, all of you—*

And then she thinks: *the gunshots.* She doesn't know about those.

Back to the elevator, then. She ducks into an elevator as a cop comes out of the other one. A crumple-nosed slob in a rumpled uniform spies her, yells, "Hey!" just as the doors ding and slide closed. She stabs the button to go back down.

Once more, ground floor of the courthouse.

She heads for the exits.

If anyone knows—

It's the guards.

Her breath slides cold through her teeth as she goes to Hugo, the old white guard, and she thinks: *Act normal, don't act like an animal, like a freak, like some weird tweaker who jills off every time she catches a whiff of morgue stink.* And she says, trying to keep the tremors in her voice invisible and contained:

"I just want to thank you for doing such a good job here." And she thrusts out her hand, and the liver-spotted old white gent reaches out and takes and shakes her hand—

Three men in full camo, face masks, vests, the whole militarized enchilada—they've got black rifles tricked out, and they march forward and spread out, firing into the foyer. A pasty white woman with four Starbucks coffees in a carrier sees her hairline torn back by a .223 bullet. A black man in a fringed denim jacket yells, starts to run, catches a bullet right through the throat and out the back of his spine, his head flopping around like it's just barely stitched on. Hugo reaches down, feels his heart thundering in his chest like the drumbeat hooves of a cattle stampede and he feels for the gun at his hip, but one of the men turns, points the rifle, and one shot—*pop!*—and that fast-beating heart has its pulse cut quick by a hot lead injection at eleven hundred feet per second. The old man drops, barely holds himself up by the metal detector. One of the shooters now winds through the detector, and as he does, the old man sees the shooter has his arm exposed, and ink crawling up it—the name JANICE in flowery script along the forearm, and on the bulging bicep, across skin bumpy with earthworm veins, another tattoo: a dead tree with lightning striking it, four words painted indelibly underneath, A STORM IS COMING. Beneath that tattoo, an uneven oval scar, like a cigar burn—or a bullet wound. Then the shooter points the rifle right at the old man's head and the gun goes off and so does the top of the old man's head—

Miriam cries out and steps back—

The elevator at the other end of the downstairs dings.

A cop yells.

The old security guard up front hasn't caught on yet, hasn't heard the yelling, and he offers Miriam a soft smile and says, "Why, thank you, miss."

And then she's hurrying the hell out of there.

TWENTY-THREE

ROASTING MARSHMALLOWS

Miriam orbits the courthouse a few times, just to make sure the cop isn't following her anymore. When she's sure, she goes back to the van, opens the back, finds a ratty old loveseat back there, and curls up on it.

She sobs like a hurricane. Gulping gale winds and floods from her eyes.

In three weeks, this building will be destroyed. At least partly. And many of the people inside will die. Either by the explosion or at the hands of the gunmen in the lobby. Bullets and bombs. A mass murder. A terrorist act.

And it all starts to wind together. A coil of barbed wire around her wrists, forming a pair of handcuffs, shackling her to this thing raw and bloody. She wants to say, *This isn't my business, this isn't my problem, it is neither my circus nor my monkeys*, but that is no longer true. Mary Stitch—Mary Scissors, Mary Skizz—is in there when it happens. Which means she dies in three weeks. Worse, the men in the lobby? Same tattoo and motto as the rifleman in the desert. The one who tried to kill her and tried to kill that boy's mother, Gracie. The one tied to the same group that killed Wade Chee in looking for her.

Miriam wants to leave. Her greatest desire right now is to reach up, pull the ripcord, and eject way the fuck out of this burning, guttering plane. Before it crashes. Before it kills them all.

But now? She can't.

"You know you like it," comes a voice from the front seat.

She startles, rolling off the couch and into a crouch. Already she reaches for the knife in her back pocket, opening it with a flick—

Wade Chee leans around the front seat, stares into the back.

He looks the same.

Except for his eyes. Those are like crispy campfire marshmallows. Black charflake on the outside. Gooey, goopy white on the inside.

"Fuck off," Miriam spits.

"Come on," Not-Wade says. When he speaks, little embers cough from his mouth—tiny fiber optic filament points glowing bright before going dark. "This is your jam, Miriam Black. This is your bread and butter; this is your sweet spot. This is your circus and"—here he spreads his arms out, and she can hear, if not see, the crinkly sound of burned skin breaking, like potato chips under a stepping foot—"these most certainly are your monkeys."

"I don't want any of this."

Wade's melting, ruined eyes narrow. Forcing tacky white rivulets to run down his cheek, bubbling, steaming. "Really? *Really?* Reeeaaaaally? I think you do. A part of you knows this is where you belong. Right in the middle of the shitstorm. Your heart races. You feel awake and alive in ways you never did before. When you got wrapped up with saving your big trucker boyfriend a few years back, you woke up. You found you had *power*. Riverbreaker—the stone that parts the waters. Fate's foe—the one who can slap away the Reaper's hand. You got used to it. You started to like it. And you like all of *this*, too."

Miriam lurches up. She hard-charges to the front and jams her knife in his neck. "I don't. You're lying."

Wade giggles and gurgles. "So violent. Like a feral cat. We

like that about you, Miriam. You get things *done*. We hope you stay on board with us for a long time. We'd hate to see you go. Though we do have one helluva severance package for you when the time comes—"

A sound comes up out of her like she's dead-lifting a refrigerator, and before she knows what's happening, she's plunging the knife in and out of Not-Wade's face, stitching the blade from chin to brow—

Her eyes refocus.

She's just stabbing the seat.

Because the Trespasser isn't real. Or, at least, isn't a *physical* being. Maybe a hallucination. Maybe a ghost, or a demon, or some part of herself projected. Maybe her dead child, stolen from her by a woman with a red snow shovel, a dead child grown up into a proper specter and haunting his terrible mother.

Miriam paws for the keys in her pocket and starts the van. If she's going to have a conversation with somebody, it's going to be someone real.

KEY WEST

"You're fucking kidding me," Gabby says.

"Not so much," Miriam answers. A bottle of Blue Moon beer, slick with condensation, hangs in Miriam's hand, her fingers forming the spider legs that cling to the neck of her prey. Gabby watches her drink it. Every time she takes a sip, she makes a face. Miriam does not seem to like beer.

"You think I'll go with you? Are you out of your gourd?"

Miriam shrugs. "At least a little. Maybe all the way out of my gourd."

The two of them sit on the porch of Gabby's house, asses planted on white wicker furniture like they're a pair of genteel ladies instead of the two *un*natural disasters that they are. Miriam just showed up here. She just fucking *showed up*, and did she go for the small talk, *Hey how are you what have you been doing sorry about your scarred-up face, Gabster*? Hell, no. She jumped straight into the piranha waters with *Hey, wanna go on a road trip with me?*

Thing is, any time Gabby looks at Miriam, all she sees is her own life reflected back in a mocking reminder: a dog-eaten puzzle with half the pieces missing, a world broken by the earthquake that was Ashley Gaynes and his knife. Ashley Gaynes, made who he was because of Miriam. And now Gabby, made who *she* is because of Miriam too.

Every cell in her body is trying to free itself from its prison and run the other way. Miriam once said she was like a poisonous animal with all its strange colors acting as a warning sign: Gabby looked it up. It's called aposematism, which she thought had something to do with Jewish people, but it's a scientific term for exactly what Miriam described—bright colors painted in warning.

"You want a cigarette?" Gabby asks suddenly. It's weird to feel like *Oh, I'm being rude*, because Miriam is the spiritual manifestation of rudeness. Maybe Gabby is trying to do the opposite thing and show Miriam what it's like to be an actual human being. "I don't smoke, but I might have a pack around here. Weed, too. Or a Cuban cigar if you want to chomp on a dog turd—"

"I don't smoke anymore." The way Miriam says it, though, all her body seems to shrivel up like a dying bug. Maybe it's not a lie, but Gabby thinks the woman wants a cigarette bad enough to stab somebody. "I'm trying to do better. To be better."

"Oh."

"*Oh?* You said that like—"

"I said it like what?"

"Like you're not hopeful."

"No, it's just—you're you. You don't seem like the type to change. You were pretty comfortable with who you are. Or were. Or whatever."

"Well, I'm trying to fix some fucked-up stuff." The way Miriam says it, she's angry now. Defensive. If she were a dog, the hair between her shoulders would be bristling like a brush.

Gabby feels unexpected disappointment. Which is twisted, isn't it? She should applaud Miriam's efforts to be a better person. She should be throwing her a parade with big trumpets and crashing cymbals and a whole float that says THANK YOU FOR NOT TRYING TO FORCE THE WORLD TO DEAL WITH YOUR TOXIC BS. And yet, Gabby admired Miriam for knowing exactly what she was and leaning into it, even if what she was happened to be a drunken clown car crashing head-on into a tractor-trailer carrying beehives.

"I'm here to see Mom," Miriam says. "Deal with some of her stuff. Then I'm back on the road again and . . ." She swigs at the beer, makes another face.

"You said you're looking for someone?"

"A woman named Mary."

Gabby arches an eyebrow. "What does Mary have for you?"

"Mary is going to fix me."

"Fix you?" She almost laughs. "Okay. Sure." Her hand instinctively moves to her face, feeling the puffy ridges of scars there, like the solder in stained glass. Gabby stands up suddenly and says, "The last time we did this thing, it was fun and—you know, *whee*—but I don't want to Thelma and Louise with you again. I can only go over so many cliffs."

Miriam stands too. "I don't need you that way."

"What way do you need me, then?"

"I need—I *want* a friend. Okay? We could be friends."

"When you and I get together . . ." Gabby frames her scarred face with her hands like she's a film director framing a shot. "Ta-da."

"Yeah. No. You're right. Totally right. I don't blame you. I'll leave you alone. Have a good rest of your life, Gabs." With that, Miriam starts to step off the porch. Gabby says to Miriam's back:

"Good luck with this . . . woman you want to find. I hope she fixes you." Her brow wrinkles up. "Though I'm at a loss how another woman will fix you."

Miriam turns slowly. "You don't know, do you." A statement more than a question. "Of course you don't. I never told you."

"Told me what?"

"I have this . . . power. A gift, a curse. And this thing?" A long sigh escapes Miriam's lips. She bares her teeth—the signs of a nic-fit, maybe? "This thing has rules." Then she tells Gabby a story. A strange story. An *impossible* story.

And a story that helps it all make sense. A special kind of sense. But it's like scattered pieces brought together to make a picture.

Soon as Miriam's done telling the story, Gabby decides. She makes the decision because she has to know more. She has to know if it's really true. And if it *is* true, then what Miriam Black goes through on a day-to-day basis is a horror show unlike anything Gabby could have imagined.

Gabby tells her that she hates Florida and she wants to leave.

"Let's go on a road trip together, Miriam Black. As friends."

"As friends."

And their fates are sealed with a handshake and an awkward hug.

TWENTY-FOUR

SWEPT UP IN A TERRIBLE WIND

She parks the wizard van at the Motel 6. The sorcerer cooling his heels, the dragons frozen in place, the battle between them ongoing and eternal.

She takes a moment to compose herself. An odd action for her. *Since when do I care what other people think of me?* Is that what this is? Is it a strength or is it a weakness? She can't tell. Fuck it. She heads upstairs to their room.

Already as the door starts to drift open, she knows something's wrong. The way it feels. The air in the room: still, too still, too strange. Every molecule unsettled.

Before the door is all the way open, she's got the knife back out—blade flashing with the snap of the wrist.

A man sits on the edge of the bed.

Broad shoulders. A two-day beard growth—scratchy and rough, like you could clean your boot on his chin. A disarming smile in the midst of it.

He leans forward, hands on knees. "Miriam. Come in."

She knows that voice. The man from the phone.

"Where is Gabby?" Miriam snarls.

"Your friend is fine," he says. A pistol sits on his knee, covered mostly by the flat of his hand. She curses herself: the other gun, the one she stole, is still in the damn van. *Shit.*

"How'd you find me?"

He hesitates. "That's my little secret."

"Fuck you and your secrets. You'd better talk quick because I'm rattlesnake-fast. You'll point. You'll shoot. But by the time I flop over dead in your lap, you'll have *my* knife sticking in the side of *your* neck." Everything feels like it's pulled taut—a choking rope, a fraying wire, a bow dragged slow across violin strings. She points the knife at him with a shaking hand. She cuts the air with a castrating swipe: *swish swish*.

"Settle down. I want to be friends. My name is Ethan. Ethan Key. Why don't you close that door so we don't attract any other new friends?"

She hesitates. A part of her thinks, *Just run*. Stable door is still open. She could bolt like a coltish horse. Gabby will be fine. Once they know she's hit the trails, they'll ditch her. *Or cut her throat and dump the body. Or burn her up like they burned Wade. Goddamnit. Goddamnit!*

With her heel, she gently eases the door shut.

The lock engages.

All parts of her hum like wasp wings.

Ethan says, "Things have changed. I figured you for a fly in the ointment, but now I'm thinking different. Wade seemed to think so. Said you knew things about people. Things nobody else could know."

She stiffens. "Wade told you that."

"In a manner of speaking." That disarming smile flinches a little. Twitch, twitch. "I have an interest in people like you."

"Bitches with knives?"

"People who can change things. Change the whole world, even."

"You got the wrong girl. Whatever he told you, Wade was just selling you a story. Maybe if you wouldn't have tortured him and killed him—"

The man stands. Hand curled around the gun. "Wade was

not a good man. I don't blame you for letting him die the way you did. He once raped a girl; you know that? High school. The school covered it up, no conviction."

Through clamped teeth she says, "You're lying."

"Telling you the facts as I know them. I believe in being straight with people. Honest to a fault." Ethan shrugs. "Truth is hard. Most people who you think are good often aren't, I suspect you already got that part figured out."

You have no idea.

"And I'm supposed to trust you?"

"No. Not yet. But you are going to come with me."

"Eat me. You try to take me anywhere, I'll scream. I'll cut you. I'll scream. It won't end well for anyone."

"Including your friend Gabrielle."

It's just Gabby. Asshole. "Here you're trying to sell yourself as a white knight, then you go and threaten my friend."

He takes a step closer.

"No," he says. "I'm not a good man. I am, in fact, a bad one. But even bad people can do good things, and I'm hoping you get that. You'll see it in time. You're going to come with me because we have your friend, and if not that, because amongst my friends and my family are others like you. People with powers. People who can change things."

And then he turns the gun around, lets it swing loose with his finger curled around the trigger guard. Ethan urges the gun toward her, grip thrust first.

She sees the round knobby curve of his thumb knuckle thrust up. A tantalizing piece of skin. *Touch it. See how he dies.*

"What is this?" she asks.

"It's my gun."

"No doy, asshole. Why would you give it to me?"

"A peace offering of sorts." Then he laughs a little. "That's a strange offering, I suppose. A gun as a symbol of peace? These are curious times and we are unusual people, you and I. So, maybe it's fitting."

She takes the gun. He pulls his hand away before she gets that sweet skin-on-skin contact. No vision. No death. But that's okay, though.

Because she already knows how he dies.

She spins the gun around.

Points it at him.

Pulls the trigger.

TWENTY-FIVE

BREAKERS

Click.

Click click click.

Shit!

"If I had that pistol loaded up, you would've jeopardized everything. Your friend. My life. Your own, inevitably. Just because you can't control yourself." Ethan sighs, clucks his tongue. "You are indeed a wild horse in great need of breaking. That's all right. We'll get there. I have a gentle hand."

"I do too," Miriam says, and gives him the finger.

His smile finally falls away.

"Let's take a ride," he says.

PART THREE
THE BAD LANDS

YOUNG MIRIAM

Miriam is eight years old.

Lightning flashes. Thunder rattles the old house a half-second later. Rain hammers the window glass like it's desperate to come inside, like the only thing it wants is to drown them all.

Miriam cowers under the covers.

She tries not to cry. But sometimes, she makes this sound in her chest, a sound that rises up out of her lungs and her heart, a sound like an injured animal—a bleat, a cry, a wail she has to cut short and bite back.

Another pulse of lightning. Another teeth-rattling bang of thunder. Like dynamite going off on a too-short fuse. Flash, *boom*. Flash, *boom*.

The thought, tantalizing and forbidden, keeps circulating like a dog chasing its tail: *Just get up. Go tell Mother. Tell her you're scared*.

No, no, no, no.

That won't work.

That *never* works.

Flash, *boom*.

She cries out again. A throat-cut sound.

Before she even knows what's happening, her bare feet are landing on the cold wood floor of the room, and the blanket is trailing behind her and she knows, *she knows*, no, no, no, stop now, turn around, no good can come of this, no way, no how, but still she keeps going. Past the one teddy bear on her shelf with the dangling button eye, a shelf with books she hates to read: the Bible, Aesop's Fables, *Crime and Punishment*, *A Tale of Two Cities*, and some old Russian children's book, with monstrous Constructivist humans showcasing their weird Russian jobs (and smoking), none of it in English, all of it in Russian. Past the crucifix on the wall with the poor, scary man named Jesus who hangs there, bleeding. In the hallway, past the mirror hanging there crooked, past the heating vent on the floor that *tink*s and *tonk*s and bangs when the heat comes on.

To Mother's door.

Don't knock don't knock don't knock.

She raises her hand to knock but holds it there in the air, like she's holding onto something invisible and just can't let go.

It won't work. It never works.

Deep breath, in and out.

With no small amount of sadness and fear, she decides to go back to her room.

But Mother's door opens. Suddenly, swiftly—startling her.

And there stands Evelyn Black. Scowling down, each of her hands clasping its opposite elbow, rubbing the skin there. A black shape, blacker against the dark room behind her. Her mother utters a disgruntled *hnnh*.

"Don't think I didn't hear you," Mother says.

"I'm sorry."

"In your room, caterwauling like a cat. You should be ashamed. It's just a storm. You're eight. Not four. Not a diaper baby."

"I just, I just . . ." She hears herself stammering and it makes her feel even more shame and more embarrassment that she can't even manage the words. But somehow they tumble out: "I just want to see if muh-maybe I can come in? And sleep with you. Just tonight. The lightning is really—" As if on cue, a flash hidden in part by the lack of windows in the hall, but a swift splitting of the air afterward. The mirror down the hall rattles against the plaster. "It's close."

"And you're scared."

"Uh-huh."

"Scared as if the lightning might grow hands and reach in through the window. Snatch you up. Drag you out into the rain." Miriam hadn't quite thought of it that way, before, but now that she was . . .

"I don't know. It's loud and scary."

Mother grunts. "Life is loud and scary, Miriam, dear. The dark comes every night. Storms come every season. No comfort I can give you will change what's coming. It is up to you to stand against it because it is what it is, always and forever. We must trust in God to grant us the steel and the salt to push back fear. If we are good to God, then He will be good to us and give us shelter and courage."

Tears well. "But, Mother—"

"No. No more crying or I'll take your blanket away and give you nothing to hide under."

"Can I . . . can I have a flashlight, at least—"

"The lightning will be light enough. You have a roof over your head and God's plan. You need nothing else." Her mother stiffens. "Don't make me angry, Miriam. Go. Go now, and let me sleep."

Miriam hurries back to her room, trying not to weep.

The lightning flashes, and thunder booms.

In the morning, they will discover that lightning hit a tree in their front yard. Thirty feet from the house.

The tree stands split down the middle, as if cleaved by an axe.

TWENTY-SIX

THE VALLEY OF THE SHADOW OF DEATH

The mountains sitting at the base of the sky look like torn paper—ripped into jags and peaks by untrained or uncaring hands. Or maybe it's the sky that looks like paper. Miriam can't tell, her gaze swallowed by the horizon. A brown world the color of a grocery bag. Little scrub bushes here and there: creosote and palo verde shouldering their way up and out, branches reaching for one another (but never touching), like a kingdom of doomed lovers.

Miriam's hands grip the steering wheel of the wizard van, knuckles gone bloodless. Fingertips tingling, the tension all the way down the elbows.

Ethan sits in the passenger seat, staring out. He made her take the van to get it off the road—said cops other than his friend might be looking for it.

The highway ahead is long and mostly empty. A car or truck passes on the other side every couple of minutes. A horse trailer. A pickup. A Jeep.

"I could drive this car off the road," she says. "Just cut the wheel, hit some Mack truck coming on the other side. Wipe us both out."

Ethan shrugs. "You want to do that, that's your right." But he sits up straighter, probably because he remembers how *handing her a gun* went. The gun that once again sits on his knee, this time its barrel almost nonchalantly pointed at her, his finger curled around the front of the trigger guard. "I figure you won't. You're in this deep already. Might as well at least take the ride to its end, see what waits on the other side."

"I want you to know, if you hurt Gabby . . ."

"We did not hurt her."

"But if you did. Hypothetically. Or hell, maybe you hurt her *feelings*. Maybe she stubbed her toe on the way in. That happens, dude, I will repay the slight a thousandfold. You picking up what I'm putting down?"

"We're not so different," he says.

"Oh, god, here it comes. Classic villain talk."

"You protect your loved ones with tooth and claw. So do I. That's what all this is about. Protecting what we love. You'll see."

A sedan passes going the other direction. All the muscles and tendons in her arm ache to jerk the wheel. Head-on collision. *Maybe I'd walk away from it.* She's a survivor. But maybe this guy is too.

"You all say the same shit. *We're not so different.* You justify what you do as something good because nobody thinks they're the bad guy. You all think you're the heroes of your own story— misunderstood underdogs who know how things *really* work, and if only the world bent to your horrible will, everything would sort itself out. Truth, justice, and McDonald's cheeseburgers for all."

He laughs—a genuine thing, that laugh, as disarming as his smile. "I bet you think you're the good guy too."

"I dunno." Hell, yes, I'm the good guy. "I don't think about it." *Am I the good guy? Oh, shit.*

"Here's what I think," he says. "I think that *good guys* and *bad guys* is too simple a thing, Miriam. I think we're all on a spectrum of gray, and each of us is capable of very good things and very bad things, and we are sure to do both in our lifetime.

Best you can do is have a code, a set of rules, and stick to it. I am willing to do bad things to achieve good. That's my code."

She rolls her eyes. "Here's a wacky idea. Why not trying to do *good* things to achieve good? Give to the poor. Save a kitten. Say nice things to old ladies. What a kooky code *that* would be."

"That what you do?"

"What I do isn't send snipers to shoot a mother in front of her child."

He sits up straighter. "I was wondering if we'd get to that."

"What I do isn't burn a man inside his own gas station."

Ethan shrugs.

"What I do isn't blow up buildings."

There. That one. A little arrow plucked from the future and fired right into his eye. *Thwock*. But there he gives pause. His brow furrows like a plowed field. "That woman we were pursuing, she was a danger to her own child, and I cannot abide danger to children. Wade, well, I already told you: he was a rapist at the college where he worked. But that last thing? We haven't blown up any buildings."

Yet.

Though he does seem genuinely bewildered. That's a kink in the hose she can't quite work out.

He says, "We're not terrorists, Miriam."

"You keep saying that. *We*. Who's *we*, Key? The Coming Storm?"

He sighs, and the smile slowly returns to his face: slow as a sunrise, slow as an ice cube melting, slow as cold honey.

"That," he says, "you'll see soon enough. Keep driving."

TWENTY-SEVEN

LIMITED PATROL AREA

She drives for a couple hours. South through a few small towns of shitty little houses and boarded-up churches. Eventually, the afternoon sun hangs in the sky, its head hung low, the bleach-smear of a star drifting sluggardly down toward the horizon like it just can't do it anymore—as if even the sun is tired of the heat and it just wants to find a shadowy place to hide and sleep.

The two of them don't say much. Occasionally, she catches Ethan watching her. Smiling. Thumb drawing circles on the outside of the pistol.

He tells her to take a turn off the highway—a highway that's increasingly lost to disrepair, a highway now where they haven't seen another car in five, maybe ten minutes. At the turnoff, a sign. White sign, green text:

HIGH CLEARANCE VEHICLES ONLY

4-WHEEL DRIVE RECOMMENDED

ROAD NOT MAINTAINED

DO NOT CROSS FLOODED WASHES

SERVICES NOT AVAILABLE

LIMITED PATROL AREA

The sign's got bullet holes in it.

"Down this way," he says.

"I don't think the van has four-wheel drive."

He tilts his head in a half-ass shrug. "It'll be fine. I've driven this road many a time. We'll make it."

Miriam turns the van onto the road—which is less of a road and more of a car-width dirt path carved through the desert. Ahead, the land rises up in berms and hills. A few trees here and there. Cholla catching the late-day light in silver cactus needles. "This road have a name?"

"Grave Gulch Road," he says.

"You're fucking kidding me."

"I am not. Story goes that a century ago, a great gullywasher of a storm came down so hard, it dug up all the graves at the cemetery—what town, I don't know—and washed all the bodies out of their graves and down into the gulch. Stories say a lot of things, but I'm inclined to believe this one."

The van judders and groans on the uneven, unpaved road.

"Limited patrol area," Miriam repeats from the sign. "What's the deal?"

"Ahead is some of the most lawless land in America," he says. "The Wild West but a whole lot worse. Might as well be the mountains of Afghanistan. Here in the Valley, the cartels send up drug smugglers, human traffickers, stone-cold killers—and nobody knows how to handle it. Not the government, not the people who actually live here. Then you get rip crews trying to hit the drugs, the money, the slaves. Then you get coyotes—other smugglers—trying to sneak through without being noticed, and then it's a shooting war. Innocent people get hurt."

Way he says that last thing is different from how he said all the things before it. *Innocent people get hurt*. A fire stoked in those words. Hot ash poked with an iron prod.

She senses a scab. In true Miriam fashion, she decides to pick it.

"Someone you know got hurt."

He nods. The van bangs and bounces along. "My wife."

"What happened to her?"

"You'll see. At dinner tonight, you'll see."

TWENTY-EIGHT

CAMP LIBERTY TREE

The sky goes purple: spilled wine and black eyes. The rumbling road winds through a pair of hills, and then Miriam sees: two telephone poles, thrust up out of the desert ground. Wire strung between them, flags hanging upside down—Ethan advises her to drive underneath. One flag: tattered, washed-out, showing a green pine tree with the words APPEAL TO HEAVEN underneath. A second flag: yellow fabric, coiled rattlesnake, DON'T TREAD ON ME. A third flag, instantly recognizable (and Miriam's middle twists like an earthworm when she sees it): lightning forking toward a dead tree, a tree with stars in its branches.

THE COMING STORM.

Ahead, a cattle gate. A husky man with a big round belly stuffed in camo fatigues stares ahead into the van's windshield, then jogs over, the rifle at his back bouncing with each step. He unhooks the gate, lets it swing wide.

Ethan rolls down the window. The man comes up. Guy's got an ogre's nose and a thatchy golden beard that looks like the hay sticking out of a scarecrow's sleeve. Each of his cheeks is a moonscape of pockmarks. He says, "'Sup, hoss."

"Bill," Ethan says. "We got a guest here."

The man peers in and grins. "The girl."

"Jesus Christ with the *girl* shit," Miriam hisses.

Bill says: "Got some venom, this one. That's good."

"Everything quiet around here?"

"No louder than a lizard fart."

"Let's keep it that way. See you, Bill."

Bill tips his cap.

Miriam pulls the van through.

The gate closes behind them with a squeak and a bang. Each sound makes her jump—just a little, she hopes, so Ethan didn't see. But she knows: *This is the point of no return.*

What the hell is this place?

Ahead: buildings. A few little ramshackle houses. Maybe a half-dozen trailers and, beyond them, twice as many tents. Folks around, doing work: A man in a white T-shirt and jeans carries a case of what looks like Gatorade. Another woman in a long ponytail pulls a handtruck loaded with heavy square boxes, boxes marked with green and yellow bands and with a logo that reads REMINGTON. Ammunition? As if on cue, somewhere off in the distance, the *pop-pop-pop* of guns going off. She recoils.

"Relax," Ethan says. "Just range practice."

"So, this is some kind of what, cult? Militia? You're Jonestown but with Gatorade instead of Flavor Aid?"

"I thought they drank Kool-Aid."

"Nope. Flavor Aid. The Kool-Aid Man is a patsy."

Ethan nods. "You're a smart girl."

"Smartest motherfucker in the room," she lies, bold with false bravado.

"Good. We need more people like you."

She sneers. "I appreciate your optimism, but I'm not really the *joining* type. I won't even stand for the Pledge of Allegiance—I fade out in the middle. Shit, I just quit smoking—I'm so bad at commitments, I can't even stay addicted to something. So, if it's between you and me, I'll just grab my friend and head back to some place where a bunch of fucking screw-loose crazy-brains aren't marching around with automatic weapons in their little pretend army."

Ethan's smile drops. "Stay one night. I want you to meet my wife."

"I don't give a raccoon's red cock about your wife. I just want to go."

He tightens his grip on the pistol. She'd almost forgotten about that. He says, "The request is polite but firm. Less a question, more of a command, Miriam."

"You like ordering people around, do you?"

"When it gets the job done."

"You know who else liked ordering people around? Hitler. Probably."

"You got the wrong idea about us. But you'll see. Here—" He points ahead, toward a little avenue tucked between a trailer and a massive tent. "Pull back there and park. I'll get someone to take you over to your girlfriend, maybe give you a quick tour. Then dinner with me and mine. How's that sound?"

"Like a nightmare."

He shrugs as she pulls forward, finds a patch of rough-but-even ground to park the van. "The nightmare is what's outside these fences, not what's inside of 'em. Go see Gabrielle—sorry, Gabby. And we'll hook back up. Oh, one more thing—" And here, as they park, he grabs the keys out of the van. He gives a wink and a nod as he yanks his hand away before she can touch him. "Just making sure you'll keep your dinner date, not skip out on us."

TWENTY-NINE

THE VIEWER, THE DOER, THE WHOO-ER, AND THE TOO-ER

For a moment, Miriam feels unpinned—a lawn chair blowing around in a tornado. Ethan is gone. And she's alone. In this strange little half-town, way out in the desert, in a state she doesn't know, in a part of the country she doesn't know. She wants to find Gabby, but suddenly, everything seems big and she feels small.

Then: a young woman stands there. Dusky, smooth skin, long black hair drawn back in a ponytail. All parts of her stand at a tilt: head cocked, arms crossed, upper torso tilted left, hip and left leg going right. A human zigzag.

The woman sucks air through her teeth.

"What?" Miriam asks.

"I'm your guide."

"Guide. What is this, Disneyland? I want to see my—" And here she catches herself because she's about to say *girlfriend* but that's not right. Is it? "I want to see Gabby. My friend. So, let's hurry that along."

"Yeah, yeah, but she's at the far end, and we gotta walk it. So: a tour."

In the distance, as the sky bleeds from purple to red like a gut shot, she hears those rifles and pistols going off not too far away now: *pop pop pop*.

Miriam feels unsettled. This place is—she doesn't know how to describe it. Uneven, somehow. Sound crackling from a broken radio. In discomfort she seeks comfort, or at least her own sick and twisted version of it. And given her inability to see how Ethan Key was going to take a desert dirt nap, here's a chance to satisfy the craving that lives in her tingling fingertips, in the hinge of her wrist.

She thrusts out her hand. "I'm Miriam."

"I'm Ofelia."

Ofelia takes the hand and—

A red crimson wash. A pulsebeat drumming. A breath, deep and gasping, in and out, in and out, inhale, exhale, all the world a throbbing heart, a palpitating lung, a great artery flush with blood . . .

Miriam gasps, pulls her hand away.

"You," she says.

"Me?" Ofelia asks, cheeky. Because she knows.

"You're . . . You have a power."

Ofelia sticks out her tongue and she seems proud as the cat that not only caught the canary but ate its head clean off its body, too. "Maybe."

"What can you do?"

"You'll see. C'mon. Tour time." And with that, she starts walking.

Here, Miriam's stubbornness wants to rise up from the dirt like an iron beast and plant its immovable feet: she doesn't want to move. She wants to pout, spit, hiss until she gets her way. *I don't follow people.* She leads the way. Others trail after in the wake she leaves behind. But? Fine. Gabby is at the end of this yellow brick road, so with reluctance so strong it's painful, she hurries after.

Because now she's playing catch-up.

And she hates playing catch-up.

Ofelia, she's already talking. "Mostly, the trailers are houses. People live there, sleep there, got kitchens. The trailers are for special people. Like me. Like you, if you decide to stay." That last sentence doesn't sound welcoming. Miriam detects a bitterness there—jealousy like battery acid burning. "Tents got more beds—cots one after the other, but that sucks because it gets pretty cold at night. There's a few actual houses here too—and the ranch house at the end of the drive is Ethan and Karen's place."

"Karen. His wife?"

Ofelia gives a dismissive hand gesture as she walks, like *yeah yeah whatever, bitch, I'm talking here.* "You take that little road there, you get the greenhouse, the storage locker, the mess tent, the honey buckets—" Ofelia turns around, preemptively irritated, eyes narrowed. "Honey buckets are, like, Port-a-Johns. Where you do *your business.*"

"I'm road trash, bitch, I know what a honey bucket is."

"I bet you do."

There, a look that says—what, exactly? Somehow, this little twat thinks she's better than Miriam? "Don't sass me, hooker."

And there: the girl's face falls. Like she's reeling, like somebody just slapped her. "Who said I was a hooker?"

"Uhh." Miriam scrunches up her face. "This is seriously the easiest game of Clue you'll ever play. It was Colonel Miriam. In the desert. With my *mouth.*"

"But who *told you* that?" And here she pokes Miriam right in the breastbone, prod, prod, prod. "Who said that's what I did around here?"

Blink, blink.

"Jesus, don't get hostile. Is that what you do around here?"

"I'm an escort." More poking. Poke, poke, poke. "Not some hooker."

"Hey, fuck off. I don't care—" She catches Ofelia's finger, holds it there. "I don't care what you call yourself, hooker, ho, escort, courtesan, Scheherazade—"

"Schuh-hur-a-what?" And then Ofelia gives her a hard shove

and comes at her. Miriam staggers back, looking around like *Is anybody seeing this? Does anybody even care?* Ofelia shoves her again. "What's that mean? What'd you call me? You fuckin'—" She cocks a fist at Miriam's head, and Miriam thinks: *I'm gonna have to take this cuckoo cunt down, right here, right now.* But then the fist just falls apart like a loose snowball and the girl shakes it off. "You're not worth it. You wanna see your friend? Fine. Let's go."

She marches off. Arms stiff, swinging at her side. Petulant.

Miriam, again, catches up. "Hey, hold up—"

"Shooting range is over there. Ammo and gun closet nearby. Got a few general-use vehicles like Jeeps and shit in the back lot—"

She reaches out, catches Ofelia by the crook of her arm. The woman's hand curls back into a fist. Miriam, in a rare moment, holds up the flats of her surrendering hands.

"I get it," Miriam says. "You're a psycho psychic with a chip on her shoulder the size of a perching pterodactyl. We're practically *sisters.*"

Ofelia looks her up and down. The distrust and disdain come off her in waves. If this were a cartoon, she'd be giving off *stink lines* of the stuff.

"We both have powers," Miriam says. "What can you see?"

"See?" Ofelia asks with a hollow laugh. "I don't see a thing. You're a viewer. But I'm a *doer.* I don't see shit. I *do* shit."

"Like what?"

Ofelia grabs Miriam's chin. Tilts her head straightaway. She meets Miriam's stare—a hard stare returned, two eyes like iron pokers gone hot cherry orange. And Miriam feels a twinge— something deep inside her, some hunger, some lust, some whipping and lashing thing like an eel caught on a fishing line, and something between her legs coils tight. Even in the dry desert, she feels wet—wet there, wet under her tongue, wet under her armpits—

Miriam pulls away.

Then she shoves Ofelia.

Ofelia laughs. "That's what I do. I make people want me. Can't do it to women too much—works a little better if they like chicks." She holds up her two fingers in a V and waggles her tongue between the valley of digits.

"I didn't say you could do that." Her jaw locks. *Hit her. Just hit her.*

"You didn't say I could do a lot of things. I don't need your permission."

"This is what you do, isn't it? You make men want you. Then they pay you for the privilege. That's about a hundred miles away from hooker."

"You just mad because some little Taw-haw-naw bitch took control away from you. Maybe you need to be a little out of control."

Miriam narrows her eyes. "Trust me. If I'm any more out of control, I'd be a fucking F5 tornado. You don't get to tell me who I am or what I do. Now—point your finger to where they're keeping my friend."

"Your lezzie girlfriend?"

"Point your finger."

Ofelia licks her lips. She looks half-mad, half-embarrassed. After a few moments of moping, she sticks up her hand and extends a finger. "That tent over there—the red box tent. She's in there."

"Good."

Miriam pops Ofelia in the stomach. The girl *oofs* and doubles over, dropping to her knees.

Then Miriam says, "Thanks for the tour."

She marches toward the tent as people in the street rush toward Ofelia. Miriam sets her jaw. Doesn't look back. Someone wants to come for her?

Let 'em come.

THIRTY

THE RED TENT

Nobody stops her. Someone yells but she keeps going. Fist throbbing from the hit, Miriam pushes the flap of the tent back, and there, ten feet away, sits Gabby. Staring down at her hands folded in her lap. She's not alone. Big guy behind her—a muscle-bound freak with a crooked jaw and an ink-black military buzz cut. Ink scrawled up both arms. He steps forward, lifts his chin not by way of a greeting but like he's looking down his nose at her, inspecting her.

Miriam skirts past him. Gabby sees her suddenly. Launches up. Her face, already lined with crisscross scars, already like a puzzle that a child forced together, now sits streaked with makeup. The two of them succumb to gravity and pull together in a hug.

Gabby cries softly.

Miriam rubs circles on her back. "Shh. It's okay." Then she pulls back and holds Gabby's face with both hands. "Did anyone hurt you?"

A gentle—and hesitant—shake of Gabby's head.

"No one?" Miriam asks. "Nobody laid a hand on you?"

Gabby flits her eyes toward the big guy only a few feet away. "He . . . slapped me." And now Miriam can see it—that little crust of blood, a little line of it, down the center of Gabby's lower lip.

That's it. That's all she needs. Miriam leans in, hugs her again, and whispers in Gabby's ear: "I'm gonna kill them all for you. And I'm going to start with that fucking meatsack over there."

They share a look then.

What shines in Gabby's eyes, Miriam can't quite tell. She thinks it's fear. Maybe pride, too. Like she loves Miriam, but she's scared of her too.

That's probably fair.

"C'mon, girls," Musclebound Meatsack says. He reaches for them, but Miriam pulls away. "It's dinnertime."

The temptation to touch him is an overpowering frequency. But Miriam just offers up her most vicious, vulpine grin and says, "I don't need to touch you. Because I already know how it happens."

Her words, though, trail off. Because as he turns, she sees something written across his forearm. A tattoo. *Janice*. Above that, the tree, the lightning, the warning about the coming storm.

He's there. In the courthouse. When it all goes to hell. Musclebound Meatsack will be the one who shoots the old guard in the face.

"Just fucking move," he says.

Miriam thinks: *I'm going to kill him here. Now.*

Her gaze flits. He's got a gun slung over his shoulder—a rifle. Miriam's no expert, but it looks like an AK-47: brown stock, metal everything else. She thinks: *Grab the gun.* Or maybe there's something nearby. A knife. Scissors. Christ, if she could get a pair of *tweezers,* she'd use them to pull the tip of his dick up through his chest and out his mouth. He turns his back, waves them out of the tent. And then she sees it: a metal stool. Gabby was sitting on it.

Miriam's hand reaches. Her fingers curl underneath.

She's gonna dash his brains all over this tent.

Gabby puts a hand on her arm. She says to Miriam, "Let's just get out of here. No trouble. Okay?"

The sheer potential for violence crackles off Miriam like

supercharged static electricity—just seconds before the sharp snap of shock.

The plea shines in Gabby's eyes.

Miriam gives her a small nod.

"Let's go, girls, come on, come on, Jesus." Meatsack waves them on, lifting the tent flap. Miriam ducks underneath but pauses next to him.

"What's your name, soldier?"

"Jade."

"Jade and Janice. Janice your girl?"

"Janice is my *mom*. Now fuckin' move."

Miriam bares her teeth in something resembling a smile.

And, like the man says, she moves.

THIRTY-ONE

BREAKING BREAD

They don't go through the house. Meatsack Jade ushers them around the side, past a couple rusted rain barrels, past stacks of crates, to a patio out back underneath an off-kilter pergola. In the far distance, the last light of day doesn't fade so much as it's shoved down below the horizon by the great expanse of night-time sky: an infinity of stars flung across the uneven black like glitter.

He indicates the table and chairs—a couple of picnic tables shoved together, joined by a red-checkered tablecloth and surrounded by a mismatched set of white plastic patio chairs.

Miriam and Gabby share a look.

Jade goes behind them—there's the familiar sound of a Zippo lighter clinking. Then the crackle of flame to paper. Miriam turns, see him throw a wad of newspaper—a tongue of flame dancing off it—into a rusted barrel.

Whatever's inside catches fire fast. The smell of lighter fluid hits her nose before vanishing. Smoke rises from the barrel like desert ghosts.

Miriam shrugs, pulls out a chair for Gabby, then one for herself.

Let's just get out of here. No trouble, okay?

A small, and possibly impossible, promise, Miriam thinks. Part of her wants to get this over with and get the hell out. The

other part of her? She wants to know how it's all connected.
Because some strange, hard-to-see thread ties this all together:
the woman, Gracie; her son, Isaiah; Mary Scissors; the explosion
and gunmen at the courthouse. Miriam's feeling for a rope in
the dark. Something, anything to help guide her through this
moonless maze.

Her fingers rattle an impatient drumbeat. There's a flicker of
movement close to her—

Thunk!

A combat knife slams down two inches from her hand. She
recoils, reeling in her grip lest she lose a pinky.

Jade frees the knife, tilts it toward her.

A tiny scorpion twists at the end of the blade, the knife tip
stuck through its middle. Meatsack leers, grinning. "It's the little
ones you gotta worry about. The smaller the scorpion, the deadlier the venom."

He pinches it, plucks it, and flings it over his shoulder.
Laughing.

"Thanks," she says.

"All kinds of shit out here will kill ya. Black widows. Rattle-
snakes. Killer bees. Gila monsters." He leans in close. She can
smell his breath: rank, like rotten food stuck between his teeth.
"I hear tell even *vultures* can end you."

She sniffs. "You know? I've heard that very thing. But you
know what else I hear? That *no* animal is deadlier than man. Am
I right?"

"Hand to God," he says, and chuckles. "Hand. To. God."

Sounds like he's about to say more, but there's movement
inside the house—and, half a second later, a sliding glass door
opens. Out comes Ofelia, carrying a long plate covered by
tented foil. Steam escapes and the smell of good food is like a
fishhook in Miriam's mouth. Ofelia stares daggers, then sets the
plate down. She goes back inside, passing a young man coming

out: he's got a boyish, maybe even girlish figure, and he walks like a puma pacing its cage.

He sets down a pitcher of lemonade. With arched eyebrows and an exaggerated, almost cartoonish sneer, he surveys Miriam and Gabby. "Lemonade," he says. "Need glasses. Hold still. BRB."

Then he slinks back into the house as Ofelia comes back out again—two plates in each hand. Each swaddled in foil. More smells: cooked meat and something spicy. Miriam's salivating mouth reminds her she hasn't eaten all day.

The lad comes back out, drops some glasses, then sits. He meshes his fingers together, rests his chin in the cradle.

Miriam's about to say something—she doesn't know what, but smart money's on something snarky and inappropriate—when their hosts come out.

Ethan wheels out a woman in a wheelchair.

She's thin. Too thin—her skin is like gauze draped loosely around a skeleton. Her mouth hangs open, showing a pale tongue and long teeth popping out of pasty gums. Makeup adorns her face: a peachy blush, pink lipstick, mascara, and eye shadow ladled on with a heavy hand. Her hands are brittle things, not holding each other so much as placed near one another. Her head lolls around on her neck, controlled by forces that do not seem completely her own.

As Ethan wheels her closer to the table, Miriam sees the woman's face more completely by the firelight—

A puckered scar like a cat's asshole decorates the space just above her eyes.

"Thank you all for coming," Ethan says. "I appreciate your time. Especially yours, Miriam and Gabby. Got a humble feast here today. Tamales. Some skirt steak. Squash blossoms and zucchini. And the lemonade there is made with a cactus syrup—Ofelia's people, the Tohono O'odham make it."

"Taw-haw-naw," Ofelia says. When she says it, she's staring

at Miriam, not at Ethan. Ethan seems to ignore all of that and keeps talking:

"This is my wife, Karen."

The woman's mouth stretches into some crass mockery of a smile. When she speaks, her tongue clicks sticky against her teeth and her voice is a dry, stuttering croak like a frog choking on a marble: "Hello. Everyone." She pulls in a deep breath: a long wind-tunnel wheeze. Then she adds, "Please . . . eat."

And with that, Ofelia and the young man begin to pull the foil off the dishes and pass out paper plates. The smell intensifies; Miriam's hunger dogfights her anger inside her middle. Hungry, she can handle. Her anger, though, is a straight-up lava geyser—no getting her hands around it.

"What the actual fuck," she says.

The clinking of dishes, the crumpling of foil—it all stops.

Everyone stares.

"Miriam," Ethan says. "Something on your mind?"

She lets her mouth hang open like a broken porch swing, just dangling there in the wind. "We're not pals. We're not family. We're supposed to just sit here and eat and pretend that nothing weird is going on? No guns, no dead Wade, no rifleman in the desert, no wife with what appears to be a bullet hole in her head?"

Ethan sets his fork down. It has a steaming slice of tamale on it. He licks his lips and says, "You're not one to just enjoy a moment, are you?"

"Not so much. In fact, every moment I sit *here* feels like me trying to rescue a pubic hair stuck somewhere in the back of my mouth. It's gross and uncomfortable and I just want to pluck it out so I can move on with my life."

His face shows a moment of barely controlled rage before a wall of smiles contains it anew. He nods. Pushes the plate forward. "Okay. Talk first, eat after. Everybody okay with that?"

"No," Ofelia says, pouting.

"Fine," the young man says.

And when he does, Miriam says, "Who are you?"

He smirks but says nothing.

"That's David," Ethan says. He reaches over, rubs his wife's shoulder. "So. Miriam. Gabby. What would you like to know?"

The laugh that bubbles out of her is so loud and so fake, it might as well be a Prada purse sold on the street in New York City. "Are you fucking kidding me? This is like pulling teeth out of a pissed-off dog. What the hell is happening? Why am I here? When can we go? How about you pick one thing—anything, really—and just fucking *explain* it. Explain that one thing, and then? Explain *everything*."

"The universe was born into darkness," David starts to say, but Ethan shoots him a look and a short, sharp shake of the head. He laughs but stops.

"This is my land," Ethan says. "My father owned this before me. Used to be peaceful enough out here, but this became a real hot zone over the last twenty years. Like I said: this is the Wild West now. They bring drugs in. Take guns out. The war goes on." He sips lemonade. "Coyotes smuggle in people, too—lotta times, people who think they're coming to a land of freedom but are really gonna end up as heroin mules or sex slaves. You got smuggling paths up through Mexico to here, then here to Nogales or to Las Cruces. I hated seeing that happen to my land. To my *father's* land. And there were others out here too."

Miriam snaps her fingers, impatient-like. "Right, okay, so you formed your little desert army and—great. Can we go?"

"That's just the start of it. We did form a militia. Lot of militias in this state—some by right-thinking folks, some by wrong-thinking folks. But we held our ground. Did work that the government was too afraid to do—"

"*Still* too afraid," David says. "After 9/11, they started to send drones. Sometimes you see them. Flying up there. Quiet as a vulture. Watching. But even still, that's all they send out here. Drones."

"Nah," Ofelia says. "They got the Shadow Wolves."

"What are the Shadow Wolves?" Miriam asks.

"The Shadow Wolves are bullshit," David says. "If you're like, one sixteenth Tohono, they let you join their little group of mostly-but-not-quite-white-guys—"

Ofelia elbows him hard in the ribs. He hisses at her like a cat. Ofelia says, "They're ICE guys. You know, immigration? They're trackers who hunt this valley, looking for smugglers. Couple dozen of them at best. Buncha badasses, I'm telling you. Every one of them is like, fuckin' indigenous. Not just Tohono but like, Navajo, Yaqui, whatever."

"She's not lying, but ugh," David says.

"Children," Ethan says. Stern voice. Daddy voice.

"Sorry, Ethan," David says. Ofelia just holds up her hands in surrender.

"Point is," Ethan continues, "we fought back. We watched the hills. Took shots at those we saw moving through the dark. Sometimes, they shot back. Point wasn't to hurt anyone but to scare them off, let them know we weren't letting our lands get taken over without a fight. But then—" And here there's a break in his voice, a small tectonic shiver. He pauses, a callused hand along his scratchy beard—a sound like sandpaper smoothing out a splintering board. He clears his throat. "Then came the day that Karen went on a run up into Tucson for supplies. Simple enough. We don't have a lot out here, so you gotta stock up. She took this little white truck we had, a pickup, and she drove it out and drove it back, but by the time she came back, evening had come on. Painted the sky with the coming darkness. And as she turned down our road, three men ambushed her. Shot out her tires. Dragged her out of the van. Kicked her. Beat her. Then one of them . . ." He's barely keeping it together now.

His voice has cracked apart like a clod of dry earth in a closing fist. "One of them took out his pistol and shot her in the head."

Silence. Spreading out from this table and these six people and all the way out across the desert, too—like a rolling wave of it, a soundless empty nothing. Callous and consumptive. As if on cue, a coyote howls somewhere. A dog barks soon after. A small wind nudges tinkling chimes.

"I . . . died," Karen says, suddenly focusing. Her head tilts back on her neck even as her eyes—big and bold and white as moons—stare at them all.

"She was . . . technically dead," Ethan says, pulling himself together. He reaches over and brushes a lock of hair out of his wife's eye. Then he takes her hand and holds it, almost like they're praying. "The bullet went in through her skull and took out the connective piece between the two halves of your brain—the corpus callosum, they call it. They must've been using a lower-caliber weapon because the bullet is still in there. In the back of her skull. The doctors didn't want to take it out. Thought it was safer to leave it in."

"I'm sorry," Gabby says.

Miriam follows with: "Yeah. What she said. It still doesn't explain—"

Ethan holds Karen's hand to his forehead. His eyes, shut. David and Ofelia sit stock still and watch.

Karen's head begins to roll on her shoulders, moving faster and faster as she speaks: "Columns of fire burning the corn. Red infection eating the flesh of man. We eat dogs. We eat each other. Tumors bursting. Cancers in the dirt like black worms." She cries out, a ragged moan like from a woman giving birth, and her words come more quickly now: "An invasion. Death in the streets. Machine guns cutting children to pieces. Mass graves. White masks. They're speaking a language now. Some strange tongue. Orientals and Islams. Lions in clouds. Lightning strikes. Everything is fire. Everything is sickness."

Then—

Her head slumps. Chin to chest. A low whine like from a hurt dog rises in the back of her throat. Ethan kisses her hand. Places it back on the table.

"Best we figure it," he says, "Karen had a vision of what's to come. Not the end of the world, maybe. But the end of us. The end of America. Something nuclear and maybe biological, too. A one-two punch that takes us out."

A long, sad breath escapes Miriam's lips. "So. You're a militia turned doomsday prepper group? Visions of the end are a dime a dozen, dude. I mean, no harm, no foul, but people see shit all the time when they're dying. I've sat with dying men, women, children. Sometimes they see loved ones. Sometimes they see heaven or hell. One guy saw—and this is no bullshit—a giant spider on a nearby wall and it had a LEGO guy head on it. Like a yellow barrel with a painted-on smile and snap-on hair? People see things. Doesn't mean it's real."

Ethan leans forward. "We're not just a prepper group. We're active. We're trying to change the future. Trying to change this nation's fate."

It's Gabby that asks, "What does that mean?"

"This government has to be shut down."

And here the tumblers of the lock start to click in place. They attack the courthouse because they don't care for the law. Or the government that makes those laws. It adds up to a narrative that is as pathetic as it is obvious.

"That's fucked, and you know it," she says.

"Is it? You ever open a newspaper? Things are broken, Miriam. Almost irrevocably. Police shooting unarmed people and getting away with it: no indictments. Our own government torturing people—the wrong people—and getting away with it.

They send drones to sovereign countries and blow up weddings, funerals, schoolhouses—innocent women and children torn apart by nineteen-year-olds half a world away, sitting at a computer screen, pulling a trigger. We pay taxes that sanction the rape, torture, and murder of people inside and outside our own borders." He shakes his head. "And one day? One day we're going to knock over a domino that starts a whole line of them falling. It'll be like the bullet that hit the Archduke Ferdinand—the one that started the First World War. When we do that—when we light that fuse and start it burning—then there is no turning back. I don't know who: Russia? China? Some Arabs we've already armed? And I don't know how. They launch nukes and then hit us with some new super-flu, maybe. This country is going to be destroyed by its own government. We can't let that happen. So, that's why we're here. We're not the coming storm, despite what our name says. We're what stops the storm from rolling in."

"And you're going to help us," Karen croons.

Panic crawls through her like a colony of ants. She thinks: *I have to get out of here. Have to get to Mary Stitch. Have to call the police. Have to do something, anything, to get the fuck out of here.* She just needs an opportunity. "Ethan, you know this sounds loco bananapants, yeah? You're basing all this on a vision that is more likely to be a delusion at the moment of death—a hallucination, not a psychic vision. You know how many people think they're psychic but—"

Karen's head ratchets up.

Her eyes stare right at Miriam. Through her, even.

"Mary Stitch," the woman croons. "Mary Stitch, Mary Stitch."

Miriam's heart clenches.

"What?" she asks.

Ethan says: "Mary Stitch. Who is that, Miriam?"

But it's Karen that answers.

"A name. A shadow across her mind. I pluck it. Like the cat catching the mouse. Dangle dangle, tail in my mouth." She laughs: a sound like mad music, music that doesn't make any sense— laughing at a joke nobody gets.

"She can read minds," Ethan says. "If they're alive, just a little. Thoughts at the surface. Like a child catching leaves floating on a pond."

The question is a terrible one, and Miriam hates to ask it.

But her words form it just the same: "And if they're not alive?"

That smile. Ethan says, "That's how we found you. Wade wouldn't tell us what we wanted to know. And he buried the thought deep. But . . ."

"Dead minds are easy to see," Karen says. Staring up at nothing when she says it. Tongue sliding across the dry slug that is her lower lip. "For a time. They linger. Like a smell. And then they fade. . . ." Her head slumps, this time to the right—her neck forming a sharp, miserable right angle. Her teeth clack together and her eyes shut. She hums a little discordant song. *Hmm hm hmmm mmmmm.*

Ethan says, "Wade got us to your old motel. The new clerk helped by explaining that his van—his very conspicuous van— was stolen. I have a friend on the force. Was easy enough to find out where you'd gone." The look on his face says he likes this, at least a little bit. He may be sad about what happened to his wife, but Miriam thinks a part of him likes what she's become as a result. What Miriam sees in those eyes is pride, buffed to a bright and troubling shine. "You still think we're not the real deal, Miriam? That we're just some . . . loony-bird fringe group? We're serious. We're motivated. We aren't messing around."

Underneath the table, Miriam feels someone grab her hand. Gabby.

"What's your plan, then? Why am I here?" Miriam asks.

Ethan leans back. Like he's suddenly comfortable. "I want

this to be our family. Special people. Different. Folks who can see how things really are, and then move to *change* them."

"And everyone here is . . . like that? They all have the curse?"

David's eyes twinkle. "We sure do."

"But nobody said it's a curse but you," Ofelia says.

"You're different too," Ethan says. "Isn't that right, Miriam?"

She wants to say: *You don't know me*. But in a rare moment of restraint, she keeps her lips zipped and the words tucked. "The boy. What about him?"

"Isaiah? Oh, he's very special, indeed. Isaiah, the child that never should've lived. The premature child of a drug-addicted prostitute mother." Way he says these words, it's like the boy is some kind of prophet. Some *savior*. "Died twice in the NICU at Cardon Children's Hospital. Brought back to life both times. In and out of foster homes until he came to us via a very kind set of foster parents: Darren and Dosie Rubens. But his mother . . . Grace." He clucks his tongue, shakes his head. "She came to take him back. We invited her to join us, but." He shrugs.

"What can the boy do?"

He grins. "I would hate to spoil that for you. We'll get him back. And then you'll see. But he's a very powerful child."

"He is a . . . weapon," Karen says, her voice muffled as she stares down at her lap. Her shoulders hitch and twitch as she speaks.

"Well, *I'm* no weapon," Miriam says. "Nothing I can do will help whatever . . . *this* is. I think we're done here."

She stands up. Gabby follows suit. And then the two of them just stand there. Ogled. Ofelia snickers. David frowns. Miriam feels a presence behind them—it's a good bet it's Jade, Ethan's soldier. Gun ready.

Ethan picks at his teeth with a thumbnail. "I have not yet returned your keys. I think before I even consider giving them back, you ought to do us the favor of enjoying the food we've cooked. I hate to waste it. And I don't want you to sell yourself short, Miriam. I think what you can show us will be profound. To peer into our lives. To see our deaths. That's powerful business."

And there. An opportunity.

"You want to know," she says. A statement, not a question.

"Know what?"

"Don't play coy. You act like you're a straight shooter, so shoot me straight, cowboy. You want to know how you die. It's okay. Everybody wants to know. It's like the world's most morbid party trick."

Ethan licks his lips. It comes off him in waves: the eagerness, the interest. She knows it well. He has a taste for something he hasn't even tasted yet. The most forbidden fruit—rotten and sweet. A glimpse at the end of the road and what waits there in the last light before darkness.

Good. She can use that.

He stands up. "How's it work?" he asks.

"I can't do them." She points to the others at the table. "I can't see what becomes of others with the curse. Their fates are on a roulette wheel that's still spinning. But for you? Oh, for you, it's simple. Skin on skin will do it. A little touchy-touchy. I see *how* you die. I see *when*. I don't see where, so that's one variable in the equation that will have a big blinking question mark over it. But the rest is on me. You really want to know? It'll shake you up like a soda can."

Ethan kisses the top of his wife's head. Karen moans. He nods.

Miriam pries her fingers from Gabby's. Poor Gabby. She doesn't know what's coming. Maybe she can sense it, though. *Hopefully she does, because I'm going to need her to be ready.* But she can't risk giving it away, so . . .

Everybody's flying blind here. Everyone but Miriam.

She steps around the back of Gabby.

Ofelia and David watch her with dark eyes. Ofelia looks

bored. But David—he gets it. He understands that something's happening. He just doesn't know what.

Miriam creeps around the table, stands on the far side of Karen's wheelchair. Ethan opposes her. He puts out his hand.

She starts to put out hers.

Karen's head lolls back and she stares up at Miriam with white eyes gone suddenly bloodshot—spider webs of little red veins. "You," Karen says in a loud whisper. "Death touched you. Killed something inside you. And now. Now he's passed you by. He can't see you at all."

Killed something inside you.

Somewhere out over the desert, Miriam's sure she hears a baby screaming. A loud squall like from an infant that's starving, cold, or hurt.

It's not real. She knows that. It's the Trespasser fucking with her. Well, fuck him. Or her. Or whatever the Trespasser is. She grits her teeth and looks down at Ethan's waiting hand.

Miriam takes it in her own and—

THIRTY-TWO

BROKEN KEY

Ethan Key stands naked and alone in a cement block room. No lights above. Just a small Coleman camping lantern sitting nearby. His mouth is taped shut. He is bound to a pipe above his head. His fingers are broken. His toes, too. His nose. He's been like this awhile, and his nude body shows dozens of bruises. Bruises like the shadows cast by clouds drifting lazily overhead.

A murmur of voices somewhere nearby. Spanish. Ethan speaks it but can't understand what they're saying—too far away, behind too much cement.

Footsteps. Coming closer.

A door opens. Metal. Ratchets open with a squeak, shut with a bang.

A man enters. He's tall, handsome, in a bold white suit. The way he walks is almost rigid, robotic, like he's a department store mannequin. When he speaks, he does so with a voice of burned caramel, with words of warm whiskey. An accent waits there: Central or South American, maybe. The man saunters forward. Something's in his hand.

That something flits and flips from finger to finger. A card, like a playing card. Bowing and arching as he moves it from knuckle to knuckle.

With a flourish and a flip of the wrist, he faces it forward. Toward Ethan.

On the card is a crude drawing of a spider. Inked in, all the way black—all of it except for a circle on the spider's back. A circle with three lines spinning out from the center. "Is this your card?" the tall man asks.

"Wuh. Wuh. Who. Who are you." Ethan's words are mushy, muddy.

"You know who we are. You had to know the cartel would be coming for you eventually."

"Please. No. Let me go. We left you alone . . ."

The man draws a deep, satisfying breath through his nose. "Life. Existence. Presence. It is decided at the moment of inception. A length of string carefully meted and measured out, then cut. All things, predetermined. Destiny: from the Latin, destinare. Meaning, to make something firm. To establish its permanence. As if carving it in stone. Fate: a thing ordained. Fate. Fatal. Death. Nona, Decima, Morta. You established your fate when you built your little town."

A low animal whine rises from Ethan. A whine of fear and uncertainty. Tears run. He's a man broken: a stick snapped over someone's knee. "Puh—puh—lease. Lemme . . . just lemme . . ." He doesn't finish. He can't. Words swallowed by the whirlpool of tears.

"Creation is thought to be a gift, but it is not," the man says, barely paying attention. He stares up into the shadows of the ceiling. Or past them. "It is not a thing given but rather a thing bought. Purchased. A debt incurred at the moment of becoming. All things must end."

The man flips the card and it disappears.

He pivots now, walking from Ethan to the door and back again. Feet echoing.

"I don't I don't I don't understa—"

"It is not just a person's life that incurs this debt. All things that exist must make the purchase and owe the payment. Everything that exists will one day not exist. That can be troubling for some, but I find it freeing. Our presence here is given margins. A start and an end. Everything in this way has a story; some stories are long and boring. Others? Short and exciting. Yours was exciting, I think. And good for you. But it will be shorter than you like."

"My wife. Just leave her alone."

"She is with us now. She will be kept safe. I think she could bring some value to our organization. Don't you?"

"You fucker. You fucker."

"You toyed with things you did not and do not understand. You played with the length of string. All because of some . . . what? Visions? Delusions? Well. You interrupted our business. The cartel can only stomach so much troublemaking. Things were going to go the way things were going to go; fate was to have its course, and yet here you are, acting like you didn't expect this."

The man's hand flips again.

A knife is in it now. Out of nowhere? Or always up his sleeve?

He drags the tip of the blade up Ethan's thigh. Past his balls, his cock, up his belly. Drawing a tiny line—like a thorn-scratch. Circling a nipple. Up the neck. Under the chin. Ethan whips his head around now, an eel on a fishing line, but no struggling will change what's about to happen.

The man turns the knife so that the hilt is down and the blade is up. He cups his hand almost lovingly underneath the hilt. And he slowly begins to press upward. The blade enters the rough skin there under Ethan's jaw. Ethan's eyes go wide. He struggles, shakes, but it only makes it worse. Blood on the man's hands. Blood wetting the rim of his white sleeve. Up, up, up the blade goes. Into Ethan's mouth. Spearing the tongue. He gurgles. Screams. Legs kicking. Elbows locking.

A little resistance now.

So, the man drops his hand and jams the knife back up again with the heel of his palm. A crunch. The resistance is done. The blade into the brain.

Ethan Key is dead. Body slack. Naked. And bleeding.

THIRTY-THREE

BUSTED LOCK

Time is a fraying ribbon. Cut up into loose threads. Every second on the clock a strange and uncertain misery. Her hand slides out of Ethan's grip. She hears him asking, eager, needy: *How do I die?*

Karen stares up. Eyes wide. Mouth frozen in a silent moan.

Ofelia sneers. David looks bored. Gabby tenses—she knows.

With every blink, Miriam sees Ethan Key's death. Cement room. Spare lantern. A playing card with a spider and a circle. The knife. And she tries to feel the strings of this thing and where they lead: Mary Stitch and a little boy named Isaiah and the Trespasser. None of that means anything in this moment.

She tells Ethan: "The cartel kills you."

It's not a lie. She just doesn't tell him all of it. Devil in the details, and all of that. Why give him the details? Why offer him the Devil?

The look on his face is one—oddly—of comfort. Like he always knew this was the way. Well, fuck him for that. Fuck him for his *satisfaction*.

She plays it up:

"You're naked when they do it. They kill your wife in front of you. They cut off your dick and your balls and make you eat them—"

The look on Ethan's face is like hot chocolate on a cold day:

so pleasurable to watch his mask of satisfaction crack. His smug mouth turns down and his eyes go wide and she sees his eyes actually get wet from coming tears—

But then David, pouty fucking David, ruins it all.

"Liar," he says. Singsongy.

Ethan turns toward David, who gives a small nod. Anger and disappointment war on Ethan's face.

What, then, is David's curse?

Best guess: he's a human lie detector.

Shit.

Ethan's hand moves. She sees the gun at his hip—the pistol from earlier, sitting there in an unclipped holster.

It's time.

She gives a hard hip-bump to the table. Glasses spill. Lemonade all over. It's a distraction—small but vital. Everyone's eyes turn toward the thing that's moving more than she is. They're all looking at the pitcher and the glasses and the table shaking, and as their eyes move, Miriam's hand darts out—

The steak knife, Ethan's steak knife, is in her hand.

She moves backward, bringing Karen's wheelchair with her—and just as everyone turns to see what's happening, she brings the knife to Karen's throat.

Jade is screaming, rifle up.

Ethan is shaking his head: *no, no, no.* Hand waving to Jade: *put it down, put the fucking gun down.*

"I'll kill her. I'll kill your goddamn wife. Your *prophet.*"

"I can take the shot," Jade barks. "*I have a clean shot.*"

"Don't!" Ethan yells at him. "Don't you dare, Jade. Put it down."

"Better yet, give it to Gabby," Miriam hisses.

Jade, though. Jade's a maverick. He doesn't give a shit.

He gives her the gun, all right. He raises the rifle, points it at the back of Gabby's head and—

No, no, god, what have I done, no—

But Ethan points his own pistol.

At Jade.

"You shoot her," Ethan says to his soldier. "Then I shoot you."

"Let me play this my way, Ethan," Jade says—not angry but pleading. Like he thinks he can do this. Gabby cries out. Her face scrunches up as she tries not to sob. She's holding it in, keeping it together, but barely. She's ready to come apart at the seams. Miriam is too, but she can't let that happen.

"Jade, goddamnit—"

Miriam yells, "Shut the fuck up! I count to five. Jade, give Gabby that rifle. Ethan, I want that pistol. If I get to five, I cut Karen's throat."

David, from behind clasped hands, says, "She's not lying."

Miriam: "One—"

Jade: "Ethan, let me pop this bitch."

Ethan pulls back the hammer on the pistol. "Pop her, I pop you."

Miriam: "Two!"

Ethan: "Karen, baby, it's gonna be okay."

Jade growls. But the rifle stays pointed. He jabs it into the base of Gabby's head and she almost breaks—her teeth clench, she whines through them.

Miriam: "Three!" Her hands tighten around the blade. Karen bleats.

Jade roars.

He throws the rifle on the table.

Ethan exhales.

But Miriam, she's still on the clock: "Four!"

"Whoa, okay, now, okay." Ethan sets his own pistol down, nudges it toward Miriam. She reaches over Karen's arm and wheelchair wheel and snatches up the pistol. She points it at Ethan and flings the knife to the side. Karen gabbles and screeches, her head whipping around on her neck like she's a parakeet on fire.

"Gabby, point that rifle at that muscle-bound sack of meat."

She does. She gulps and turns. The gun rattles as her hands shake.

Jade sees it. He knows she's not ready for prime time with that thing. He presages his movement—all parts of him tense up. Gabby doesn't see it. She doesn't see him roar and reach forward, grabbing the barrel and stock and turning it away, raising a fist—

Pop.

His brains disappear into the darkness.

The recoil from the pistol vibrates Miriam's arms.

He drops. Gabby screams. Ethan starts to move but Miriam trains the gun back on him. "I told you I was fast like a rattlesnake." Grotesque satisfaction fills her, blooming like a heart full of black flowers. She thinks the courthouse will still suffer an attack in three weeks' time, but at least that fucker won't be there. He won't be the one to put a bullet in that old man's head.

"Miriam, you have made a terrible mistake," Ethan says. He's mad now. Nostrils flaring like a bull seeing a matador. "This is gonna come back on you. Like the recoil of that pistol."

"I can handle the pistol. I can handle you. Keys. To the van. On the table."

"What if I say 'no'?"

"Then it all ends here. You. Your wife. Those two mental midgets—" She gestures toward Ofelia and David. "You have a chance to keep your weird fires burning, but me and mine, we're getting the hell outta here. So: *keys*. Now."

He holds up his hands. "I don't have them."

"Lying," David says. Then gasps and covers his mouth.

"David—" Ethan snarls.

Miriam pulls back the hammer on the pistol. "Last chance."

Ethan Key roars and then acquiesces. He fishes the keys out of his pocket with a jingly-jangle and slams them down on the table.

"Good," Miriam says, and reaches forward.

But as she does, Karen looks up and whispers:

"Death doesn't see you. *But I do.*"

Miriam growls: "I don't need to see how you die, Karen. Way I figure it, you sneeze too hard one day and that bullet lodged in your brainmeat will pop free and come back out the hole it came through." She shakes the keys. "Gabby."

Gabby, still holding the rifle, gives a terror-struck nod.

Together, they flee.

PART FOUR

DEAD BIRD DON'T FLY

THE TITMOUSE

The titmouse is a friendly bird, the park ranger said.

Miriam just laughed, because, c'mon. Titmouse. *Titmouse*. The ranger just stood there, annoyed—blink, blink, blink—and Miriam of course explained because Miriam *of course* enjoys digging holes and jumping in them. She said, "Because first you imagine a mouse, a little squeaky mouse, and then you imagine a tit—a boob, a breast, a sweater monkey that has escaped its underwire cage—and now it's attached to the mouse? Like, on its back? Or the top of its head? Flopping around like a damn Jell-O mold? Huh? Right? Oh, come on. That's funny. That's just . . . that's just good humor, lady."

And the ranger—a woman with a dour, sour-milk face and red hair pulled back in a no-nonsense, zero-fuckery ponytail—said rather humorlessly, "They have genetically engineered mice to grow human ears, you know."

Miriam explained that this was gross and the ranger ruined a perfectly good joke. The ranger shrugged and continued on her litany of titmice talk: blah blah blah, they're friendly birds, they might even eat out of your hand, they sometimes flock with birds of other kinds like chickadees, juncos, flickers, woodpeckers, and nuthatches. Miriam snorted at wood-*peckers*, and then lost it at *nuthatches*, at which point the ranger encouraged Miriam to either go out and enjoy the state park there in Chattanooga or leave the park.

All that from asking: I want to go bird-watching, so—what kind of birds should I be looking for here?

Because it was time to practice.

Now she's here, in the park. Surrounded by tall oaks and warm September air. A stream pops and bubbles nearby, carving a narrow channel between some rocks. She's been walking now for . . . what? An hour? Nobody around. Blue sky. Beautiful day. Nothing can ruin it. She just needs to find a bird and . . .

Sure enough, there, on a nearby stump—a stump as tall as she is, a stump that sits crooked like a hooked finger—sits a titmouse.

Big black eyes. Tiny head shoved into its plump soup-dumpling body. An ostentatious tuft of feathers sticking from the top of its head like a nasty case of *just-been-fucked-in-a-gas-station-bathroom* hair.

The bird whistles and whoostles and chirps.

Stupid, cute little jerk.

Miriam is not one to be drawn in by cuteness—it is, after all, a trap. A trap engineered by nature so that you want to take care of such ittle-bittle-widdle critters, or at least so that you don't ditch them in a hole somewhere. Small head and big eyes? A ruse. A clever, careful, evolutionary ruse.

And she feels herself getting suckered in.

She wants to whistle back. She wants to hold it because the feathery little dum-dum looks cute as all fuck. If she could, she would reach out and grab it and hug it and squeeze it until it pops like a grape.

The desire to hug adorable things until they are dead is strange, she decides. Best not to shine a light in that dark corner and just *get on with it*.

"All right, boob-rat," she says, cracking her knuckles. "Let's do this."

She draws a deep breath. Closes her eyes.

She hears the bird's whistle.

Its little claw-scrape on the sawn wood end of the stump.

She reaches out—with her mind, not her hands. *There*. A little something in the dark behind her eye. Something in the three-dimensional nothing beyond her. A tiny light, a life pulsing there like an M&M-sized heart—

And then it's gone.

She opens her eyes. The bird isn't there.

What the— Well, fuck.

But then: she hears it. The whistle. Not far. Just over there—on a rock covered over in creeping five-leaf ivy. Hopping about. Like it just doesn't have a care in the world. Pecking at something. A seed, a black seed. Peck peck peck. Break. Flip seed into beak. Chomp chomp.

Miriam can feel the cuteness seeping into her. Like a disease.

Again she shuts her eyes. Too hard, at first—like she's wincing, like she's trying to block out all the light. *Relax. Just lie back and think of England*. Her walnut-cracker of a tight jaw loosens. Her breathing mitigates. In. Out. Ah.

There it is again. That tiny heart.

She reaches out for it. Feels along its margins. Pries at it like a toddler trying to peel an orange—clumsy, ineffective, impossible. *An opening*. Small. But she reaches in, pushes her mental thumbs downward and—

A shrill, sharp trill.

Miriam's eyes jolt open. The bird is on the rock. Flopping about. She hurries over to it—the wings flap, the claws are balled up and clutched close to the bird's white, downy breast. It's crying out—an alarmed chirp, panicked. Something's wrong with it. The thing's middle is—it's almost like the bird has a new joint. Oh, god. *I broke its back*.

She did this to the bird.

"I did this," she says. Voice just a breath. Before she even realizes what she's doing, she reaches out, grabs the titmouse's head, and twists. The bones pop like bubble wrap. So easy to snuff out its life.

Miriam leans her back against the rock. Slides down to the grass. Tearing ivy off the rock, ivy that drapes across her brow like a garland. She thinks back to a time when Uncle Jack took her out and she used his BB gun and shot a robin. Killed it. *Nicely done, killer. That was an ace shot, little girl.*

She cries like she's dying. Stupid, stupid bird.

THIRTY-FOUR

THE DEAD BIRD BONEYARD

The wizard van sits parked between the rusted, gutted husks of two old airliners—wingless, dented tubes with broken windows, the rust on them like a disease: metal eczema, steel scabbing. The moon sits at the peak of the sky, bright and full and staring down. Hopefully, Miriam thinks, it is the only thing that sees them here tonight.

When they pulled out of the compound—Jonestown? Keystown? Whatever—her foot was mashed hard against the accelerator, and the whole time, she knew she was going to hit a hole too hard, bust the tire, dent the rim. But the motel clerk's mighty wizard van had real magic pumping in its pistons, because somehow, it managed.

She expected the gate to be closed. Every part of her antici-pated some kind of shootout with someone manning the exit— blond-bearded Bill or whoever—but to her surprise, nobody was there and the gate was wide open. She didn't think much about it: a way out is a way out. You don't stop at the doorway of a burning building to think about what it means. You jump out with flames licking at your heels.

They drove for almost an hour—first back out of the raw and dusty road that took them to the compound in the first place. Then north, then east. Sometimes she'd see headlights ahead of them or behind and every cell inside her body would tense up—a string tied into too tight a knot—and she'd think, *Here they come; they found us.* But the truck would pass on the other side or the car behind them would turn off and it'd just be her and Gabby again. Alone on the dark desert road.

Finally, they saw something. A series of shadows and shapes like dinosaurs walking, like buildings that fell. Miriam thought: *This is it; we can hide here,* and she pulled off the road. They found themselves in a junkyard for old planes: big ones, little ones, Cessnas and jets and whole airliners from decades past. A few helicopters, too, sitting at the edges, rotors wilting like the wings of dead dragonflies. Nothing military—all domestic, commercial aircraft.

Now she paces. Outside the van. Gun back in her hand.

The back doors of the van hang open. Gabby sits at the edge. The rifle is flat across her lap. She stares down at it like it's a scrying pool.

Miriam talks. The adrenaline is still there, chewing through her like a hive of wasps hungry to make their nests from her— and right now, she burns it off by walking and by talking.

"They let us go," she says. "That's wrong. That's fucked. Why? Why let us go? Maybe they . . . maybe they put a tracker on us. I didn't find one but it's night. And what would I be looking for, anyway? Jesus. Shit! *Shit.* Maybe they let us go because he realized we were too much trouble. The fire got too hot to hold, so he let it burn somewhere else. That could be it. We did kill his man."

Gabby says, "You killed him. I didn't . . . I didn't kill anyone."

An uncomfortable red flare of anger fires up inside Miriam's gut. She wants to say: *I would not have shot him if you had stayed frosty, sweetheart.* But she tamps it back down.

"Maybe I should've shot them all. Left a pile of corpses. Set 'em ablaze like a bonfire. Everyone would've thought it was the cartels."

"That's horrible."

"Yes," Miriam says, coldly. She stops walking. "It is." Deep breath, refocus. Back to pacing. Desert stone and scrub crunching under her boots. Somewhere, a coyote howls. "You know what, they're gonna try to find us. Shit, they found Gracie out there, had a sniper lined up and everything. They got the curse like I do. They'll find us. Somehow. Shit!"

She roars and kicks the side of an old Boeing. The thing *gongs* like a metal drum. Rust flakes rain down on her and she shakes them out of her hair.

"What is it?" Gabby asks.

Miriam wheels. Feeling manic. She realizes now it's another nic-fit, this one strong enough that it feels like she's going to vibrate apart—fingers falling off her hands, arms out of their sockets, uterus plopping out like a muffler knocked off the bottom of a truck. She'll crash and burn like one of these old planes. Wingless. Ruined. A rattletrap husk. *I need a cigarette I need a cigarette I need a goddamn cocksucking motherfucking hell-shit of a cigarette.*

"I need a cigarette. It'd help me . . . *see* everything. It'd help me focus. I can't—nnngh, okay. *Okay.* I don't want to be drawn into this, okay? I don't care what Ethan does, I don't want to march in his little parade, I don't care. This isn't my job. It's not my life! He wants to try to take on the US government, he wants to try to blow up the courthouse, more power to him—" .

"Wait, what? Blow up the courthouse?"

Right. *Right.* Gabby doesn't know.

She catches Gabby up. Mary's file—of which she only saw a birthdate, 11/7/63. The bombs at the courthouse. The gunmen with the same tattoos seen on the flags at the Coming Storm compound. And, puzzlingly, the presence of Mary "Scissors" Stitch at the scene—apologizing for what? The bombs? Maybe. Or something else? Could she have been talking right to Miriam? Through the vision? It wouldn't be the first time. Ashley did the same thing.

There—the look on Gabby's face. Shell-shocked. Electrocuted by all of this cuckoo cracker factory narrative. Christ, she's locked up like a fritzing computer.

She's been through so much.

Ashley Gaynes cutting her up.

Miriam showing her face again.

Road trips and drug dealers and the emotional hurricane that comprises Miriam's many ugly feelings. And now: kidnapped, dragged out to the desert, forced to hold a gun, made to watch a man's brains evacuate his head.

And now all this crazy talk.

Miriam thinks, *This is it*. This is when Gabby breaks down. She can't hack this. How could she? Who could abide these things and keep it all together? Miriam can barely manage—and, frankly, the fact of her togetherness is debatable.

But Gabby says, "You're wrong."

"What?"

"This is your job. This is your life."

"Bullshit. I didn't ask for it."

"And yet you have it. This . . . curse, this gift, it's real. You can help people. So, you need to help them. The . . . the people at the courthouse? The little kid, Isaiah? You have a responsibility."

"Oh, fuck you. What do you know about responsibility?"

Gabby looks stung. Then pissed. She shoves Miriam backward. "Don't you *dare*. I've been keeping your shit together this whole trip. I'm responsible for *you*. Guess what? You're a mess. You're like a forest fire and I'm out here with a hose keeping you from burning down the rest of the world and everyone in it."

"No. I can handle my life on my own. You need to go. I'll go find Mary. I'll go get rid of my curse all on my own. You just . . . just go home, Gabs."

Gabby throws up her hands and barks a hollow laugh. "Oh, hell no. You don't just get to discard me, Miriam, because I'm saying things you don't like to hear. You condescending little cunt. You can't just push me away. I know you. I *get* you—"

"Please. Nobody *gets* me."

"Oh, *right*. Because *nobody* can understand you, can they? Poor Miriam. The cryptic cipher—a mystery wrapped in an enigma. If nobody ever understands you, then anything you do is fine, everything is permissible because they just don't *get it*. How *convenient* for you. Well, I get it. I get you. I fucking *understand* you whether you like it or not. And what I understand is that you have a gift and you need to use it to do the right thing. To be the person I know you are."

Miriam jabs her in the chest with a finger. "Fine. You want to know the kind of person I am? Here it is. *I know how you die*."

"Wh . . . what?"

She hears herself saying the most horrible thing, the thing she never wanted to say, but the reverse peristalsis cannot be stopped, the words refusing to be bitten back and choked down—

"You kill yourself."

"I wouldn't . . . I wouldn't do that."

"Except: You do. Only a couple years away now. You go into your bathroom. You grab pills. And you eat a lot of them. An epic amount. And then you go and you die. You do it to yourself." Her voice shakes as she tells it.

Gabby is staggered. Left standing there, blinking. Her hands flexing into fists and then going slack again. All these little micro-movements—little flinches and tics—pass across her face as she struggles to contain what are probably tears.

Then she marches up to Miriam, stares her down like a gunslinger.

"That's a problem for another day," Gabby says. "Today, we have other problems. Problems you can help fix. You're responsible for them, and I'm responsible for you, so that's that. We need to figure out our next move. *We*. Not you and me separate. You and me together."

Miriam swallows hard.

It strikes her like a slap:

I thought Gabby needed me.

But maybe I'm the one who needs Gabby.

"Our next move should be to run. Drive far away from all this."

"No. We're in this."

A sound by Miriam's ear. A squeak, a stutter—like a thumb rubbing across the surface of a latex balloon. A red balloon, she imagines. Gabby doesn't see it. It means it's not real. She *knows* it's not real.

But just because the balloon's not real doesn't mean there's not a very real message it's carrying. *Damnit*.

"The boy," Miriam says. "You're right. He's in danger. I can't—"

"*We* can't."

"We can't let him go. We have to help him be safe first."

"And there it is."

Miriam sighs. "There it is, yeah."

THIRTY-FIVE

GAS, SNACKS, ABANDONMENT

The wizard van idles in the parking spot. The passenger door pops open, and Gabby starts to climb in, her arms loaded for bear with snacks in bags and a dangling four-pack of Monster Energy drinks in her left hand.

Miriam is conspicuously silent.

Gabby must notice that, because as she's about to drag her seatbelt across her chest, she pauses, her eyes collapsing to suspicious squints.

"You were going to drive away, weren't you?" Gabby asks.

Miriam clears her throat. "I already did. I got about a mile out and felt super shitty about it. So, I drove back."

"You're impossible."

"I'm *very* possible." Miriam starts the van, then says, "By the way, Monster Energy tastes like tweaker piss. But it'll do."

She whips the van out of the parking lot, tires squealing.

THIRTY-SIX

SNIPE HUNT

Noon. Hard and bright: the sun like napalm sprayed on and left to burn. Four crumpled cans of Monster Energy form a small sacred cairn in the center of the wizard van: a sacrifice to modern gods of get-up-and-go. The drink makes her sick and buzzy. As Miriam drives, her skin buzzes like she's touching a live wire. Gabby slumps in the passenger side. Blearily staring out.

"I told you, go in the back and lie down," Miriam says.

"No. Nope. I'm in it. I'm not going soft. You roll hard, I roll hard."

"What's the next place?" Miriam asks.

"Uhh. Ahhh." Gabby leans forward, grabs a piece of paper with a bunch of writing hastily scrawled across it. "Westgate Heights. No! No. We just did that. Trumbull Village. Which means—ooh, oh, turn here."

"Right or left?"

"Right. No! No—*left*."

Miriam cuts the van hard. Tires squeal. The whole thing feels like it's gonna roll over like a kicked log. Gabby grabs the oh-shit handle above her head and cringes.

And suddenly, Trumbull Village. They pass a set of storage units: orange like a hunter's vest, the fences around them bent and warped and falling down. Ahead: a few condos and town-homes. Bars on the windows. Everything blasted and bleached and sucked dry by the vampire sun. Beyond them: a series of little houses. Square and utilitarian. Shoeboxes behind chain-link. The lawns are either dead or just gravel and dust. Some have pools that even from here look toxic: bright green, like the whole thing is a giant science experiment.

People mill about. Old folks stare through slatted blinds. Gangbangers sit on lawn chairs—little brown paper baggies underneath those chairs. Shirts just barely covering the pistols that hang tucked in their shorts and jeans.

Eyes stare as they pass.

Probably at the cool wizard on the side.

"Nice neighborhood," Gabby says.

Miriam shrugs. "Looks like most of America to me."

Gabby just makes a sound: *hunh.* "So," she says, and Miriam can detect the subject change the way a sea captain can predict the shifting wind. "I'm surprised you wanted to go after the kid."

"I don't want to go after the kid. But you convinced me."

"It's the right thing to do."

Miriam sighs. "Jesus, I know. Okay? I get it. He's a kid. Nobody's looking out for him. Children are routinely fucked over. Ignored or abused or otherwise ruined by their terrible parents. Parents who are terrible because, ta-da, they were once the children to terrible parents. An endlessly spinning carousel of awful people."

"Do you want kids someday?"

Miriam gives her the side-eye. "What, with you?"

Gabby flinches. She tries not to show it, but that question—or worse, the way Miriam asked it—must've hurt.

"Someday," Gabby says, defensive. "I mean . . . *eventually.* With someone."

"I . . ." Miriam really, really doesn't want to get to the next part, but oh, hell, here it comes: "I was pregnant once."

"What? Oh."

"Uh-huh. High school. I was Little Miss Repressed and I

found this boy I liked, Ben, and we got smashed on my mother's liquor and banged like awkward squirrels in the woods. Just once. Ah. Young love. Turns out that can make a baby, who knew? Obviously, my school didn't, nor did my mother, since the only thing *they* preached was *don't fuck anybody*—and since fucking somebody is the first and last thing a teenager thinks about every day, not a real valuable approach in terms of sexual education. It's like telling people to not go outside instead of preparing them for what they find when they're out there."

"Turn here," Gabby says. Miriam eases the van down into a little subdivision. More shoeboxes, fences, nuclear pools, dead lawns. "So. What happened?"

"My mother wanted me to carry to term. I did, too, if only because I wasn't really aware that *abortion* was an option and because I grew up kinda cuckoo religious and I guess even though I didn't believe it all, I didn't want there to be a chance that my tiny little non-baby would go to Hell—because there's a God I want to believe in, the kind who sends aborted babies to dwell in eternal misery."

"You had the baby?"

"I . . . did not. It's, ahh. Complicated?" What's complicated about it? Ben shot himself. His mother lost her mind. She found you in the bathroom at school and beat you half to death with a red snow shovel. "I lost the baby."

"Oh."

"And I got . . . all this." Miriam sweeps her arms out over the duct tape–wrapped steering wheel. "I almost died, and when I woke up, I had this *thing*. This way to see how other people were going to bite it."

"Jesus."

"I don't think Jesus had anything to do with this one."

"I'm sorry."

Miriam shrugs. This is one of those stories she wishes she

was telling with a cigarette hanging out of her mouth. "Don't be. Probably a good thing. Er, in the universal sense, at least. Me, with a kid? Even back then that was a recipe for a nightmare. Even at my nicest, I would've made a wretched mother."

"Don't say that."

"Why not? It's good to realize that. Not everybody is meant to be a mother or a father, and the more of those assholes figure that out, the better. But for some reason, our biological urge to reproduce is given this gross social weight. *Oh, are you pregnant? When are you going to have a baby? Are you? Will you? Won't you? What's wrong with you?* It's like if you're not a breeder, you're a nobody."

Gabby holds out her fist. "Lesbian fistbump on that one."

Miriam goes to bump it.

But.

Whoa.

"Look," she says, staring ahead.

"I don't know what I'm—*oh*."

The pickup truck.

Her pickup truck.

Parked dead ahead.

THIRTY-SEVEN

GOOD NIGHT, GRACIE

Pay dirt.

Before coming out here, they stopped at a local library in Phoenix, just as it opened. And they—well, let's be honest, *Gabby*—did some research. With the help of a reference librarian who, according to Gabby, was a wizard with far greater magic than that Nordic douche on the side of the van.

Didn't take long to track a trail of breadcrumbs through the newspapers: First, the boy who lived, Isaiah. Died twice, yet lived. Then the mother: Grace Baker. Arizona streetwalker. Or was. Arrested. Multiple times for prostitution, and a few for drug charges, too.

It's the drug charges that give them the thread to pull.

Found across police blotters in the newspapers: Grace's last arrest was two years ago. She was found at her boyfriend's house in, sure enough, Albuquerque, New Mexico. The boyfriend: Hermes Vela. Probably also her pimp and/or her dealer. Trumbull Village. Utah Street.

Which is where they find Miriam's pickup truck.

She lets the van drift past it.

"Where are you going?" Gabby asks. "That's your—"

"Yeah, I know. I wanna park down a ways. Just . . . in case."

"Oh. Good thinking."

Miriam winks. "That's why I'm not dead yet."

Though it's been close, hasn't it?

She eases the van up to a decrepit playground. A sandpit, really. Most of it gone to rust, though the slide looks recently replaced—the metal shines so bright in the sun, it looks like it's gone molten.

Miriam kisses her hand, presses it against the dashboard.

"What's that for?" Gabby asks.

"We won't see this brave wizardly steed again." She sees Gabby's quizzical stare and answers it with: "I'm gonna get my fucking truck back."

Then she grabs the pistol out of the glove compartment. They both get out.

The heat hits them like a slamming door.

Global heat death is on its way, Miriam thinks—though, at least, not in her lifetime. (If it were, she'd have seen it in the death visions by now. So, the planet gets at least a century to survive before it bursts into flame.)

Together, they head to the house. Shattered sidewalk underneath their feet. A little brown lizard hurries to and fro in front of them, fleeing them and scurrying from one dead scrubby shrub to the next. Like Godzilla in reverse.

The house is tan. The yard matches it in color: just pebbles and dirt. A junker Toyota sits in the driveway, the back windshield blasted out. Tossed off to the side: a kid's Big Wheel, crushed. As if by a tire.

"Looks like a kid lives here," Gabby says.

"Looks like a kid could learn the alphabet by going through all the varieties of hepatitis that live here," Miriam counters. *A through Z and 1, 2, 3,* she thinks. "No idea what to expect," she adds. "You ready?"

Gabby nods. She's not ready. That's as obvious as the sun in the sky. But nothing to be done now. Miriam goes to the front door.

To knock, or not to knock. That is the question.

Fuck it. She tries the knob.

The door opens.

Huh. Okay.

Inside: a smell hits her.

Oh, no, no, no.

Spoiled food. But something else, too: the smell of death. And death isn't just the stink of a body gone south. It's all the things that come with it, too. The waste, the fluids, the life *leaking* out in drips or gouts.

Gabby covers her nose. Miriam just steps in. Thinks: *Please don't let it be the boy. Please.* A shadow passes in front of her. A red balloon, floating. She pauses, shuts her eyes, opens them again. The balloon is gone. Never there.

The carpet at the fore of the apartment is ragged, torn. They turn left into a shitty living room. A flatscreen—newish—sits on a coffee table pressed against the wall. Opposite that: a couch that looks like a sagging old man. Broken down so far, it looks like any minute the whole thing could just disintegrate into dust mites and floating fibers. A little tray for kid's food—Disney characters on it, fading—sits on the cushions. No food there. Pills. A needle. A satchel. A Ring Pop, of all things. Just sitting there. Still life in drug culture.

Three ways out of this room. One is the way they just came. Another looks like a short hallway going to—where? Bedrooms, probably. Next to that, a small door. A door that's open just a crack.

Miriam holds a breath. Creeps gingerly toward it. Gives it a nudge with the flat of her boot and—

There sits Gracie Baker.

Her T-shirt slick with vomit. Mouth hanging open. The whites of her eyes gone liver-yellow and blood-black. Gray lips. A couple flies take flight, disturbed from their prize.

A needle hangs out of her dead arm.

It's like the color's starting to go out of her skin. Ashen and fading.

"Hey," says a voice behind them. Gabby starts to scream but clamps it down with a cupped hand. Miriam wheels, reaches for the pistol—

A lanky guy with broad shoulders and ribs showing underneath a too-tight white tee comes in from the hallway, picking his teeth with a chopstick. He walks right past them. Dude doesn't sit so much as he just lets all control of his body go: his frame collapsing onto the couch like an emptied bucket of chicken bones.

He stares at the TV—or past it, really—and reaches into the couch cushions to fish out a remote control. TV goes on. He starts talking, still looking a million miles away: "Yeah, yeah, you need, ahh, whatcha need? You here for pills, I got pills. Oxy, Perks, Vikes. Don't, uhh, don't got the new diesel yet, the stuff from Sinaloa, but, you know. You know. Unless you're here to work."

It's Gabby that says it: "There is a dead woman in your bathroom."

"Mm-hmm, mm-hm. That's a shame, that's a cold shame, but she couldn't hang, and so we'll figure that out, that's okay." He blinks. His pupils are big as slingshot marbles. "So, whatcha need, huh?"

"We want the boy," Miriam says.

"Huh? What boy?" But he shakes his head. "Oh. You want Gracie's boy. Izzy. Voodoo child. That one's in the back bedroom. Second door down. You can have him. State won't pay me for him. Paperwork, man." The man—Hermes, Miriam is guessing—lifts his hand and, in a limp, frittering gesture, points toward the back of the house.

Then he reaches down and pops that Ring Pop in his mouth. Sucking on it noisily. Eyes pointed at nothing.

Miriam gives Gabby a look. Whispers: "Come on." Gabby

gives a short nod and the two of them duck down the hallway. Together, they creep toward the second door. Even in the dry heat, Miriam's palms sweat. Just as she didn't want to see the boy dead, now she's afraid of what she'll see.

That one's in the back bedroom, Hermes said.

Children in the bedrooms of strange men is not something she wants to think about.

But what choice is there? She opens the door.

. . . and nobody's here. Just a messy bed. Old snacks strewn about. A dirty cereal bowl growing a brain-shaped bloom of mold over it. Dirty clothes. A rank smell.

Then: a sound. Movement. From inside the closet.

She hurries in, moves the sliding door—

Isaiah. The boy in the Superman T-shirt. Sitting there next to a half-collapsed set of drawers. "He told me if I left here, he'd shoot me," the boy says. He smells like piss. His pants are soaked through.

"Come on," Miriam says, holding out her hand.

But he doesn't take it. "I know you. I saw you. You're the truck lady."

"Yeah. Yeah." She tries to smile. It feels forced. "I'm her."

"Where's my momma?"

"She's dead." Those two words come out of her mouth like a pair of hammers—*clunk, clunk*. She can't take them back now.

The boy blinks. His eyes, wet. But tears never fall.

"Okay," he says.

From the front of the house, Gabby hissing from the hallway: "Miriam! *Miriam!*" *Shit, what now?* Miriam leads the boy to the door of the bedroom but tells him to stay there until she gets back.

Gabby points toward the living room, and at first, Miriam doesn't see it.

"A car just pulled up outside," Gabby says. And sure enough, past the living room to the window beyond—not a car, but an SUV. Black. Smeary with rust-red dust.

Two men and one woman are getting out. One of the men, she's seen before. She saw him at the Coming Storm's compound.

None of them have guns out, but she can see the bulges: they're all packing.

Did they follow the same trail Miriam and Gabby found? Or is this something else? Does Karen Key have some way into her head? God, this is making her paranoid. No time to worry about that.

Now they've got to get out. With the boy.

Think. Think.

"Hermes?" Miriam asks, hoping that's really his name.

He blinks, then finally looks at her. "Whuh?"

"You got a gun?"

"Somewhere. Shit. Where'd I leave it?"

She hates to do it, but she has to give it up. She turns her own pistol around and hands it to him. "There are people outside. They're coming to take your drugs. Right fucking now."

His slack mouth tightens up. His shoulders surge forward.

"Protect what's yours," she hisses.

"Damn, yeah," he says, licking his lips and standing up.

Miriam grabs Gabby by the elbow. Drags her back into the house. She fetches Isaiah and his hand touches hers—

The feeling of being crushed and smothered by dirt, grave dirt heaped upon her, pressed around her, soil in her mouth, packed in her ears, until all she tastes is filth and all she hears are the cooling sounds of the earth and her own galloping heartbeat and everything is noise and pressure and breathless death—

There. Not a proper vision. He's got powers, like Ethan said. She doesn't know what. But whatever it is—it's real.

No time to think about that now.

Together, the three of them hurry toward the last door: another bedroom, Hermes's bedroom, a worse mess than anywhere else. Clothes strewn. Two bongs. The skunk of spilled bongwater. Condoms new and used strewn about like holiday decorations.

A window in the back. Barred, but those bars open from the inside—they hang on a hinge. Miriam with one hand opens the window and then helps Gabby undo the locks of the bars.

At the front of the house: a door kicked open.

Yelling.

Then: gunfire.

"Go go go!" Miriam says, and Gabby clambers out. She helps Isaiah climb up and out—Gabby assists from the other side. Then Miriam goes.

They hit the ground and bolt.

A stray thought, absurd and disappointing, hits Miriam like a rock from a slingshot: *I'm not getting my truck back, am I?*

THIRTY-EIGHT

ANGELS AND DEMONS

The boy sleeps on the motel bed. The motel is a rat-trap and cockroach party—one of the few that let them pay with cash.

Miriam stands over the bed as he sleeps curled up around a pillow.

She imagines that he thinks it's his mother. That may not be true. He looks like a tough little peanut, this kid, and turns out that Grace Baker wasn't much of a mother to him. Maybe she wanted to be, but life isn't kind to people at their level. Miriam knows that because she's seen it, been in it, lived it.

Gabby comes up behind her. She rubs Miriam's shoulder. Outside, the bright red-and-orange neon of the tepee-shaped motel sign blinks. Casts the room in a kind of strange, hellish hue.

"I don't know what to do with it," Miriam says.

"It? You mean Isaiah?"

"Uh-huh."

"First, you might want to call him 'him' instead of 'it.'"

"I guess." She scrunches up her face. "He's going to want to eat. And he'll need clothes. Ugh. Do they take baths? They probably take baths." She sniffs the air. "He smells like bongwater and piss, so he's going to need a bath." Pause. "Shit."

"It'll be okay."

Miriam wheels. She whisper-hisses: "No, it fucking will not! I don't—I'm not a *caretaker*. This is not my bag. I don't understand

children. I barely understand adults." *I barely understand myself.*
"He's not my responsibility."

"So, whose, then?"

"I dunno! The system's."

"The system did *such* wonders for him already," Gabby says, hands on her hips. "The system is how he ended up with Ethan Key and his cult in the first place. The system routinely fails people."

"So, what are you proposing?"

"I'm not proposing anything. I'm just saying we keep him safe. For now. When dark skies clear up, we'll figure out the best place for him."

Miriam chews on that but nods. And here, a voice in her ear, a voice not hers, a voice that belongs to dozens of others—Louis, Uncle Jack, Ben, Melora, even her own mother: *Don't you wonder what he can do? He has a power like you. And still you don't know what it is. Can you trust the world to handle him? Can you trust him to handle the world?*

"I need to sleep," Miriam says.

"That's a good idea. You can take the bed with Isaiah—"

"No," Miriam says—too abruptly, she realizes. "You take the bed. I'll sleep on the floor. Then, in the morning, we need to figure out our next steps."

THE TRICKSTER

A coyote sits on a rock. It is plainly dead, and yet there it sits. One eye runny like an over-easy egg. Fur coming off in wet, sloughing patches. Bits of rib showing. A gray tongue panting.

Miriam sits across from the coyote. She is also on a rock.

Around them: the desert at night.

A bird shrieks somewhere. Crosses the moon. A big thing: massive, blotting out the light, sweeping across the stars like a hand in front of a projector's beam. Somewhere, thunder tumbles like falling rocks.

"Dreaming," she says.

"You always do that," the coyote says. Voice raspy. An old man's rheumy rumble, like hard phlegm rattling around in the well of his chest. "You always like to assess whether what you're seeing is real or a dream."

"Given my life, it's a smart play."

On her knee sits a pack of American Spirit cigarettes. Her hand moves—almost of its own volition—to the pack. The thumb toys with the flip-top.

"What if you're wrong?" the animal asks.

"I don't follow."

"Oh, you follow me just fine. I mean: what if your waking life is the dream, and this dream is what's real?"

She holds her hand to her mouth in mock existential shock. **189**

"What if my color blue is your color red! What if this is all a computer simulation! What if we're all just in the snow globe of a little handicapped boy!" She rolls her eyes. "Spare me the philosophical wank. You have something to say, so say it."

The coyote leans forward. Its mangy, slick muzzle inches from her nose now. She can smell the dead stink coming off it. The sour-sweet pickled smell like when you pass roadkill on the highway. "Consider this, then. What if all this—waking and dream—is just an illusion? Just a moment before dying."

"As my mother says, *It is what it is*."

"Maybe you're dying right now. Maybe you're a young girl, still, on the floor of a high-school bathroom. Bleeding out of your broken womb. A red snow shovel clattering nearby. A little light inside of you *winking out*, like a star gone dark—and all this has been a fever dream at the cusp of your own demise."

Her mouth goes dry. Her hand shakes. The fear is unexpected: *Am I really afraid of dying?* She sticks out her chin in faux defiance. "Fuck you," she says. Her thumb flips open the cigarette box.

Spiders spill out. Black spiders with tickling legs. Little tarantula babies running up the back of her hand and—

She shrieks, hops up, shakes them off her hand.

They're gone. So is the pack.

The coyote's one good eye blinks lazily.

"Or maybe," the coyote says, "when that little star inside you collapsed, something else filled the vacuum—a purpose, however dark, filled the void. A power. A power you have since failed to appreciate. A power you have only recently come to see fully. You change things, Miriam. You are chaos: necessary so that order does not calcify all we see. Vital: free will shattering the mirror of fate, a mirror that reflects *the way things are* rather than *the way things could be*. Why do you resist? Why do you *run*?"

Above, the massive winged thing swoops again—the shadow

in front of the moon. The night is suddenly cold and a chill skitters up her spine.

"I run because I'm done," she says. "Because I want the choice to work for *me* this time. Not for—"

"The boy? Isaiah? Or Louis? Or Gabby? So many you've saved."

"So many I've *hurt*."

The coyote gives something approximating a shrug—as much as a canine can. "If you say so. Go on, then. Save yourself. Find your way to the door in the dark. *This way to the great egress*. Go. Find Mary Scissors. Pull the stitch. You run because you're a coward. You shun your gift because you want to be normal? Now, after everything? Bah. You will never be normal, little bird. But fine. Cut the thread. Begone. You'll never see how much you can do. You have only found a part of your reach, a fraction of your power. But you plainly don't *deserve* it."

"Eat balls, coyote."

The bird shrieks.

The coyote laughs.

The dark shape swoops for her—from high in the sky to suddenly right above her. The stars, swallowed. The moon, eaten. Talons in her back, her shoulder, puncturing her head like a fork through a grape, and—

THIRTY-NINE

PULLING STITCHES

Snort. *Wuzza?* Awake. Miriam lurches up from the floor, suddenly panicked. *They're gone, Gabby is gone, the boy is gone.* And it's true. Nobody's there. The bed is a rumpled mess. The bathroom door is open; the lights are dark. Sunlight in through the crack between the curtains: like fire through broken stone. And she thinks an absurd thought: *That massive dark bird came down, stole them from me. Took them away in its terrible claws.*

But then the door to the motel room rattles. Unlocks. Miriam feels around under the bed for the pistol and *damnit* she gave it to that whacked-out-of-his-gourd dealer, Hermes, while poor Grace Baker sat dead ten feet away.

Miriam thrusts out her claws.

My talons.

The door opens and Gabby walks in. Holding Isaiah's hand. He's clean. So is Gabby. Seems like they had bath-time while Miriam was out cold.

They have a bag from Conoco. A white paper bag with what looks like grease soaking through. The smell of something spicy hits her nose.

As they enter, the boy says, "I think your scars make you look pretty. Momma broke a mirror once and I thought it was cool-looking after that."

Gabby looks like she's going to cry. A sweet smile. She runs a hand across his close-cropped hair. He pulls away—a shy move, not a defensive one.

"I'm gonna go wash my hands." As he skirts past Miriam, he says, "Hey."

"Hey," she says, giving him a nod.

Into the bathroom. She hears the faucet running.

"What was that?" Miriam asks.

Gabby gives her a quizzical look. "What do you mean?"

"He's . . . I dunno." She really doesn't know. Being around kids makes her uncomfortable. They seem so fragile. Like a stack of teacups you *know* you're going to knock over because it's sitting right there in the room. "He seems okay."

"He's not, probably. But he'll get there. I think he's processing. Or just shutting it all out, maybe. What do I know?" She shakes the bag at Miriam. "Breakfast sandwich. Chorizo and egg."

"Oh, fuck. I'm gonna need that in my body right now."

"Language," Gabby says.

"What language?"

"As in—" And here Gabby lowers her voice. "Watch the f-bombs."

Miriam blinks. "Why?"

Gabby's voice drops to a whisper. "Because of Isaiah."

"I think he can handle a few naughty words." Miriam gets close so he can't hear her. "His mother was a prostitute drug addict who just died. He may or may not have psychic powers, the truth or myth of which means he was in the care of a cult of patriotic weirdos. Or maybe they're anti-patriotic? It kinda seems like both, somehow. And now he's stuck in a hotel with a pair of cuckoo bitches who stole a wizard van. Either way, I think hearing me spout vulgarity is the *literal* least of his concerns." Footsteps behind her, and here he comes. As he sits on the edge of the bed, Miriam turns to him and asks: "Do you care if I say 'fuck'?"

He shrugs.

"Is that a noncommittal *no I don't care* shrug, or are you scared to say to me that you do care?" she asks.

"You are scary," he says in a small voice. "But I don't really care."

She sizes him up. He's wearing a different shirt. Gone are the Superman duds. Now it's a green shirt with what looks like the symbol of a ring in the middle. She recognizes it back from when she read comic books. "Green Lantern, huh?"

"Yeah."

"Cool."

"I like the John Stewart Green Lantern."

She clicks her tongue. "I only remember, what's his name? Barry Allen?"

"That was the Flash."

"Right. Shit. It's been a while."

"Hal Jordan, maybe."

She snaps her fingers. "That was it. Hey. How old are you?"

"Eight."

"Eight years old. All right. Cool." The conversation suddenly hits a wall. "Good talk, kid." She pats him on the shoulder, then gets up and snatches the food out of Gabby's hands. "See? He's eight, going on eighteen. Practically off to college. Let's eat."

"We ate already."

"Oh, well. Don't mind if I do, then." She hunkers down at the rickety-ass, rinky-dink desk here in the motel room like a gargoyle and starts unwrapping the sandwich. Steam comes off it. A spicy, vinegar tang. Behind her, the boy picks up the remote control and turns on the clunky, boxy TV. Flips through channels until he gets to something that sounds like a kids' show: lots of *boings* and *gonks* and other sound effects reminiscent of Saturday morning cartoons.

"I got you another present."

Miriam bites into the sandwich. It's hot. Burns her tongue. She doesn't care—*let the scalding commence*. Around the mouthful of food she says: "What is it? Liquor? Helper monkey? Green Lantern ring?"

Gabby smiles, but it's one of those wince-smiles. "It's a *good news, bad news* situation."

Miriam frowns. Gulps. "I don't like those. I like *good news, better news*."

"Bad news first?"

"My life story. Sure."

"We're out of money."

Miriam blinks. "That is not ideal. Especially since we just had a lot of money. Like, a few hundred bucks. In a bag."

"That's gone."

"Why is it gone?"

"Remember the wizard van?"

"Of course I remember the wizard van; the wizard van is amazing. It's the best thing in my life right now."

"It no longer has a wizard on it."

"You have killed the thing that made it beautiful. You have killed beauty. The world is a dead place now. Full of darkness and devoid of wizardly hope." Miriam sighs. "Let me guess, you got it painted?"

"I got it painted. Paid extra to get it painted fast."

"That's probably smart. You're smart. I hate that you did it. So, the bad news is, no money, and the ugh-fine-whatever *good news* is that you got the wizard van painted. I am sad the wizard is gone. But I'll cope."

"I also stole a license plate. Traded it from another van at the collision place. No cameras. I checked."

Miriam nods. "I like this version of you. You saucy little criminal."

"I thought you might be proud. But the good news isn't done." **195**

An arched eyebrow. "Howzat?"

"Actually, the bad news isn't done either."

"Jesus, it's like an emotional roller coaster already."

Gabby reaches into her pocket. "I spent all the money in my account. My debit card. Burned through the last of my cash."

"Like, this morning? Buying breakfast? Gas? A cruise vacation to Puerto Wherever? Diamond-encrusted tampon holders?"

"On this." She hands Miriam a piece of paper.

On it is scrawled a Tucson address. Miriam looks it over, gives a quizzical glance. "What is this? I mean, I know what it is. But who lives here? The Pope?"

"It's her," Gabby says. "Mary."

Blink, blink.

"What? How?" Miriam asks.

"They have these websites. You can look people up—do background checks and the like. It costs, though. Given that Mary Stitch is on probation, it means she's in the system. Which means— using the birthdate you found—I was able to look her up."

Miriam holds the address in her hands. The birthdate was key. One little piece of data unlocked that door.

"There's something else," Gabby says.

Miriam waves the address around. "This is the finale. You don't get to have *more*, Gabs. Seriously, I think you're going to kill me. What is it?"

"You know what needs to happen now."

"Yeah," Miriam says, laughing. "We go after Mary—"

"No, *you* go after her."

"Me? But we're a thing. We're a team. You made me believe that."

"And now I'm leaving."

A thunderclap knocking the breath out of Miriam's lungs. "No, no, no. I need you. We've determined that. You convinced me." Then she gets it. "It's about him, isn't it? The kid."

"He can't stay."

"I know *he* can't—so we go and we drop him off at a cop station—"

"I told you. The system will eat him up. Especially here. I sat at a computer and I Googled it—Arizona is one of the worst states in the country for foster care. They got kids sleeping in agency hallways. Not enough foster families. Children ending up on the streets because the system is fucking broken."

"So he stays with us. Just for a little while—"

"You'll endanger him."

"Me?"

Gabby gives her a look that says, *duh, yes, you.*

"I have a sister," Gabby says. "She lives in Virginia. We don't talk much, but she's bailed me out of shit before. I already called her. She wired me money for a couple bus tickets. We're out of here tonight."

Miriam slumps backwards, a doll with the stuffing gutted from her, leaving her feeling like nothing more than a ratty sack that once contained something human. She stares at the carpet.

She wants to suddenly rage. Kick out. Shove Gabby. Bite at her, scream at her, throw her down on the floor and fuck her till they're both panting, but she squeezes her eyes and blinks back tears and pretends that everything's fine. She's not mad, she's not sad, this is all perfectly normal.

"You're making a mistake" is all she says.

"You know I'm not," Gabby answers, then kisses the top of her head. "I have to go pack. I hope you'll give us a ride to the station."

FORTY

TRIGGERS

Miriam stands outside the motel room. Not smoking but wanting to. Smokers have triggers; she knows that much. They say that cutting the legs off your addiction is often about something so simple as a change of scenery, a shift in habit, a transformation of context—it's why so many of those soldiers who got hooked on heroin in Vietnam came home and got clean so easily when other addicts just can't manage.

Addiction, like so many things, suffers from context.

For Miriam, the whole world gives her context. It's one big trigger—and she's the finger curled around it, ready to squeeze. Dust blowing off a highway. The sound of traffic. The smell of exhaust. Hell, just *being outside*. Walking. Standing. *Existing at all*. Those things make her want to smoke.

And somehow, she's not.

All parts of her, clenched up like a fist. Cinched like a knot.

The motel room door opens behind her. It's the boy. Isaiah. Gabby's still inside, maybe packing.

"Whatcha doing?" Isaiah asks.

"Trying very hard not to smoke a cigarette."

"Oh." He comes a little closer. "My mom smoked once in a while."

"Not just cigarettes, though, huh?"

"No."

She lets her fingers drift to her mouth. Can almost taste the paper. Can almost feel the heat coming off the cherry. Her lungs ache for it. Her fingers form little scissors. Clip, clip, clip. "So. You ever been on a bus before?"

"Nuh-uh."

"Well, let me tell you, it's a delight. Buses are basically insane asylums on wheels. A metal tube on spinning rubber barreling down hot asphalt. Full of whackaloons and kooky fucks—just last year, some homeless guy who had gotten ahold of bath salts ate the face of another guy in Miami. I read about it."

"You don't know how to talk to kids, do you?"

"Not really. Sorry. I think I knew how, once. Or maybe had the equipment to figure it out at least." *But all that's been broken and beaten out of me.* "The bus trip will be fine. You get nice people on buses too. Old folks. Soldiers going home to see their family. College students deciding to see the world for the first time. It'll be great. Don't worry, Superman."

"Green Lantern."

"Fine. Yeah."

"I miss my mom."

"I miss mine, too."

"Is she dead?"

Miriam blinks, and offers a half-truth: "Yeah."

"Oh. Sorry."

The boy reaches over, holds her hand. She looks down at it and is about to yank her hand away like she's touching a hot stove. But it feels nice, too. So, she leaves it. Gives that hand something to do for now that isn't holding a phantom cigarette. And at least this time, she doesn't feel like she's being buried alive by touching him. Who is this boy? What can he do?

"So," she says. "I'm told you have a . . . thing, like me. A gift, a . . ." She decides to frame it in a way he might get. "A super-power."

He looks up at her. Big eyes, unblinking. "It's not a super-power. Superman does good things. Green Lantern is a good guy." He looks down at his feet. "What I have is something bad. Like a supervillain. I hurt people."

"How?"

But he doesn't say. His eyes shine. He squeezes her hand.

"I hurt people too, kid," she says. Not with her power. Not really. But hurt them she does. Miriam doesn't need superpowers for that.

They stand there for a while longer, watching a car go by once in a while down the long, dusty nowhere road.

FORTY-ONE

GIDDYUP, MOTHERFUCKERS

Greyhound Station. Gallup, New Mexico, not far from the motel, and pretty close to the border between this state and Arizona. Outside the van, with the sky darkening like spilled oil, they say their good-byes. Miriam tells Isaiah to keep Gabby safe. He nods. Then hugs her. She pretends it burns like poison, but truth is, it feels just fine.

Gabby and Miriam stand there. The space between them suddenly feels infinitely unfolding—though they are only a few feet apart, the distance seems to be ever-increasing.

"What are you going to do now?"

"I'm going to find Mary. Somehow, she's . . . involved with Ethan's people. Or at least his plan. I need to get to her before she gets blown to bits at the courthouse." Mary's strange apology echoes inside her mind.

"And then? Then you'll deal with Ethan's people?"

Miriam hesitates.

Gabby continues: "You have to do something. They're going to kill a lot of people. And they'll keep coming after Isaiah."

"I know. I'll do something." But that may be a lie. What can Miriam do? She neglects to remind Gabby that to undo fate, she has to take a life. Maybe more than one. To stop the Mockingbird, she had to kill a *whole family*. What about this time? Does she kill Ethan? Karen? Or every last one of them?

What sacrifice balances the scales? Who is the engineer of the bombing?

And what if Mary offers her an easy way out of her powers? Something as easy, perhaps, as walking through a doorway. What then? Would she walk away from it all just to be rid of her power?

Like in a Magic 8 Ball—

Answer unclear, ask again later.

"You understand why I have to go," Gabby says.

"Sure. Yeah. Yes." Another lie.

"You seem mad. Or hurt."

"I'm fine." Miriam pushes a smile onto her face and props it up there like a billboard. "Go on. Bus is waiting."

"You'll come out okay. We both will." Gabby leans forward, gives her a small and tender kiss. "We'll see each other again."

Miriam keeps forcing that smile and nods. "I know we will."

One last lie. Because she's not sure she believes it.

FORTY-TWO

MOVING THE NEEDLE

Nighttime.

Miriam drives the no-longer-a-wizard van.

She crosses the border back into Arizona. The road ahead is blacker than night. The devil's tongue, tarred and slick. Painted with a forked yellow line.

Not long after, she pulls over and cries. First it's a sad cry. Then an angry one. She punches the steering wheel. Kicks the dash hard enough, she dents and cracks it. Slams her elbow back into the seat again and again.

She misses Louis. She misses Gabby. She misses the wizard.

Fuck fuck fuck fuck.

A bird passes in front of the moon. A vulture, probably.

Thunder follows it. Distant.

"Why are you crying?"

Miriam gasps. There sits Gabby in the passenger seat. Smiling. She turns slowly, and blood glistens in the moonlight. Blood seeping from cracks in her face, cracks like those in a shattered porcelain vase. Bits of her skin and skull slide together and then apart like floating puzzle pieces.

"Fuck you," Miriam tells the Trespasser.

"No, fuck *you* for wanting to be rid of me." Not-Gabby pouts. Black fluid bubbles up between a split in her lips and oozes down her chin.

"I don't want this anymore. I don't want *you*."

"Rejection really does sting, doesn't it?"

"Go away. I don't need you anymore."

"We'll see. You might need me yet."

Those last words, spoken by nothing but a red mist—a crimson vapor that seems to dissipate in front of Miriam's eyes.

Somewhere, out over the desert, a coyote howls.

Miriam sits for a while. Her fingers wrap around the wheel of the van until they've been squeezed bloodless. *Get it together*, she thinks. *You're about to go find the person you've been seeking for a year. You may finally have an answer. You may finally have a way out. Get pumped, bitch. It's time to finish this.*

She lets out a war whoop.

It feels insincere. And so, like she is both the woman onstage and the audience listening, she thinks: *I can't hear you.*

War whoop number two. Better. Louder. Giddier. Good.

She pulls off the highway shoulder and guns it.

Miriam watches the needle on the gas tank dropping. Will she make it? As she drives, she reaches down in the seats—finds some change. A rolled-up dollar bill. A rough count after five minutes of searching is she has about two dollars and fifty cents. Thankfully, she spies a gas station ahead and pays two bucks for gas, then buys a single Slim Jim. Then it's back on the road, spicy meat tube between her teeth, foot back on the pedal.

Radio on. Only station it'll get is a Spanish-language talk show. Miriam doesn't understand it. White girl from Pennsylvania. In school, they had to learn a language and she was going to take Spanish because it seemed practical, but her mother said, *What, do you want to be a dishwasher someday?* And the next choice was French but that earned her a pissy, puckered look too. So: German it was, and now the only part of that she remembers is a single line from her beat-ass '70s-era textbook: *Hallo, ich möchte Ihre Wurst essen!*

Hello, I would like to eat your sausage.

Good times.

She laughs at that, a mad cackle.

Then she cranks the Mexican talk show and floors it.

Turns the journey south. Road starts to break up here. The patched cracks in the road like a junkie's veins—black, obvious, like hungry worms just beneath the skin. The ground grows craggier too. Like broken teeth, red from meat.

The moon crests high. Fat and round, a spider's egg straining to hatch.

Now she's really feeling electric. Like she's close. *So close*. A year, a *whole year*, looking for this one woman. A woman who helped Sugar's mother many years before—told her the way out of her curse. Drew her a path to escape the maze. But Mary Stitch has been bouncing around like one of those superballs from a department store vending machine—whipped against the wall, bouncing here, there, knocking over a lamp, clipping a painting, sending a candy dish scattering M&M's. Miriam's tracked her from Colorado to Nevada, New Mexico, and now to Arizona. A psycho psychic in Collbran. A gambler in Reno. A whole crew of bikers in New Mexico. And now: here. With all this shit. With the dust and the dry air and the static-snap feeling of finality in the air . . .

(Here her mind flashes to the courthouse again—walls coming down, screams, death and destruction compacting those people to jelly. She shudders. Gabby's voice again: *You have to do something*.)

It can all be over soon.

An end to what has *made* Miriam for the last *ten years*. The dead bird around her neck. The thing that broke her.

She wants to be whole again. And her mind plays out all the possibilities: What happens when it's all different? What's the way forward? She thought it would be Louis. That's not happening now, is it? Gabby will be there, though—a part of her life, some-how. (And here, a grim voice reminds: *If you can stop her from downing the contents of her medicine cabinet. If you lose your curse, do you also lose your ability to change the fate you've seen? In this, did you ever really have the power? To stop Gabby from killing herself—who would you kill? What eye will match that eye, what tooth will repay that tooth?* She curses her own brain to shut up, shut up, shut up.)

Miriam kicks the mirror inside her own head. When she stares at herself through the broken glass, what reflects back? What does she see? Who will she become after all this is done? Waitress? One of those women who run the roulette table, spin-ning a different kind of fate? Maybe she'll own a restaurant. *Ooh, a breakfast joint.* Yeah. Fuck yeah, breakfast.

Maybe she'll be a mailman. Instead of delivering people visions of their end, she'll deliver them grocery circulars, tax bills, Christmas cards.

Her fingers wrap around the wheel. Her foot presses on the pedal harder. The speedometer ticks up, up, up.

She'll run a breakfast joint in the morning. Then be a mail-man in the afternoon. At night she'll watch bad TV. At home. Hell, not just a home—a house, a proper house with a stove and a couch and a fridge full of food.

It doesn't have to be a fantasy, does it? And here she reminds herself: *You tried this before, dum-dum. Remember Louis? Him setting you up at the Shore? You had a little house. A job. A normal life. How'd that go for you?*

This time, she thinks, *it'll be different.* It has to be.

Doesn't it?

FORTY-THREE

THE HOUSE OF GODLESSNESS

A cat sits in a birdbath, green eyes glittering as the headlights pass over it. It doesn't budge. Just sits and stares. The house beyond is not a house at all but an old church: a small white chapel, the cross long gone from the tip of the steeple, the bell gone from within it. A mailbox sits out front.

This, on the outskirts of Tucson. North. Nowhere.

Little lights in the distance. Other houses. But no neighbors here.

Miriam thinks to pull away, go somewhere else until sunup—what's she going to do? Go kick the door down at close to midnight? Demand salvation? A cure for her curse? A Hot Pocket and a shot of tequila and call me in the morning?

But then a light comes on inside the house-chapel.

Then a light outside the front door.

The cat finally scatters—hair stiffening, tail straight. Zoom. Gone.

The no-longer-a-wizard van idles. The front door of the house—a door painted red long ago, the paint peeling like sunburned skin—opens up.

And a woman stands there. Long, stringy gray hair. In her fifties. The woman from the vision at the courthouse. The woman in the photos Miriam saw when she was casing Weldon Stitch's place. There stands Mary Stitch. Mary Scissors. Mary Ciseaux.

The woman yells, "You coming in or what?"

Deep breath. *Maybe this won't fix you. Maybe she doesn't know anything. Don't get your hopes up.* But her hopes are up. Way the fuck up, so up they're puncturing the atmosphere, moon up, stars up, another galaxy up, flying so far that "up" doesn't even *mean* anything anymore.

She cuts the engine. She heads inside.

FORTY-FOUR

THE HEART OF LIGHTNING

Mary's already gone from the front door when Miriam enters. The house really is an old chapel—the room of worship still with half its pews intact, most of them crooked and half-collapsed. Where the pulpit once sat is now a makeshift kitchen: Miriam spies a hotplate, a toaster oven, an electric kettle sitting on a small table. A little college dorm–size fridge underneath. Two doors lead out of this room and deeper into the old chapel.

Mary appears again. She's got a bottle of something and two glasses. Way she walks, she has a hippie's rangy, roaming pace. Once-black hair gone mostly gray. She looks old—older than her years. Like something's been robbed from her. Or dried up and died out.

"C'mon, c'mon, c'mon," she says, waving Miriam deeper in. The woman winds her way through the jagged pews, to a small card table set off to the side. She knees a stool closer to the table, then pulls up a small chair like you'd find in an elementary school. She squats on the chair, nods to the stool. "Sit."

Two glasses down. *Thunk, thunk.* Bottle without a label uncorked—*ploomp*. She pours a clear liquid. Knuckles it closer to Miriam. "Drink."

Miriam takes it. Slugs it back. It tastes like barbequed tequila. Smoky. But smooth, too. "Mescal?" she asks.

"Hunh," Mary says by way of grunted confirmation. "Friend south of the border makes it. Some call it *the elixir of the gods*. There's a myth behind it because there's a myth behind all things, and the myth says that lightning came from the sky during a storm and struck a plant, an agave plant. Boom. Tore it open and cooked the heart of the thing—the *pina*. And the juices that ran fresh from it was the first mescal. A gift from the gods above to man below."

"It's a helluva thing."

"Mm. Mm-hmm." Mary drinks hers in one gulp. "You're usually more careful than this, Miriam."

"What? How do you know my name?"

Mary leans in, gives her a look. A look that says, *C'mon, honey.* "This ain't my first bullfight. You're young yet. Old in the eyes, maybe, but young. I've been out here doing my thing for a long, long time. And I know you've been looking for me. I wondered if you'd make it. If you had the salt. You did, and you do, and now here you are, sharing a little god-juice with me. But you didn't flinch. You took the glass and drank it. I could've drugged you. Or could've been serving you a cold glass of coyote piss. You strike me as the type who would've been suspicious, and yet—you didn't even stop a second to think that I'd do you like that. Which tells me you want something from me. And you want it very badly."

You have no idea.

"I have a . . . curse," Miriam says.

"So do we all. What is it?"

"I can see how people are going to die."

"Morbid."

"I guess."

Mary pours another glass of mescal for herself—and tops off Miriam's glass, too. "So, you think I can—what? Help you undo it?"

"That's what I'm hoping."

"Hoping hard. So. What do I get out of it?"

"I . . ."

"You didn't think about that, did you? Just me, me, me. Gimme, gimme, gimme. That's no way to be, Miriam."

No, don't lose her: don't fuck this up. Miriam does what she despises doing: she apologizes. And doubly strange: she means it. "I'm sorry. I didn't—you're right. I do think about me a lot. I want to change. I want to do differently. That's what this is all about. So. Just name it. Name your price."

Mary sniffs. Leans back. Glass in hand, swirling the mescal.

"I want you to drive me somewhere."

"And?"

"That's it. I have business to take care of—and as you'll note, I don't have a car. I worked with some chemists recently. Part of a small Arizona group. Trying to make inroads against the cartels—doing their own meth, synthetic heroin, hydroponic weed."

Miriam nods. "I talked to one of those dealers. Helped me find you."

"Huh. Well. They owe me money. You drive me there, I get paid. Then we're square, and I'll tell you just what you need to know."

Miriam watches her. Every time she blinks—every time her eyes go dark behind falling lids—she sees Mary Stitch there at the courthouse. Whispering an apology before death. And it's like the woman can tell. She narrows her eyes.

"What are you looking at?" Mary asks. "What do you see?"

"Just trying to figure you out, is all."

"I'm no puzzle, honey. Nobody is. We all just want what we want."

"But why we want things," Miriam says, "there's the rub."

Mary chuckles. "Guess so. I know what you want, anyway,

and like I said, the way you get it is by us taking a drive. So, let's take a drive."

"Now?"

"You got something better to do?"

Miriam shakes her head.

Then Mary shrugs. "No time like the right now."

FORTY-FIVE

SOMETHING ABOUT MARY

They're headed to the van, and Mary says, "Ah, shit."

Miriam turns. "What?"

"I wanted to bring that bottle with us. Gimme a second."

The old hippie takes her time wandering back to the chapel, pulling her hair back in a ponytail as she walks.

Miriam stands near the hood of the van. Staring out at the lights over the desert. Windows of houses. Headlights. All far enough away that they might as well be a world apart. Above them, the nighttime sky is a wide mouth, deep and dark and eternally hungry.

She hears the door lock up and the sound of feet crunching on loose stone and scree. Miriam says, "It's pretty out here. Maybe I'll live like this someday."

"Maybe," Mary says.

Miriam turns and it takes her a moment to parse what she's seeing. The other woman, chin up, her mouth a scowl like a twist of bitter lemon.

A gun in her hand. A little automatic.

"This is going to hurt," Mary says plainly.

Then she pulls the trigger.

Miriam twitches. A feeling hits her—like being punched in the chest.

Everything sinks. Like an anchor crashing through ice. She

turns—*I need to run, need to get out of here*, but she takes one step and it's like her whole middle is a black hole drawing everything in. Light. Sound. All her energy. Her knee jukes left and she drops. Wheezing. Can't catch a breath. Her fingers claw at the ground.

Mary stands above her. Stoops, then rolls Miriam over.

Air comes in a screaming wheeze. In. Out. A high-pitched whine. Darkness creeps in at the edges of Miriam's vision.

"Stay with me," Mary says. She holds up the gun. Gives it a little shake. "This is a .22 caliber pistol. Okay? Listen to me, now. Focus. It's a small bullet, tinier than my pinky finger's tip." She wriggles that finger like an inchworm. "That bullet just went through your right lung. Like a cannon through a pirate ship's sail. Now you got wind whistling through the gap. Feels like there's a hard pressure at your chest, huh?"

Miriam blinks through the haze. She feels it. Like . . . all of her is leaving, being sucked out of her, up into the starving sky.

Mary sniffs, nods. "That's what they call a *sucking chest wound*. Like popping the door on an airplane as it flies. Creates an effect called a pneumothorax. Won't be long now before your chest will fill up with all this bad air, start putting pressure on your heart and other lung. You'll undergo cardiopulmonary arrest. You'll be dead in about five minutes."

Miriam reaches for the air. Claws at nothing. Imagines her hands around this woman's throat. Closing. A dream. An illusion. *No*.

Tries to scream. Weep. Yell. Anything. Nothing.

Just hissing, keening air from the bubbling blood hole in her chest.

"You never asked me what my gift was. Did you?" Mary *hmmphs*. "And it is a gift. I have used it to great favor throughout my life. I can see weakness. In people. In things. In structures, systems, even ideas. I can see how you break something down. Cut it apart. A snip-snip of the scissors. I knew where to shoot you. But I know so much more. All these threads tied to you. Chains, really." She draws a deep breath, like she's centering herself, finding focus. "We need you alive for what's to come, Miriam. My new friends have made that a requirement."

A vibration in the ground. Faint. Stronger. Headlights cutting through the night as Mary straightens up, reaches in her pocket, pulls out a small, thin something. A card.

"A playing card," Mary says. "Queen of hearts."

"Fuhhh." Miriam gulps, trying to catch air the way a child catches fireflies in a jar. "Youuu."

"Such anger. That's one of your chains." Mary stoops. Flips the playing card around and around. Then reaches under Miriam's shirt—hands, ice cold and burning hot at the same time—and *pops* the card against the bullet hole.

Miriam's body rocks like it's hit by a wave.

Suddenly, she can breathe.

Still a keening wheeze, but—in, out, in, out.

"Just gotta stop the chest wound from sucking so hard," Mary says with a wink. "That'll give you about five, maybe six hours more of life. Here's my new friends. You know them, I think." Mary stands, her knees cracking and popping like bubble wrap. "Ethan. Ofelia."

Miriam hears Ethan Key's voice. "Hello, Mary. Thanks for this."

"Motherfucker." Miriam seethes.

"She's feisty," Mary says. "Dumb, too. Stepped right in it."

Ethan's face wanders into view.

That smile is there. But it's cold, empty, like a skull's grin.

"Time to go home, Miriam," he says. "We're gonna get you better. Then we're gonna have a long talk while you think about what you've done."

PART FIVE

NO SUN EXISTED, AND IT WAS DARK EVERYWHERE

THE BIG MAN AT THE ROCK DOVE RANCH

She's sitting outside a brothel in Nevada. As one does. Place is called the Rock Dove Ranch, or RDR. Post-and-rail fence lines a long driveway out to the highway—and about ten minutes north is Reno.

Miriam sits outside and smokes. Behind her is the ranch proper. She's not sure what she expected out of a brothel in Nevada—part of her kind of figured it'd have some Old West vibe to it. A bloodred parlor-house with wagon wheels in the windows and a froofy-but-also-stern madam with too much makeup and a hat made of white peacock feathers. Lots of fishnets and player pianos and the smell of spilled whiskey soaking into an oaken floor. But this place: it looks like an office building. Square, tan, plain as a pair of golf shoes.

Her target: a gambler named Dan Hodan—nickname "Dan-Dan"—comes out here every Friday night to celebrate his winnings. Or, when he loses, to weep into the snatch of some very enthusiastic lady of the evening. He's the next link in the chain to find Mary Stitch: the woman who Miriam believes possesses a Get Out of Jail Free card. Do not pass Go. Do not collect your two hundred smackeroos. Meet Mary and head straight to No More Psychic Powers Avenue.

It's Friday evening or coming up on it. She went in, asked around about him. The house madam was a frumpy thing in a **219** gray T-shirt with big-ass pink-framed cat-eye glasses. The prostitutes ran the gamut: blond hair, black hair, purple hair, thick hips, big ass, little ass, huge tits as fake as a wiffle ball, tiny tits with itty-bitty nips like cherries on a dollop of whipped cream, smooth thighs and cheesecake asses and stretch marks and bullet holes and tan and pale and makeup and no makeup and—

Well, only thing that seems to universally link these women is a tough-as-tiger-teeth attitude. Each one of them: smiley, snarky, each with bite. Like they know how to talk, they know how to walk. Miriam pointed it out to one, a tall skyscraper of a woman with blond hair all the way down past her ass calling herself Danika Dreams. Danika said, "You think we're hookers, but really? We're saleswomen. Each and every one of us could sell sand to a lizard. It ain't about these—" She shakes a pair of breasts that are nice, if a little uneven. "Because these only get you so far. It's about this."

And there, Danika tapped her temple and then her lips.

"What we think and what we say gets us paid," she said, then winked. She gave Miriam an assessor's glance: up and down and then up again. "You're a good-looking thing. Kind of a young Molly Ringwald type but like if she were on heroin instead of just some rich white girl. Got that road-trash vibe about you, like you just blew in here on a hot wind. Guys go for that. Some of them, anyway; they all got a type. You interested? Some girls do it just for a week, just to see."

Miriam laughed. "I would, but at some point, I'm sure I'd punch some yokel in the dick and break it off like an icicle. Bad for business."

"Some guys could be into *that*, too," Danika said, a little cheeky. But then Miriam told her what she was looking for—info on a client. Danika told her that hanging around in here might be weird, and Dan-Dan was a good client, though kind of an asshole. So, she said: best to wait outside. Not inside. Particularly

since Miriam didn't want to try putting herself in the rotation—
no need to confuse the gentlemen who'll show up here looking
for a little coital comfort.

So, now Miriam sits outside. And smokes.

Sun beating down.

The fucking sun.

Ugh.

Why is it she ends up in these places? *I gotta find a place, dark
and damp. Seattle, Vancouver, some creepy inbred New England
island. Places where the sun won't show its creepy-happy face
most days of the year.*

In the distance, a car. Silver sedan. Shining bright in the
oblique angle of that horrible sky-god, that wretched day-star.

Miriam winces, stands up. This must be Dan-Dan.

Car pulls onto the pebbled gravel.

A man gets out.

It isn't Dan-Dan.

"Well, holy shit-snickers," Miriam says. "You're alive."

Agent Tommy Grosky stands there, staring through a pair of
Wayfarer sunglasses. "I got your message," he says.

"Weldon Stitch."

He takes a few steps closer, around the front end of the car,
arms crossed. She can't see his eyes but she can tell he's regard-
ing her warily. Like a kid at the zoo excited to see the tiger but
secretly afraid the big cat will jump the barrier and make him a
midday snack. Grosky knows her well enough.

"You're one fucked-up bird," he says.

"You know me well." She flicks the cigarette. "How'd you
find me?"

"We're Big Government. Got a lot of eyes. Once I had your
location in Colorado, was easy enough to follow the trail of
feathers."

"Feathers. Cute."

He grins. "I'm a cute guy. Like a teddy bear."

"Uh-huh. Adorable. So, is it you following the trail of feathers, or is it Big Government? You here to bring me in again?"

He brushes some crumbs off his chest, off his tie. "No, just me."

"Why track me down at all?"

"Because you're amazing."

"Aw, thanks. I love you too, big guy." That spoken with as much sarcasm as she could muster: a sponge drippy with it, squeezed hard.

"I mean it. You have a real gift. People want to know how they die, Miriam. It's the one thing most of us never know until it hits us out of nowhere, like a brick thrown from a passing truck."

She sniffs and shrugs. "Yeah. Well. I know, and it's basically awful. You know how people die? Poorly. *Badly*. No dignity in death. It's all pants-shitting, drooling, barfing, bleeding—it's not just resting your head on a pillow and having an angel scoop you up into heaven. It's fluids and disease; it's bleats of pain as you piss yourself. It's ass cancer and burning alive in a DUI wreck and an old lady dying alone on her kitchen floor as man's best friend, her woozhy-woo-woo pet Chihuahua, eats her feet once one missed mealtime comes and goes. So: it's a question people shouldn't want answered. That's a box nobody should open. But for me, it's always open." *And I want it closed so badly. Right? Isn't that why I'm here? Or is it just that I can't help but pull a hangnail until it bleeds?*

"I'm just saying. You could be such a service. Imagine: Taking the hands of every FBI agent. Telling them if they're going to die on the job. Or someone in protective custody—are we going to fail them? Are they gonna get dead? God, you touch a kid born today and find out he dies in a hundred years, you can tell the future. You can see what waits for us all a century down the pike."

"Hoverboards," she says. "They're coming. Just you wait."

"I want you to join up. Be a part of something bigger."

She licks her lips. "Sorry, Grosky. No can do. I'm trying to go
the opposite way. I want to be a part of something smaller. Something as small as my life and my death, and that's it. I'm trying to
turn this thing off. Right now, I'm a broken faucet, but maybe I
can get fixed."

"That's a shame."

"For you, maybe. Not for me."

"I could try to force you. Make a threat. Bring you in again."

A wicked grin cuts her face in half. "Yeah? How'd that go for
you last time? Nah, you're too smart for that, Tommy."

"I am." He nods and sighs. "I am, I am. Well, I guess this is it.
For now."

"For now."

"You ever want anything, you call me."

"Uh-huh." As he starts to turn back toward his car, she calls
after him: "Hey. What happened with you and Tap-Tap?"

"He got away."

"Ah. Shit. Sorry. But you lived."

"I got his guys. Goldie, Jay-Jay. Shot Goldie, arrested Jay-Jay.
He rolled over on Tap-Tap and a bunch of other local criminals.
Tap-Tap went to ground. That nightclub in Miami—Atake—it's
still a haven of whatever little empire he built, though. FBI can't
quite crack it. Maybe one day."

"Best of luck with it all."

"It's not really my bag. I'm on leave for a while, anyway."

"Sorry to hear that."

"It's been good. Anyway." He nods, pops the door to the
sedan. "I'll see you around, Miriam."

She gives him the finger.

He laughs.

Then he's gone, and she goes back to waiting for Dan-Dan.

FORTY-SIX

SHOCK TREATMENT

"You're going through shock," Mary says. The world bounces and shudders. Every bounce sends a spider web of pain through Miriam's body—like a bullet hole in a mirror, cracks everywhere, everything gone wonky. Her heart flitter-flutters like a moth around a porch light. She tries to lift her arms, her legs, but it takes too much out of her. Tears crawl along her eyelids, creep down her cheeks. Everything shudders, judders, tumbles, bumbles: bump, bump, bump.

I don't know where I am.

Mary stands over her. Staring down.

Someone behind her, too.

Louis.

Not-Louis.

Trespasser.

He puts a finger to his lips. "Shhh," he says. "You're in a van. The no-longer-a-wizard van. And you're dying."

Mary Stitch doesn't flinch. She can't hear or see him. He's a ghost.

I don't want to die.

He grins. Mealworms play his teeth like piano keys. "Good."

She closes her eyes. Feels her whole self dip down into darkness, like a ladle into black broth—

Hands pull at her. Teeth bite at her. Beaks clack and squawk.

The tile floor is cold underneath her. Blood pools out from between her legs. A red snow shovel clatters nearby. Above her, Mary Stitch says, "You killed my boy. That awful thing inside you, that worm, that demon, it should never be made. You're a rotten girl. You deserve pain. You deserve a womb like a mummy's tomb: dusty and dead and sealed away so no one else can have it."

Breath stinks like snowmelt and rotten food.

A red balloon bumps along the ceiling. Bump, bump, bump. A scorpion scuttles around inside the latex. Squeaks and clicks. Bump, bump, bump.

She's running now. Boots in mud, every step making the bottoms of her boots bigger—boots like bricks, feet like cement blocks, and she thinks, *I've been running, I've been getting better, stronger, faster, why can't I do this*. But the hole in her chest whistles like a teakettle. Then it sprays blood. *Pbbbt*. A spit-take of crimson. A lung collapsed, house of cards. She goes down.

And falls not in the mud but in a river. Bubbles pop. Slick weeds suck at her ankles, pulling her down into the soft bed of the river. *The river is rising. The storm is coming.* Louis swims down. Reaches for her. He's dead, too. His lips are gone: fish-nibbled. Gums pull back, yellow teeth, and through them he keens:

"Where's Wren? What did you do to her? Don't you know what she'll do?"

Then his head shudders, and in the center of his head is a hole, and blood clouds the water, grows thick like squid ink, drops her down in the black once more. Eyes open. Gasping for air.

Above, blue skies. Morning skies. Streaked with fingers of fire across washboard clouds. The world shifts. Bump, bump, bump. Faces above her. Mary. Ethan. Ofelia. Feels like she's in a hammock.

Please make this stop. Please let me wake up.

"You are awake, dum-dum," the Trespasser says, this time with her mother's face, joining the other three. Helping to carry her. "Did you think we were your pallbearers?" Her mother laughs. Fire dances in her eyes.

A bed. A cot. Something beeping. A tugging at her arm. Someone says in Mary Stitch's voice, "We're gonna go ahead and leave that bullet in you. Karen said to keep it there. Let it be a reminder to you. A souvenir of your cruelty." Then someone else says, "This is morphine."

She floats away. Then pops like a balloon and then drowns. Swimming. Flying. Falling. Drowning. Again and again.

Somewhere, something probes at her margins. Teasing at the edges of her awareness, like fingers trying to sneak a taste of pie. Miriam grits her teeth and wills those fingers away: throws up all the walls she can, slams down every portcullis. Anything that comes to touch her, she bites at it—

Snap, snap, snap.

The feeling recedes. Water moccasins sliding back through murky water.

This goes on again and again, and Miriam looks up from her bed at one point and sees a sight that at first comforts her and then destroys her:

Isaiah. Standing at the edge of a bed in a tent. Wind ruffling the edges. He's wearing the Superman shirt again. His shoulders are wet with blood, turning the fabric purple. He says, "I'm sorry."

And she asks him why.

And he says, "Because Gabby is with my momma now."

It's then she realizes. This isn't a vision. This is happening. Clarity strikes her like a hammer on a bell: those fingers poking around, that was Karen. She was looking for something. She was looking for the boy. And somewhere in Miriam's surface thoughts, she found them. Miriam, lost to morphine. Broadcasting a signal she never meant to give off—oh, god, Karen got what they wanted. They know that Gabby went off to be with her sister. Took Isaiah.

They killed her. They took him.

Miriam failed.

A sound somewhere, like a car. Coming closer. Loud highway sounds. Miriam strains, tries to cry out—

But it's too late. The SUV tears through the tent. Strikes Isaiah. The red balloon he was holding—Was he holding a balloon? Where did that come from?—floats up into the sky as Miriam sinks down beneath the earth once more.

And then one day, Miriam wakes up for real.

FORTY-SEVEN

SHELLS CRACKING ON BLACK PISTACHIOS

Crunch, crunch, crunch. Mary Stitch sits there, prying apart pistachios with her fingernails and, occasionally, her teeth. The pistachios are covered in something: cinnamon or maybe chili powder. So red, they're almost black. Mary pops the meat in her mouth, crunching them up in little bites before tossing the shells in a nearby coffee cup.

Miriam, gray and pale and clammy, stares. Like watching a nearby mountain lion casually lazing about. Her hand slides underneath a gauzy white sheet, under a white T-shirt, finds a bandage covering the hole in her chest. She winces.

Around her, a machine beeps. An IV drips into her arm.

The older woman peers down at a pistachio. "Are these nuts or not?"

"What?" Miriam says, or tries to. Her voice is broken and dry— the sound of two tombstones rubbing together.

"Peanuts are not nuts. They're like peas. Legumes. Wasn't sure if pistachios are nuts too or what. A tomato isn't a vegetable; it's a fruit. Strawberries aren't berries, though I don't know exactly what they are." She licks the outside of the pistachio before cracking it and eating it. "All kinds of things aren't the things we think they are. We get ideas in our heads about the essential nature of a thing and don't know how to be wrong, so we just assume we're right even though all evidence, well, it's to the contrary. Like me. You thought I was going to be Little Miss Helpful, didn't you? That I was someone with a code. A twisted code, maybe, like you have, but a code nevertheless. But I don't. Not really. Only thing that matters to me is me, and even then, I'm getting pretty goddamn tiring to myself." She shrugs. "You bet on me, and you bet wrong."

"You . . . shot me."

"Mm-hmm, and the sky is blue, the desert is dry, and trickle-down economics are complete horseshit. We can make factual statements all day, Miriam."

"Wh . . . why?"

Mary looks around. The tent flutters in the wind a little, like it's restless, hoping to take off the way a kite does. "Oh. Well. That is a puzzle. One with very few pieces, as it turns out. First reason? These very nice people in the desert have chosen to make use of my services. They have money to share, and in return, we've concocted a little plan. Like I told you before: I am very good at highlighting the weakness of things. Not just people. Systems. Structures."

The realization strikes Miriam like a car slamming into her: *At dinner, Karen took Mary's name right out of my mind. Snatching it like a fly in an open hand. They're going to destroy that court-house with her help.*

But only because I introduced them.

Once again: Miriam ties the noose she fought so hard to unravel.

Miriam tries to cry, but her eyes are little deserts all their own. Her brow is damp, but everything else is dried up—her fingers like pumice, rasping against each other, the skin pulling away from her nails. Her lips are that way too: cracked and crispy and ready to split.

"But"—and here Mary leans forward—"the real reason is, you killed my brother. You killed Weldon, you nasty little cunt. That I cannot abide."

"He was a monster."

"He was my *brother*."

"He raped you. Molested you."

A sharp bark of a laugh. Mary says, "You think that's how it went, do you? Oh, honey. See? I told you: you think you know a thing, but then it turns out you got it all twisted. Weldon never touched the kids. He paid me to do that. Like he did to others throughout his life. He just watched. It was God's job to sort him out, not mine, not yours, not the law's. You're the monster. Not him. Not me. You think you do good things. You think you're righteous. But you're not."

"You . . . you're an animal. So was he. I'm glad I pulped his head like a fucking *blood orange*." Miriam starts coughing, hacking, body wracked. Every inch of her tightening up, shuddering. Everything hurts.

When she's finally done and left panting, Mary stands up.

"I'm going to make this threat one time, and I know I'll have to make good on it because I can tell you're not the type to listen to good sense. But they've hired me to help them, and one of the ways I'm going to help them is that I know all your pressure points. I don't just mean physically. I mean, I know what hurts you. I know how to make you bleed and cry and die inside. I know how to break you down, whittle you like a stick. So, here's the carrot: you tell them where Isaiah is, and I'll give you what you want. I'll tell you how to get shut of your curse, your power. How to pinch that artery off for good. You don't do that, then it's adult swim time, honey. All kids out of the pool."

A surge of hope: *Isaiah is not here.*

And then, a secondary feeling: how tantalizing that offer sounds.

Grapes hanging above her head, plump and juicy. All she has to do is reach up and *pluck* them off their branch. And her mind goes through the mental calisthenics, the justifications:

They don't want to hurt Isaiah. They'll consider him family. His mother is dead. Gabby and I can't take him. Foster kids are routinely abused. Who cares? That old Polish phrase again: *Not my circus, not my monkeys.* She can taste it. Taste those sweet grapes.

"You a woman of your word?" Miriam asks.

"You bet I am."

"You won't hurt him? Or the people he's with?"

"Not in the cards, as I understand it."

Miriam shuts her eyes. Takes a deep breath.

And then she tells Mary the address.

Mary just nods. Then starts to walk away.

"Wait," Miriam cries. "You were going to tell me. You made a deal."

Mary Stitch shrugs. "One I'll honor if they tell me to. But I've gotta tell Ethan first. Then he can sign off on if you really get a bite of this carrot or not."

"Fuck you."

Mary chuckles, then ducks under the tent flap and is gone.

FORTY-EIGHT

RETURN ON INVESTMENT

Time slips like a bad transmission.

Nights pass by. Two? Maybe three. Days stretch out before her like a long highway. Sun up and over the tent. Creeping under the fabric—a hot line of magma at the right of the tent in the morning, on the left at night. Or is it the opposite? Miriam can't tell. Can't remember. Can't anything.

Tries to move. Or pretend she can. One wrist handcuffed to a bedrail.

She feels hot and cold. Shivers. Coughs. Her heartbeat is fast as a cricket one minute, then slow as molasses the next. People move in and out of the tent. Shapes in fast-forward. Mostly men in camo pants, dark shirts. Like they're military, though they're not. There's a doctor, too, a tall woman, Latina, hair cropped short—she says little as she checks bandages, takes temperature. Miriam tries to talk to her, but the woman, she says nothing. Here and gone again.

In the black behind her eyes, dreamless sleep. A formless void. The Trespasser is gone: even it, the specter beyond everything, has abandoned her.

Then something tugs on her hand. Not something. Someone. She opens her eyes and sees the young guy—David. The human lie detector. He clasps her hand and says, "You fucked up. You know that, right?"

She manages a weak nod. A groaning: "Unnh-huh."

"They're coming. Soon. To deal with you. But first, here." He presses a napkin into her hand. "You have an infection. They won't do anything for you. But I got you a few antibiotics. The doc won't give them to you. Not yet. Here." He helps her swallow two now, then shows her another bunch of them folded up in a napkin—a napkin he then explains he's hiding underneath her. "She might change your bedding or check you for bedsores at some point—you'll need to hide them better before then. I don't know how. I'm sorry." He looks over his shoulder. "Take two today. Two tomorrow. If I can, I'll get you more, but . . ." He doesn't have to say it: *no promises*.

Then David is up.

"Wait," she says.

"I'm sorry."

"Wait, please. Don't fucking go anywhere. Hold . . . hold still."

"I can't."

And then he's gone.

She can feel the pills in her hand. She tucks them farther underneath her. Hand back out just as the tent flap opens again. A young soldier-looking kid with a mop of ginger hair and a starry band of freckles across his nose and cheeks pushes in a wheelchair, in which sits Karen Key. Behind them both comes Ethan.

"Sir?" the boy says.

Ethan cocks his head and dismisses him. The ginger scurries off.

He sighs. Pushes Karen closer—but not too close. Still five, six feet away. For his part, Ethan reaches over, pulls a chair over, and sits in it.

Miriam tries to focus on him.

And then she can see: he's pissed.

And she can't help it. She laughs. Laughs so hard she's red in the face, and the red in his face matches her, and soon it's a race between his rage and her hilarious anger—each of them a thermometer whose glass is about to pop.

Her laughs break down into hacking, wheezing, coughing.

She coughs into her hand.

The hand comes away flecked with red.

"Two of mine are dead," Ethan says, finally.

Miriam says, "That's your own fault, dickhead." She coughs again. "How dumb do you have to be? I tell Mary where the boy is, and while you don't trust me, somehow you trust her to get the right info? And all the while, you have David, a *psychic fact-checker*, under your nose, and you fail to deploy him?"

The address she gave Mary—and to Ethan, by proxy—was the wrong one.

She said to Mary, *Gabby's from Florida. She went home. Took him home to Miami. There's a nightclub—Atake. They're upstairs. Hiding out.*

Of course, that's also the nightclub where Tap-Tap ran, or still runs, his little empire of drugs and awfulness. The one that once belonged to a man named Ingersoll. A legacy of terrible people, and she sent two of Ethan's people right into that squirming nest of venomous things.

Ha ha ha ha ha.

Asshole.

She coughs again. More blood. But the smile on her face is huge.

"You're a monster," Ethan says.

She swallows—it's like a cactus is sliding down her throat. "I see you're a fan of irony."

"You shot one of my men. Sent two more into the lair of an *illegal immigrant's* drug den, got them killed. You failed to save Wade Chee. You don't care about this country or the people in it. I've tried to be fair. I've *tried* to give you chance after chance after chance. Every time I reach out my hand, you smack it away—"

"Try again and I'll bite each of your fingers clean off." She clicks her teeth together—but she's too weak to sell it. The gesture of a gentle nibble, not a chomping shark.

"You think we can't hurt you."

With that, he's up, standing over her. His tosses the sheet off her, a sheet she tries to catch and rescue. Ethan takes his thumb, presses it down against the gunshot wound in her chest.

She screams.

The thumb pushes the bandage deeper into the wound. Until soon, his digit wears the gauze like a condom, and it plunges straight into the hole.

White light. Electric and blinding. The pain so strong, it's less like pain and more like *sound* and *heat*—it's all-encompassing, enveloping her like the river that once threatened to drown her. This, a river of fire. Burning her alive.

"This hurts," he growls through gritted teeth. "And yet, Mary told me: pain, physical pain, it isn't one of your weaknesses. You can take a hit. You're too stubborn to care, too dumb to die, and so I'm just doing this *because I want to.*"

Then he yanks the thumb out. Slick with blood like he had it stuck down in the goo of a cherry pie. He shakes his hand.

Miriam tries not to sob. Tears don't come. But her whole body is wracked with them just the same: dry-heaving, trying to vomit up something, except here it's trying to cry, because at least crying would feel good.

"Just let me die, then," she says. "Your bullet-head wife can . . ." She stifles a yelp of pain. "She can just read my dead brain and tell you what you want."

He nods. "We may get there yet. But she's not sure what lurks up here"—he raps on her head with his knuckles—"will be an open door for her. And once you are dead? There's no going back. But you have an infection and it'll take you sooner than later. So, you may get your wish. In the meantime, we've got ways to make you hurt. Mary says she knows your chains. She knows where you're soft—where to stick the knife. Want a tease? Like a preview for a movie before it comes out? She saw a name. One name."

No, no, no.

"Louis Darling."

"No." All the heat rises to her cheeks, her neck, her underarms—she can feel it coming off her in hellish waves. Her hands clutch the bedsheets and she tries to sit upright. *"No!"*

"Oh, yeah. We've got his name and won't take long to find out where he's living. Some of us are police, military, ex-IRS, ex-census. We'll find his address. Then we'll march up to his front door, and we'll hurt him. Worse than we hurt you. And then you're gonna give us the location of little Isaiah, or we'll kill him."

And there's Ethan's smile again.

Big and broad and terrible and full of callous certainty.

FORTY-NINE

THE STORY OF MOCKING-BIRD

Ants crawl along her arms. She can feel them but only sometimes can she see them. Little red ants, red as licorice, red as jellybeans, marching over her arms and arm hair in winding, trickling paths—when she swats at them, they bite, and she cries out and somewhere nearby, someone laughs. Someone on the other side of the tent. She tries so hard not to pay attention to the insects. Miriam wills herself to pretend they're not there but they are—and then she thinks, *Why are they here?* She can't feel all the parts of her body. Her feet seem like slabs of flesh lying at the end of her, like roasts of cooked meat. Are the ants hungry? Has she been abandoned? Is the camp deserted and she's been left here to die?

Then she remembers: *pills*.

I have pills.

I need to take them.

I need them to survive.

She reaches under her body with a sliding hand, the hand not cuffed to the bed. The rest of her body is numb, without sensation—she can't feel her own fingers probing.

Worse, she can't find the *pills*.

Someone took them.

I'm going to die.

But then—her fingers touch something.

The edge of a napkin. There. She slides over it. Tugs on it. Eases it out. Feels the little bumps inside the napkin. Four pills. *Take*—how many was it?

Two. Take two pills.

She starts to fumble. Unwrapping the napkin carefully, with picking nails, nails that are bitten and broken. Between thumb and forefinger she presses two flat, round pills together like a sandwich, an ice cream sandwich that contains nothing sweet— but also nothing so sweet as an extension on her life, perhaps— and she extends her tongue. Like unrolling sandpaper. Pills onto the tongue. They stick. Gummy, gluey. She tries to swallow but they won't go down. And then they start to taste sweet. Too sweet. Sugar sweet like candy.

David lied to me. These aren't pills.

They're goddamn stupid shit-ass candy. Tic Tacs or something.

Shit shit shit shit.

They're just fucking with her now. They do know how to hurt her. How to break her down to little bits: a mortar and pestle turning her to *powder*.

But then the sweetness gives way to sharp bitterness—the medicinal bleed on the tongue. *They are pills*, she tells herself. But she's not sure.

Miriam swallows them anyway. They make a miserable journey down her dry throat. And somewhere in the middle, they get stuck. She's sure of it. They feel huge in her esophagus. Like pebbles crammed in a drinking straw.

She whimpers like a dying puppy.

She *hates* that she whimpers.

"You're weak," Wade Chee says. Standing there, all his body burned like a hot dog left too long over the charcoals. Flesh crispy and coming off, splitting in places (and in those splits and fleshy fissures she sees the bold red of blood and muscle). His teeth are bright. His eyes too. He says, "I was strong for you and I shouldn't have been. You're weak. You need to be strong."

"I can't. I don't know how. Not anymore."

"Then you're going to die here. And then what?"

He laughs and is gone.

Voices outside the tent. A conversation between two people, maybe three:

"Bird's down."

"Flight 6757. Crashed in the desert. Pick its bones clean."

"The corn will do it. The corn is thirsty for blood."

A laugh. "This isn't just blood. This is metal. These are souls."

"Souls are like pennies: they number so many, they're basically just garbage. Plentiful and cheap." A cough. Wet and fungal.

"Cerulean warbler."

"Crimson tanager."

More laughing. Another cough.

"I think she's listening."

"Little chickadee." Then words uttered through a mush mouth. Gibberish.

Laughter. She tries to scream. Can't. Her jaw feels wired shut.

"Welcome to Hell, right?"

Ha ha. "Right."

"Does she know we have Louis?"

"She will soon."

"He's practically dead."

Miriam thrashes. Seizes up. Ants biting her. She thinks: *This is how I'm going to die. An infection. Or maybe anaphylaxis. From ant bites. In the desert.*

"Hey." Pause. "Hey." Beat. "*Hey.*"

Miriam feels the hand on her shoulder. There. Ofelia. One of the psychics here. The one who can . . . What can she do? Sex. She can increase the sex drive. Or make herself wanted. Or something. "You," Miriam bleats.

"There's a story," Ofelia says, either biting her thumbnail or using her thumbnail to pick the space between her teeth. "It's not a Tohono story; it's, like, Hopi, maybe. I dunno." That nail scrapes teeth. Like a shard of glass scraped down a blackboard. Miriam stiffens.

"What . . . what are you talking about?"

"Just sit there and listen. So, in the time before time, the people—that's humans—were stuck in this dark place deep within the earth. The Underworld. Yeah? Like, Hell, but not the Hell with the Devil. A Hell for the living. So, they're down there, and some of the people are good but a lot of them are bad. They're driven mad by serpents. And they're abusive. Bullies. Monsters. Rapists and killers. The bad people hurt the good people, and one day, the good people say: *We have to get right the fuck out of here.* You follow me?"

Miriam tries to say something but her mouth doesn't work and those pills jammed down in her throat make it hard to speak—and then she thinks: *Oh, fuck, the pills.* She's still got the napkin and the two pills held in her hand.

Quickly she closes her hand over them, a Venus flytrap catching a fly. She can't have Ofelia see; she'd take them away.

These pills might be all she has to stay alive for a little while longer.

Ofelia seems to have not noticed. She keeps talking: "At this time, no sun existed. It was dark everywhere. So, it wasn't like you could just look up and see the way out. They looked and looked, couldn't find anything. Tried to grow trees and tall sunflowers to climb, but the plants were withered and weak and not tall enough. So, then a little bird came along. The Mocking-Bird. And the little bird said, like, *I know I'm tiny, but I can help because I have these wings.* And they did not believe the bird could help, but it's not like the bird could *hurt* them, so they said, yeah, of course, sure, you go, little bird. You go, *sinsonte. Volar alto*, fly high. And the little bird did just that. And then was gone. Right? Time passes and all seems lost as the bad people continue to hurt the good ones. And then . . ."

Here, Ofelia spits something. The crescent sickle of a nibbled fingernail.

She continues: "And then the bird returns. Tells them it has found a way out. A hole in the Underworld. Too high up for anyone to reach, so Mocking-Bird teaches them a song to sing—all at once—that makes the trees and sunflowers grow so fast and so tall that they can climb out. And they do." She sniffs and shrugs. "That's just the beginning of the whole thing, but I thought you could use it. A little bird helps them find their way out of Hell."

Miriam coughs. "Cool story, bro."

Ofelia shrugs. "Yeah. I think you're being a judgey bitch to me, which is cool because that's sort of my jam too. We understand each other. I kinda hate you, which means I kinda dig you—like, I hate you because maybe we're close. We're more than a little alike. Survivors. So, can I give you a tip?"

"Just the tip?"

Ofelia makes a face. "Whatever, shut up. The tip is: you're a survivor, so fucking survive already. Comes a point when you decide you gotta kill and eat the people you're with if you're gonna stay alive. *Es hora de comer*. Okay? Give us the kid's location. We don't wanna hurt him. He's family. I love him. We all do. We'll make sure he's safe here."

"I'm stubborn," Miriam croaks. "Not happening."

"Stubborn enough to die?"

Miriam manifests as much of a shrug as she can muster.

"I bet maybe you are," Ofelia says, standing up. "But I'm telling you. You need to find your way out of Hell. Because the way out is gonna close, and when it does, you'll be trapped in here with the rest of us."

She starts to walk away.

Miriam thinks: *Now hide the pills*. Then: *No, no, no, just wait till she leaves, she hasn't noticed anything yet*. But Miriam's hand twitches—

And the pills roll off the napkin against the ground.

They *tick* and *click* as they land.

Ofelia stops.

Her head slowly turns. Her gaze casts downward, sees the napkin in Miriam's hand. Then her eyes drift farther down.

"Huh," she says, walking over, picking up the pills. "You drop something?"

"I need those," Miriam says, feeling her lip shake.

"What are they?"

Trying not to cry, Miriam says, "Dick pills. Keep boner strong like bull."

Ofelia laughs. "That's good. Funny, bitch. Funny. These are, what, antibiotics? Somebody give these to you? Somebody here sneaking you pills, huh?" She rattles the pills in her palm.

Miriam shuts her eyes. Shit.

Ofelia walks over. Holds them out in her palm. "Here."

They're right there.

Two little pills.

Miriam reaches over to take them—

Ofelia tilts her hand so they slide back to the ground. *Tick click*.

"Oops," she says, then kicks them under the bed.

"You fucking—"

"Find your way out of hell, little birdie. Or the bad people gonna get you."

FIFTY

BONE BROTH

The spoon touches her mouth. It's warm but not hot. The broth slides down her throat. "Bone broth," Mary says, feeding Miriam. "Trendy now, I'm told. But this is old school right here. This is grandmother food. Boil bones until they break down. All the goodness of the animal—all of its barest components—here in this warm liquid. Now, let's be clear: I'm not keeping you alive because I like you. Though I hear you snuck a couple pills—your fever is down, and maybe that's why. We're keeping you alive long enough to get to this last part. I'm moistening your throat so it's easy to talk. Because soon, you'll talk. If you want me to help you, then you have to help us."

She hates that the broth is good. Her every cell, every molecule, says: *Spit it out.* Blast it in the woman's face. Blind her. Then claw at her—scratch her face off and make bone broth from the skull underneath. But her arms are weak. Her resolve: weaker. The broth is good. *You need your strength*, she tells herself. She makes a move too early, and it's curtains for her.

Miriam says after sipping another spoonful: "How long have I been here?"

"Two weeks now."

The words come out of her before she means them to: "One week left."

"Hunh? One week till what, exactly?"

"You know," Miriam says, voice cold and steely.

"Ohhh. I do know. The courthouse. Question is: how do *you* know?"

"I'm in your head."

Mary squints. "No, that's not it. That's not how you work. You saw it in someone's death." She leans back. Puts the spoon back in the Tupperware container she's holding. "Helping to dig people's graves for them is all you're doing with that power. Now," Mary taunts in a singsongy voice, "if only you had a way to get rid of that curse. If only, if only . . ."

"Why? Why the courthouse?"

"The easy answer is that it's the first domino. A match flung into a fireworks factory. The more complicated answer is that a trio of bad men will be there that day. A judge with no soft spot for the American patriots, who is always eager and willing to punish men like Ethan Key for standing up for one's God-given Constitutional rights. A state senator with a song in his heart for helping immigrants at the same time he tries to rob the common man of his right to bear arms. And a state district attorney responsible for green-lighting a SWAT attack on the Cochise County militia two years ago in a botched raid that saw three children and two women get dead. Killing those three is a strong signal."

Miriam groans as she tries to sit up. "Bullshit. You don't actually believe all that, do you? I don't think you do and I don't think you care. I think you're a gun or a pair of scissors for hire." She grunts, suppresses a cough. "Something else is going on here. Some other reason to jump in with these people."

"You don't know me."

"I know how you die."

"You can't. I know your power doesn't work that way."

"Maybe you don't know as much as you think, Stitch."

"Maybe not." Composure returns to Mary's face. She seems to

chew on what Miriam has said the way you'd chew on a stubborn piece of jerky. "Maybe you do get me. I look at you and I think I was like you, once. Maybe had good ideas. Maybe thought about being a nice person. *Help* people fix the things broken inside of them instead of just breaking them down further." Her face twists up, like a dog gone feral. "But eventually, I figured out who I really was, and then I just went with it. If you live through this, you'll get there too."

"I already know who I am."

"Doesn't sound like it to me. I can see the weakness in people, and I can see what it takes to cut that weakness out. And in you I see all these gaps and voids, like holes in Swiss cheese. And boy howdy, can I see them all. Stick my fingers in, wriggle them around. Louis. Gabby. Your ego warring with your self-hatred. You're overconfident and yet never really sure. Then there's your mother, what she did to you, what happened to her. The boy with the red balloon. And Wren. And Isaiah, too. Got a thing for children, do you?" She *hmmphs*. "I see all these threads you've tied to yourself. Suicide. Miscarriage. Death. And *people*. Other people. It's them that make you weak. You're tethered to them, like that string on that little boy's balloon. The balloon bobs and you chase after it. This power makes you *care* about people. And you hate that, don't you?"

Miriam scowls her way to a grim rictus of a smile. She winks and says, "Hasn't made me care about you any."

"I wonder if that's true." Mary nods. Stands. "You wanna know why the courthouse? For real? Ugly building. Quintero's a cunt. I'm tired of having to show up there. I'm just tired."

"You don't have to do this."

"I don't have to do anything. That's the freedom folks like you and I have. But it's also a burden, too, isn't it?" The woman's face is haunted. By what, Miriam cannot know. The things she's done, perhaps. The people she knew, or the people she hurt. Ghosts holding her own ropes and tethers. Mary stands up straight, suddenly, and sniffs real loud. "Well. This'll all be over soon. Then I'll have a surprise for you. A surprise that'll have you doubling over and whistling 'Saints Go Marching In' right out of your cocky little ass, honey."

FIFTY-ONE

SCYLLA AND CHARYBDIS

The taste of bone broth on her tongue, her brow slick with sweat, Miriam waits. Eyes shut. Hands clenched up. *We'll push on that one spot soon.* She has to be ready. For what, she doesn't know. But she can't compromise. She has to thread the needle. Can't crash against the rocks. Can't get eaten by the monster.

Evening settles in. The light of day receding from under the edges of the tent like the sea gone out to its consumptive tide.

The tent flap moves back. She keeps her eyes closed. The squeak of an axle on a wheelchair. Footsteps crunching, thudding. More than one body. More than just Ethan. They keep coming.

She shivers, and opens her eyes.

"Is this my intervention?" she asks, weary. The crowd that has gathered stares on. Ethan. Mary. Ofelia. David. Karen, of course, her head tilted at a right angle, using her jagged shoulder as the world's most uncomfortable pillow. Nobody else. No armed men. They feel safe. She's sick and dying and handcuffed to a bed. What can she do? "I mean, I already quit smoking."

It occurs to her: she hasn't had a nic-fit in weeks.

A silver lining on the blackest cloud.

Ethan steps forward. Wordlessly, he holds up a bottle of pills. He rattles it like she's a cat or a baby and he's trying to entice her. Then he holds out his hand and Ofelia passes over a knockoff

247

iPad. With his arm lifted, Miriam sees the gun hanging at his hip: something shiny, nickel-plated.

He keeps the screen pressed to his chest.

Finally, he says, "It's dark on the East Coast. It's about eight o'clock there. We found your friend. Louis. We have him." Fear rips through her like barbed wire through a closing hand. Now Ethan turns the screen toward her. He flips through photos: what looks like the darkened interior of a townhome illuminated by bright flashlights. She sees the dark shadow of a rifle barrel, like something the military would carry. Each picture shows things that make her think of Louis but might not be his—a calendar hanging on a refrigerator showing a tractor-trailer, a set of big boots by the front door sitting below a big brown coat, a set of keys in a dish by the front door. A front door that's broken open. Glass glittering on the ground. A picture of a living room where it looks like there was a struggle: a flatscreen television knocked off the wall, a coffee table tipped over. She thinks: *I still don't know that this is his place. They're just messing with me. Like I messed with them.*

But then, the photos show the upstairs.

A bed, empty. Sheets torn off. Pillows, too. Blood on the bed.

Next to the bed, a photo.

It's Louis. And another woman. He's got a full beard—soft and sandy, grown in from when she last saw him. Dark hair, big smile, bright eyes. Him wearing a big Hawaiian shirt, her with a loose white blouse—palm trees behind them. Could be Florida. They're kissing. She's his fiancée. Samantha, right?

That's them.

Her blood goes slow and cold.

Ethan rattles the pills again. "Last offer on the table before we jump this car off the cliff. This is a good offer, a *kind* offer, so please: open your fucking ears. Last chance to tell me where the boy is, Isaiah. And then two things happen—or, rather, don't

happen. First, you don't die, because we start giving you these
pills: gentamicin. Strong, horse-kick antibiotics. Second, your
friend *Louis* doesn't die. And his wife to boot."

"She's not his wife," Miriam says through quivering lip and
gritted teeth.

"Well, be that as it may—"

"I want to talk to him."

"You aren't in any position to make demands."

"You want me to give you the boy, I will. But I need to know
Louis is all right, already. Okay? *Okay?* You gotta give me this."

Ethan scowls. "I don't have to give you anything. I've already
given you the sweetest offer, and it is the last. After this, it gets
ugly. You need to have a little faith for once in your awful life,
Miriam. That's an unspoken part of this deal. Faith in that where
you would tell me a lie, I am telling you the truth."

"Please," she says.

"Besides, Louis is hurting. See, the thing we did to you?
Gunshot to the lung? We did that to him, too. He's safe for
now. But in a few hours, he won't be, unless we get him to a
hospital. So, him having a conversation right now is going to
be tough. We've got him. And he's on the clock—"

"Lying."

That word, erupted from David's mouth. His eyes go wide.
His hands go to clamp over his mouth, but he's closing the barn
door after the horse already galloped away. *Lying.* Miriam's heartbeat seems to stop in her chest—

"I mean," David says. "Wait—"

Ethan draws his pistol—*bang.*

A spray of blood out the back of David's head. The body
drops like a mannequin kicked off its mount.

Miriam thinks:

This is it.

Ethan launches himself atop her. He's on top of the bed, the gun pressed to the side of her head. Any mask of civility is gone: everything is wide with rage, an open conduit for the fury he's feeling. He spits when he screams:

"Tell me! Tell me where the boy is or *so help me God,* I will shoot—"

She summons what strength she can and knees him in the crotch. He doubles over, his head dipping forward. She moves her hand underneath his wrist, launching it upward as the gun goes off right by her ear—

Bang.

A sharp shrill scream, his scream, and the screaming echo of the gunshot as his head gets close to hers, his eyes lit up like floodlights—

She opens her mouth and *bites.*

Teeth sink into the stubbled cheek. Teeth meet other teeth. Blood on her tongue. The strange, momentary taste of bitter cologne.

Ethan screams. He pulls away, leaving a wad of his face-meat in her mouth. As he reels back, she gives a twist to her hand and pushes her thumb hard into the soft, tender flesh of his wrist—

The gun drops. Half on the edge of the bed. She lets go of him as he backpedals, a spigot in his face pouring blood down his neck—

She grabs the gun. Turns it toward the chain binding her hand to the bed. One shot, *bang*, and the chain breaks. Miriam rolls out of bed, the flats of her feet landing hard against the rug rolled out on the desert floor here in the tent—

Everyone is already running. Ofelia is pulling Karen out, Karen whose mouth is now a gaping tunnel from which emits a terrible howl—

Miriam's legs almost go out from under her. Weak, wobbly, numb. Ethan darts for the door and she fires three shots from the pistol heavy in her grip, but she can barely hold it, barely aim—holes punch through the tent. Ethan escapes.

In her head, a clock starts ticking.

Her body is a fuse. Sizzling down. When it hits the bottom, she's done—not an explosion but a fizzle, a dud, and she'll drop like a rock. Hole in her chest. Weak body. Infection running through her like a California forest fire. No pills to contain it.

They'll come for her. Ethan may be escaping, but already she can be sure that his thugs and cronies will be on their way. Guns up. Ready to shoot.

She has one choice.

One word. Ringing like a crystal bell.

Run.

FIFTY-TWO

MIRIAM RUNS

She's in a T-shirt. Shitty yoga pants that aren't hers. Out in the warm evening air, she can smell herself: a musky, raw odor. Desperation and fear keep her moving. Her body is ragged. Barely even hers anymore.

She wills her feet to move.

Miriam runs. Not a real run, but an awkward, coltish trot—gravity keeps dragging her on, her head leading the way, her legs moving just fast enough to make sure that she never pitches forward, never hits the ground.

The camp and compound around her. Little houses. Tents. Yelling behind her. Gunfire. *Pop, pop, pop.* Dust kicks up around her feet. Bullets *vwip.* She darts right, between a makeshift garage and a small trailer. Ahead: a small lot of cars. A few Jeeps. Hummers. A dusty white sedan. The van—her van, the no-longer-a-wizard van, the motherfucking *magic* van. She thinks: *Yes, run, get a ride, drive.* But then, voices ahead. Men stalking the spaces between the vehicles. Guns up.

Miriam knows she should stop. Think. Consider her options. But that is, ironically, *not* an option: momentum is what she has. *All* she has. Can't stop moving or she'll collapse like a Jenga tower. She has no more fight in her—just movement, urging her ever forward, lightning loosed from its bottle.

Run, run, run.

She ducks left. Behind the garage. Between it and a corrugated tin shed. There: one of the greenhouses. Long, the Plexiglas dusty and smeary and cracked. Little cacti growing alongside. Her feet pound dirt. Pain through her heels—something cutting the flesh there. Jagged stoned, broken earth; she doesn't know and she can't pause to take a look, she can only bolt—

Into the greenhouse. More gunfire. The Plexiglas wobbles and shakes as bullets punch through it—*piff, piff, piff*. A clay pot pops. Dirt everywhere. A tomato ruptures like a popped skull. Miriam keeps her head low, and then she almost does fall but catches herself on one of the long tables. There: a woman ahead, dark, Latina, old, holding up her hands and saying, *Please, no*, and Miriam can't stop to reassure her, can't stop to do shit except shoulder hard past her.

Back out the end of the greenhouse.

Ahead, a fence.

Tall. Ten feet, easy. Chain link. Topped with barbed wire—not coils of it but, rather, angled out. Not meant to keep people in, not like at Carl Keener's serial killer playground, but meant genuinely to keep enemies *out*.

The fence, too, isn't perfect. They haven't maintained it like they should.

Warped areas in the fence leave it slack.

It won't be enough, she thinks.

She cannot make this.

But Miriam has no choice. And so she puts a little extra salt-and-pepper in her step and charges hard toward the fence, giving a hop as she nears it—

Fingers out like talons. Hands catching the chain link. Feet doing the same. And then she's clambering up the warped, wobbling fence to the top—

Pop-pop-pop-pop. Automatic gunfire. Sparks dance off the fence. Bullets clip the post just a foot away. Her hands find barbed wire. It bites into the meat of her palm. She *pulls*. The barbs tear deeper. She drags herself over the top. Rusty teeth into the flat of her belly. Then up, over. Dropping down. Landing hard on her feet. Pain jars through to her knees. Her ankle twists.

She forces the pain, or the recognition of it, back, back, back, urging it into the shadows with a mental cattle prod because she has *no time* for pain, *no time* for its distraction, and again, she does what she does best, what she has always done, what she has learned to do better:

Miriam runs.

FIFTY-THREE

LONG WALK OF THE LIVING DEAD

Sun up. Rough birth. It pulls its way up and over the horizon like a zombie clawing out of its grave.

Miriam is still going. Like that fucking battery bunny.

Walking, now, not running. No—not even walking. Shuffling. Her feet are cut to ribbons. Her middle is a stabbed-over wasteland, her belly looking like she got in between two house cats hell-bent on fighting and/or fucking.

One thought goes through her head every couple of minutes: *I needed those pills. But it's too late. She fucked that up. Then he took them.* . . .

Her entire chest feels numb. Her whole body is leaking moisture—and yet she hasn't pissed, can't spit, can't cry, can barely even bleed. Her mouth feels like a canyon full of ash. Her eyes feel like charcoal briquettes. Dried up. Bled out.

Around her, the ground rises in swells both jagged and gentle. Saguaro stand vigil. Pink blooms pop over prickly pears. Creosote reaches for the heavens—desperate fingers lined with little yellow flowers.

It's beautiful out here, she thinks. Even though this isn't her place. This is someone else's kingdom. Sun and sky and spring flowers in a dry, dead desert. Given any other day, she'd be out here, smoking and scowling and talking shit about all the stupid splendor. Fuck this and piss on that and beauty is dumb and nice things are bad and rah, rah, rah. She doesn't have it in her.

Today, she just thinks:

It's really pretty here.

It's probably because she's dying.

She knows it. The cactus knows it. The whole of the cloud-less sky knows it. It's not a secret. She has one lung that inflates, but it's like she's being stabbed by a steak knife every time she breathes. Her feet feel like she's been walking on cheese graters. The infection inside her is cooking her from the inside out. Her body feels like a rusty burn barrel. Everything charred and melting.

She has no idea where she is. She ran, then walked, and now does this undead shuffle through the wasteland. Nobody has come for her. Ahead lies something that looks like mountains, or at least really big, pointy hills. Not a city. Not a town. Is she heading north? South? East, west, up, down, anywhere at all?

No water. No food. No medicine.

I should've gotten the pill bottle.

And a Coke. And a hot dog.

And I should've just told them where Isaiah had gone. Let them all hang for it. Why do I care? She tells herself: *I don't care. I'm just too stubborn to give in.* And it's going to kill her. It's really, truly, going to kill her. Not that she even knows where Isaiah is, exactly. She was worthless to them all along.

She drops to her knees.

Chest heaving gently. Anguish sticking with every breath.

Something tickles the back of her mind. She turns her head—slowly, so slowly—and there, on a gently bobbing branch of a creosote bush, is something she thinks at first is a red flower. But it's no flower: it's a bird. A vermilion flycatcher. She doesn't know how she knows that. Over the last couple of years, she's done a lot of reading about birds, flipped through guide after guide, and maybe this is just one of those pieces of information stuck in her mind the way a splinter gets in your finger—or maybe it's something deeper than that, some deeper dive, some *psychic nonsense* that connects her with the bird. But then she wonders: Does the vermilion flycatcher think of itself as a vermilion fly-catcher? Why would it? Why would the bird care what humans call it? Unless it does. Unless birds are here for people. Maybe all things are here for people. They're the children of God and all that, and God made this place just for humans—or so the story goes—and here she laughs because if God is real? *What an asshole.*

"I need your help," she says to the bird, and her words are a scratchy whisper, barely heard. The bird chips and trills at her. "You're no mockingbird. But I need you to find the way out of Hell. Show me the way out."

Chip, chip, trill. Chip, chip, trill.

Miriam falls forward.

PART SIX

THUNDERBIRD

THE COMING STORM

Ethan Key eats oatmeal out of a tin cup. Spoon noisily scraping the breakfast—a breakfast cooked too long, so it's a little hard around the edges—off the metal sides. He sits on his back patio, staring off at the middle distance. Scanning the horizon for something, anything. He rescues a blackberry from inside the cup, eats it. Not sweet enough. Sour, acid tang.

In a fit of anger, he pitches the cup. Ten feet away, it lands with a clang and the remaining oatmeal splatters.

"You're bundled up in knots," Mary Stitch says. He startles. Flinching so hard, his neck seizes up—a kink bridging his shoulders like an electric current.

"Jesus, Mary," he says. "Warn a man next time."

Mary Stitch. Is she their savior or something much worse? He can't tell yet. She's not a true believer; that much is for sure. And he distrusts people who do things for money. Money is transitive. Barely even a real thing, just some proxy nonsense that represents not real value but, rather, measures desire.

What the hell does *she* desire, anyway?

"You're still bent up like a coat hanger," she says. "What happened, happened. You can't change that. Regret isn't worth a damn. You correct your mistakes and you move on—"

"Quit your goddamn lecturing. I don't need it. I damn sure don't want it."

She pulls up a chair, sits. Sipping at a cup of coffee. "She's dead."

They both know the *she* that Mary means.

Miriam Black.

"We don't know that," he says. "We didn't find a body."

"It's a lot of ground to cover out there. Lot of places she might've curled up and died. Under a rock. In some gulch. No way a girl survives out there. I saw the weakness inside her. Her body is strong, maybe stronger than anybody would give her credit for, but she was torn up inside and out."

Ethan grunts. He taps the center of his chest. "But she's strong *here*."

Mary laughs, and that makes him even madder. He doesn't like people laughing at him. But he lets it go because they're so close; he doesn't want to alienate her, not here, not now.

"That girl doesn't even have a heart," Mary says. "What she's got in there is just a dried, dead bird's nest sticky with waste. Blackened and foul. I should know. I got the same terrible thing in me."

"So, tell me: how do you kill something that doesn't have a heart?"

Another laugh, this one bitterer than the last. "Good question. Maybe you don't."

Ethan says what he's thinking: "Everything's gone south. She's dead. *David* is dead." And here his mind corrects him: *No, you killed him. You shot David right in the head and now he's dead.* "We still don't have the boy."

"I told you not to bluff with that truck driver thing."

"I'm not supposed to have regrets, but now you hit me with this *I told you so* bullshit? My mother was like that. She'd tell you not to worry, tell you to *be a man*, make your own decisions. Then you'd do your thing—and soon as you did, she'd tell you just how much you made everything worse. She said she was just trying to encourage us to make our own mistakes, except, truth is: all we did in her eyes was make mistakes. Maybe she saw our family as a mistake; I don't know. Doesn't matter. She's dead and life goes on."

Out there, over the desert, vultures turn and tumble in the sky.

Mary draws a deep breath and says, "That's one of your weaknesses."

"What?"

"Family."

"Family is not a weakness."

"It is for you, Ethan. You've created this idea of family in your head. Most of this started because your wife took a bullet and it changed her. So, you made this place, and now you see all these people as family, but that means they're dependent upon you and you upon them. You think that's community, but it's just weakness. It means you're not your own man."

"You're cruising," he warns.

"You thought of David as a son and he betrayed you. And this fascination with the boy, Isaiah. You don't *need* him. We've got the plan—a plan that has *not* gone south, a plan that is so close, you can almost smell the ozone before the lightning. You're going to change things. You're going to change this country."

"Maybe," he says. But they still don't have the boy. And his wife—she won't speak to him. She just sits there. In her room. Staring off. Mumbling to herself but not so he could ever hear what it is she's saying. She's frozen him out. And he knows why. Because he failed. He failed with Miriam. Failed with his bluff. Killed David. And still: no Isaiah.

"You're thinking about that boy again," she says.

"Quit that, will you? It's creepy."

She smirks. "Thought you liked us *changers*. Us fancy psychic types."

"All of 'em but you, Mary."

She's quiet for a while. Staring at him. Her eyes picking him apart like fingers pulling soft chicken off bendy bones. Suddenly, her face softens and she whistles a low sound. "That's what it is."

"That's what *what* is?"

"You lost a child."

He flinches again. "You don't know that."

"But I do," she says. "Was Karen pregnant when she got shot?"

"No," he says, mouth a firm line. "She lost the baby about a week before."

"That's a bad week."

"You have no idea."

"That's your thing with family. That's the thing with Isaiah—"

"Get the fuck out of here. Let me enjoy my breakfast—" He looks down at his empty hands. *You already threw your breakfast out.* "Let me sit here. Just let me sit here and stare out at nothing. We got a few more days left and, honestly, before that? I don't want to see much of you."

Mary stands up. The steam from her coffee rising around her like exorcised spirits. "I want to be there, by the by."

"Be where?"

"Courthouse. When it all goes up."

"No, uh-uh. I want you back here. Don't get caught up in it."

She sniffs, shrugs. "Fine. You don't want it to go right, so be it."

"What are you saying?"

"I'm saying, you want it done right, I need to be there. I know how it all goes and so I want to make sure it goes right. I got a reputation."

"Mary *Scissors.*"

"That's right." She turns her free hand into a pair: *snip, snip.*

"Fine. You help them get set up before courthouse hours. But you don't stick around. You understand? Those explosions go off and everything's going to be under the microscope mighty damn fast."

She nods. "Thank you."

"Now go on, get out."

She licks her lips, sips her coffee, then does as she's told.

FIFTY-FOUR

THE ROADRUNNER AND THE COYOTE

The vulture wheels in the sky as if a tether connects one of its wings to a central point, an invisible axis around which it turns and turns. Heat breathed up from the hot desert, exhalations of sun-warmed air, push the bird higher and higher and higher. Another vulture joins it.

The mind of the first bird jumps. For a moment, consciousness is shared between them, a single awareness spread out between them like a ribbon of warm taffy—but then the mind snaps into place. From the first vulture to the next.

For a time, the mind was part of a vermilion flycatcher. A male bird. Red as fire, red as blood, a butterfly crushed in its beak. The bug delivered to another flycatcher, a female, perched on a saguaro. A gift of mating. A gift, rejected. A butterfly, eaten. *Crunch, munch, crunch.*

Time spent lazing about, for despite its name, the flycatcher is a lazy bird. The male in particular. Most of its time spent sitting. Watching. Waiting.

Dreaming.

Dreaming of a life not as a bird, but as something else. Something with long limbs and rubbery digits—a creature without beak and talon. Pink and featherless and fixed to the ground. With all the grace of a rolling rock.

Then the flycatcher flew. Day into night and into day. Then: **265** a mockingbird, a gray and silver streak in the sky, ducking and diving. The flycatcher thought what an irony that would be, and then, not knowing what the fuck irony is except that it sought it utterly, it passed by the mockingbird and became that bird.

The flycatcher flew on. The mockingbird remained.

Stealing the songs of those it passed. Robbing the world of its sounds and repurposing them for its own: a trill, a chirp, a cell phone, a whistle, a beeping watch, things the mockingbird understood and remembered only peripherally—a distant memory that was maybe not its own. It finally settled on a song: a song that conjured new memories. A glimpse of one of those pink and featherless things flat on a table. Blood from its hands, almost black. A laurel garland of barbed wire. A larger bird-thing, leathery and reptilian, approaching.

The mockingbird pushed that song away. Then passed by the vultures, and now that's what it is. A vulture. Its beak and throat slick with rancid meat—a pleasurable sensation, death made perfect and pure because there, then, the purpose of death laid bare: death is here to feed life. A thing dies and it becomes food for other things. Fresh food or fertilizer. Broken down, chewed by teeth, smashed by beaks, torn apart by fingers of rain and claws of cutting wind, life into death into life. A purpose to the whole thing. The vulture just one part of it.

Seems so obvious now. But the pink, featherless things don't grasp it.

So, for now, the vulture is one vulture, then another, then a third. Then it is all of them at once. Circling. The musky smell of sweat and blood rising up off the desert, so it finds those invisible vapors pointing down like arrows and it follows the arrows as they fall—trailing the stink, seeking the dead thing.

There, a body.

Pink and featherless.

Its hair mostly black, but streaked with color.

A woman.

It's familiar to the vulture.

Other vultures have gathered too. Like a parliament of judges in their black robes. Standing vigil, pondering after justice.

One vulture, different from the others. Different as she is herself, different. This one has a puckered hole where its eye once was. Its other eye is not a bird's eye at all but something altogether more . . .

Human.

"The body's not dead yet," that vulture says. After every word, the *click-a-clack* of its beak. "What was it the woman in the chair said? Oh. Right." And here the vulture's voice changes to a woman's voice: *"Death doesn't see you."*

That one-eyed vulture stoops and bends its long neck, and nudges the body with its gray, hooked beak. The body twitches. The back rises and falls.

The pink featherless thing is alive.

Something pulls at the mind—at the vulture herself, like a kind of gravity, drawing her mind deeper, closer, unmooring it from the scavenger bird and toward the pink, featherless almost-corpse—

No.

The vulture doesn't want to see this, doesn't want to think about it. If this human is not yet dead, then it may fight, and right now the vulture wants easy prey. This human is not good for eating, and if it is not good for eating, then what good is it?

Angry, scared, the vulture takes flight.

The one-eyed bird calls after: "Time is fleeting. The body is dying. Death will see it soon, if it has not yet."

But the vulture doesn't care. (Doesn't *want* to care.)

It soars, pushed higher by hands of heat.

There. Another bird. Smaller, darting, ducking. A bird that knows how to eat, and now: the vulture twists and the mind stretches and—

A shrike. Small bird, lean like a laser, mean like a razor, already on the hunt. And it has a peculiar way of hunting, doesn't it? A songbird with a murderous melody in its heart, and so the shrike sees prey and sees it fast: a little lizard scuttling from one rock to the next. It dives. Talons out.

The little songbird picks up the lizard. Lifting it up, up, up— It slams it back down.

Stab. Onto the spines of a cactus. The lizard, impaled. Still wriggling. Mouth working soundlessly. The shrike is hungry, and so it eats—pecking and pulling at the helpless animal. It relishes its meal. So much so that it wants more: and so, in the remainder of the day and into the night, it captures a grasshopper, a moth, even a small mouse, and it does the same each time: up and then down, pinning it to the cactus and feasting. Its little gray breast flecked with fresh red.

She moves from hunter to hunter, then. She becomes an owl eating mice, a peregrine who flies high and then drops straight down, catching a rock dove in the air and killing it before it even hits the ground, a woodpecker tearing bugs from cactus meat, a wren plucking the limbs off a daddy longlegs, and then she thinks, *I want to eat a scorpion.* And so come morning, she finds her way into the body of a roadrunner—fast feet, sharp beak.

All day it runs and it hunts.

She—it?—kills a rattlesnake, picking it up and thrashing the serpent against a rock until its skull breaks. It spears a horned lizard, eating it in reverse so the hooks and spikes go down the bird's throat and do not catch there. And then it sees a scorpion: gold and almost translucent, legs clicking, tail twitching. The scorpion ducks and darts. The roadrunner moves fast. Head snapping forward. Spearing it. Crushing it. Eating it. The venom does nothing.

The bird is swift and deathless.

The roadrunner looks up.

There sits a coyote.

And here again: the idea of irony, though the roadrunner doesn't know what that means or why it's thinking of it.

(*Beep-beep.*)

The coyote is a mangy, sick thing. Its fur slick, its teeth yellow. Familiar to her is its one eye—the missing eye a rotten crater, the other eye unsurprisingly human. The coyote blinks and pants. Then laughs. *Heh, heh, heh.*

Behind the coyote: the body. Vulture still sitting there. Waiting. For what, though? The body must still be alive.

The roadrunner has come full circle. By accident? Or on purpose?

Above, the late-day sky darkens. Clouds gathered close over the sun. Somewhere in the deep distance, thunder rumbles like a hungry belly.

"You need to come back," the coyote says.

The roadrunner cocks its head like a bewildered dog.

"The storm is coming. Once it passes, the body is dead," the mangy, maybe-dead coyote says. A worm crawls out of its gone eye. "Death has passed you over again and again, blind to you. Ten years ago, you were marked. Death thought it took you already. You gave it a life. Not your own. Fooled it, you did. But soon, it'll figure it out. Fate will find you. Fate and Death are the same thing, you see. It hunts. Roaming closer and closer."

And the roadrunner thinks a thought that is distinctly not very birdlike: *Well, so fucking what?* The bird expects the body to die. Thought it already should've been dead, to be honest. And then it can truly be free. The roadrunner can do this forever. Go from one body to another. Bird to bird to bird. Never trapped by mere meat and bone. Flying, running, hunting, swooping, soaring, falling. Immortality, red in feather and beak.

Another boom of thunder somewhere far away.

The roadrunner turns to run—

But the coyote stands in its way. Head stooped. Teeth bared. Mealy tongue licking along its rotten choppers. "You can't run this time."

The roadrunner thinks: *Running is what I am and what I do.*

The coyote answers: "But you're not a roadrunner, are you? Miriam, it's time." Another thunder-tumble. The gray clouds have gone black. Far off, the mountains disappear behind a haze: rain falling there.

When the roadrunner looks, the coyote is no longer a coyote. It's a big man, broad shoulders. Sandy hair and a trucker hat. One eye ruined. Then it's a young woman with a carved-up face, the scars once red, once pink, now pale as the veins of a ghostly body. Then a little boy holding a red Mylar balloon. Then a little boy in a Superman costume, cape and everything. Then an older woman with a sneering face, her eyes framed by long gray hair, a pair of shining scissors in her hand with which she cuts at the air. She says, "Poor Miriam."

In the roadrunner's chest, something burns like a hot coal.

"Lying." A gunshot.

Hands around her throat. Gun to her head.

A series of explosions, above to below.

Brick, fire, death.

"Other people. It's them that make you weak. Connected to them. Tethered and chained, boat anchors holding you still . . ."

The roadrunner thinks: *I'm not connected anymore. I'm strong.*

But the coyote shakes its musky, stink-slick head.

"That isn't right," it growls. "It's not people that make you weak. It's people that make you strong. It's time to come back for them, Miriam. Not for you, maybe. But for them. Come home. Back to the meat, bones, and blood of the human condition. *Come home.*"

Lightning strikes as thunder kicks a hole in the sky. And rain falls through, hard and heavy and mean. And when it does, the roadrunner runs.

And Miriam—the body lying there, face forward in the dirt—gasps and shudders and cries out with a wordless sound.

FIFTY-FIVE

SHADOWS

Blink, blink, blink.

Miriam snaps to awareness. Nothing makes sense, not at first. Her world bucks and bangs, sending jolts up through her spine to the base of her neck. Everything is dark, and everything hurts. Shapes sit around her, to her left, to her right, across from her. *Human* shapes. But gathered there like—

Like a parliament of vultures.

Her brain, still loose and frazzled like the torn and tattered end of a shirt sleeve, thinks: *That's not the right word; it's a parliament of owls, not a parliament of vultures*, and yet that's what they looked like—a ruling body, a gathering of judges or politicians, waiting to make a vote . . .

They seem to have made their decision.

Or maybe she's the one who cast the clinching vote.

"Who are you?" she calls out into the darkness.

"Hot shit, she's awake," a man's voice says. A shadow stretches long near her, and a small light clicks on. Five figures sit near her inside some kind of vehicle—something military-looking. One person on each side of her. Three across. Four men, one woman. All in dusty desert camo. The one who turned on the light has a bristly boot-brush mustache, black as soot: "Miss?"

"Fuck. *Fuck.* What." She draws a deep, panicked breath. She feels suddenly trapped, her skin crawling. "What's happening?"

She's got a water bottle. Clutched between her knees and steadied by her hands. Quickly, she takes a long gulp. It's cold and yet it burns at the same time.

"We found you," the man says.

The woman leans forward. She's got small, dark eyes like black stones and a nose long and flat like the blade of an axe. As she leans closer, the gear on her belt—flashlight, knife, little grenades the size of Red Bull cans—rattles. "The cartel do this to you? Ma'am. *Ma'am.* You a mule? You got drugs on you? Where you hiding it? Hnnh? Start talking now, maybe we can end up friends."

"The fuck. No." Miriam coughs. "No, that's not it—"

Bootbrush says to the woman: "Nez, cool it. She doesn't fit the profile."

The woman—Nez?—shrugs, leans back. Arms crossed. Staring.

Next to Miriam, one of the men—Latino, maybe, with a pencil-thin mustache, leans forward and hands Bootbrush a little black flashlight.

"Thanks, Donnie," Bootbrush says. He clicks on the flashlight, passes it in front of Miriam's eyes—just as the vehicle they're in takes a hard hit and pulls sharply right. Miriam almost lands in Donnie's lap. Bootbrush clicks the flashlight off. "Ma'am, my name is Ken Kescoli. That's Dana Nez, Donnie Begay, Jim Lopez, and Octavio Kino." Jim's got messy hair and a huge grin decorating a round red baby face—a face so red, it's like he's not only been out sitting in the sun but is, perhaps, the sun itself. The one on the other side of her, Octavio, is handsome in ways people shouldn't be: almost too perfect, like he was formed by the wind and the water over a thousand years. "You can't see him right now, but we got Hal Curtis driving—you know our names now. Do you remember yours?"

She does.

That fact surprises her a little.

"Miriam," she says.

Bootbrush continues: "Hi, Miriam. You got a last name?"

She does. She doesn't say it. The man keeps on talking:

"We're a group of trackers working for ICE—that's Immigration and Customs Enforcement. Okay? We found you out at the edge of the Tohono reservation. You're in pretty rough shape, so we're going to take you to a hospital, get you looked at, then we'll have a chat—"

"*If* we don't get drowned in this gullywasher," Lopez says, still smiling.

Bootbrush nods. To her he says, "Got some bad weather out here. Storm coming through. Floods, so we're just trying to make our way back out."

"No," she says. "I'm not . . . I can't. I'm not hurt."

But she is. She knows she is. The pain that runs through her is—well, it's different now. Not vibrant and alive like it was before. Now it's bigger, broader, but duller, too. Hidden: buried under rock and dirt. She instinctively reaches under her filthy shirt to feel for the bullet wound in her chest and—

She finds something dry and bristly there. Dried grass, stitched in and out of her skin, sealing the wound and—

Thunder rumbles, lightning flashes. She sits up in the desert, gasping. A crow hops onto her belly, another onto her shoulder. With its beak it flips up her shirt, then crawls underneath it, its talons scrabbling to gain a foothold, and she tries to pull the bird out, but then its beak plunges into the wound in her chest and she screams. The bird's head works in and around, rooting. She feels air hissing out of her, blood rising up, and then it's back out again. The pain is like the bang of thunder, the flash of electric across the sky. The crow turns its head and something glistens in its beak. A mushroomed piece of lead, slick with red. It flicks its head and the bullet lands somewhere with a *pock*. The other crow has a wad of dried grass in its mouth, and the other pokes at it, and the two of them again approach her, and again they go to work, both beaks going stitch, stitch, stitch—

Did that happen?

Or did she just imagine it?

The grass in the wound . . .

"I'm fine," she says. "I don't need a hospital."

The woman, Nez, looks her up and down. "Lady, you *need* a fuckin' hospital. You look like you were just born. All that blood. Did someone rape you? You can tell us. Cartel men? Coyote? Bandits, smugglers, crazy desert motherfuckers, who?"

Donnie gives her knee a slight kick. "Hey, let her chill. Besides, we're not cops—let's just get her out of here."

"It was a . . . cult," Miriam says. "Not a cult. A group. A *militia*."

Octavio says with a smirk and a flourish of his hands, "A lot of those around here, miss. United States is the land of the free, but Arizona is the *land* of the fuckin' fruitbats."

"They . . . I can take you to them. They're, they're . . . north of here? High-clearance vehicles only. Road not maintained. I'm trying to remember—"Another hard bang as the truck dips. Rain hammers the roof. "Grave Gulch Road."

"I know where that is," Nez says.

"We're not doing that," Bootbrush says. "This storm is bad. You need help, and we need to get out of this desert."

She says as it hits her: "You're the Shadow Wolves."

"That's right," Bootbrush says.

"See?" Octavio says to Nez, elbowing her. "I told you people know who we are. We're famous. Basically."

Donnie says, "*Nobody* knows who we are. People in this country are about as dim as a bulb can get before it's gone dark. They don't even know where to vote, or what's in their food, or what rights they have—"

A hard brake. Everyone lurches forward. The truck dips

forward and there's a loud metal *bang* and a *ggggg* grinding sound just after.

Then everything is still.

"What the shit," Nez says.

A little panel between the back of the truck and the separated driver's seat slides open. A set of brown eyes stares out. Someone (who must be Hal Curtis) says through the slot, "Way ahead is flooded. Front end is down in a ditch, too, gonna need some pushers."

"Piss," Octavio says.

"Time to get wet," Lopez cackles.

"One of you makes another joke about my pussy," Nez says, "and I take out my knife and collect your balls as trophies."

Bootbrush stands and pops the back door. The others pull on floppy-brimmed hats and hop out as he waves them on.

Rain hits Miriam in the face. The gray day pulses with lightning, and the rain sound is a ceaseless roar. As Bootbrush goes to be the last one out, he holds up the flat of his hand: "Stay here. Won't be long. Gotta get the truck up and then scout a new way. Then we'll get you safe."

He hops out. Slams the door behind him.

Miriam sits.

Up front, the truck lurches in reverse as they push it. The engine goes. Tires spin. Their voices almost lost behind the sounds of the storm.

She doesn't want to go to the hospital.

Vultures standing around her as the crows stitch. A hawk perching on a nearby cactus as the first raindrops start to fall. A little shrike flitting about. A mockingbird mocking her. Like a princess from a Disney movie—except instead of dressing her, they're dressing her wounds. And waiting.

Waiting for what?

A dark shadow passes in front of the gray sun.

She looks across and someone is sitting there.

Louis. Not-Louis. Trespasser.

An oddly comforting sight. For now.

"Do-overs and come-backs ain't free," he says, extending his tongue. A scorpion dances on it. He bites it in half, lets the bits squirm between clamped teeth. She remembers what the scorpion tastes like. She remembers what it all tastes like: lizard, mouse, butterfly, even Ashley Gaynes as the gannets tore him down to the studs and struts, to the bones and sinew. "You owe. We got work to do."

"I know," she says.

Miriam opens the door, quiet as she can, and ducks out into the storm.

KAREN KEY

The rain has stopped. The clamor of the storm is far off, now. Karen Key's head lolls. She sits in her chair by their bed, in their little house here in the middle of the compound. Her body is broken but her mind is sharp—many shards of a shattered mirror, each a cutting weapon. Ethan kneels before her, his head in her lap as he likes to do, and he cries softly, and with one slow, shaking hand she strokes his hair as she is wont to do—or was, until recently, when she refused to touch him or even look at him. But now, everything is in motion, all pieces are in play, and one by one, the dominos tip into each other, *click, click, click*. The sound of cards in bicycle spokes, of poker chips rattling, of everything falling apart but also falling into place. Soon now. Soon.

She hears thoughts—stray thoughts, snippets snatched out of the air like music heard down a city street, like the smell of food from a faraway restaurant carried on the wind—and she takes these thoughts and brings them into her. Most stray thoughts are worthless and shallow—

why does it have to rain today of all days
stupid bitch won't let me see my kids people don't know how dads have it
am I drinking enough water probably not
this coffee tastes like shit but I'm still drinking it
gets hotter earlier every year

—because most people are worthless and shallow but they
give her comfort just the same: because she is not those things.
Karen is better now. Wasn't once. Is now. Thanks to a bullet in
her brain.

at least it's not a dust storm

ate too many donuts

Mexican pieces of shit

People think about simple, meaningless things all day:
weather, food, momentary comfort, cigarettes, candy, a pebble
in the shoe, whether you left the oven on or put the flag up
on the mailbox. But once in a while, people reveal themselves
more completely: a worry over cancer, a fear of strangers, a violent urge, a sexual thrill so strong and so secret, it threatens to
plunge Karen into darkness. Most brains are a boring soup until
a truly interesting ingredient rises to the surface, borne forth
on so many bubbles. Even insipid thoughts can be revealing: a
worry over rain or heat parlays into a fear of global warming and
an anxiety over death and control; a stray thought about food
reveals worries over cancer or diabetes, hypochondria rising like
a hungry beast, and again that familiar, persistent, universal fear
of death; a desire for momentary comfort shifts and becomes a
question of whether one even *deserves* it.

How deep the rabbit hole goes.

Karen cannot go so deep. Not unless they die. And then, for a
time, while the mind and soul linger, she can go all the way down.
Like she did with Wade Chee. Like she's done with smugglers
and mules and thieves. She did it with David when he died—not
because he had secrets (though he did), but only because it's
how she honored his sacrifice. He was a good boy. Driven to
destroy himself, though, as many are: a self-destructive urge,
an obsession, an *addiction*, to picking scabs and letting the liar
blood flow.

She wanted Miriam Black to die so that she could crawl

around that mind like a worm in the dirt. Cover herself in it. But she's never tried to dive deep into the mind of a changer, a psychic, someone with power like hers. Even surface thoughts from those never come easy—it's less *plucking moths from the air* and more *breaking icicles off gutters.* A sharp snap, cold in the hand.

Miriam was supposed to be an ally in all of this.

Though she was, in a way. Unwittingly so.

That name, Mary Stitch.

A horrible woman. But such power.

Everything will soon be different. Karen knows that now. A necessity. The world must be moved. It takes more than a small effort to do that. It takes a swift hand. Violent and strong and sure. Motivated by truth and honor.

If they cannot succeed, the end is coming. She is sure of it. The vision she saw there at her own end, upon her death and resurrection: America, burning. Cornfields on fire. Sickness in the streets. The people poisoned by their own food and by each other. Red parachutes in the sky: invasion. Dead people in the streets: plague. The stars-and-stripes cut to ribbons and burned for warmth as a long winter sinks its teeth in and never lets go. A certainty of this future lives in her heart. And she knows it's our fault. Our weak leadership. Our socialist regime. America bent over like a drooping flower, its bloom *begging* to be deadheaded.

That course of action will be long and hard, and it has begun.

They will succeed because they are just and they are right.

New people have begun to show up. People who have heard about them on the Internet or through whispers. They're a group who is really going to change things. They are the storm that's coming. A storm that will sweep through this country, cleaning out the trash, drowning the weak, washing the slate clean.

For a moment: a feeling of triumph and satiety.

But then: something tickles the back of her brain stem, something scratching there like a hungry rat. "Something . . . is . . .

wrong," she says, her mouth struggling to speak the words that come so easy inside her mind.

Ethan pulls his head off her lap—him weeping because of what he's done, what they've done, and what must come—and he sniffs and wipes his eyes and nose with the back of his hand. "What do you mean?"

"I . . . don't . . . know. Get . . . Ofelia."

A ripple out there somewhere. The thoughts of those around suddenly peaking like a sharp spire of static—

Ethan stands, starts to move, but then he's frozen in place—startled by a fluttering black shadow at the window.

A crow. Or a raven. Is there a difference? This one is bigger. Its beak, all black. The feathers at the back of its head almost squared away at a granite-block angle. The bird opens its bill. It croaks—*wawk wawk wawk*.

Then on the glass: *tap tap tap*.

Behind it, another black, fluttering shape.

The thoughts from all those around in the compound begin to focus.

They begin to find *common theme*.

that's a big bird

they're probably gonna shit on the greenhouse

look at them all

maybe the storm spooked them

The light coming through the window—gray, but tinged with the renewed sun—suddenly dims, darkens. A rush of sound like rain, but one Karen knows isn't rain, isn't storm, isn't thunder:

It's birds.

FIFTY-SIX

CHOOSER OF THE SLAIN

Miriam walks.

The rain falls hard at first—like a castigation from a vengeful God hoping to once more drown the people of the Earth and start all over again. But she knows that this storm will be over soon. Birds avoid storms—it's one of the things she knows from reading about birds but also from flitting around inside their bodies. A storm comes and birds seek its margins, traveling along the borders of it or finding shelter in a tree or under a rock.

And so, they know the margins of this storm too.

This one is passing east.

Miriam is walking north.

North is where the camp is. The compound. Ethan's people. She knows this because the birds know this. They go there sometimes for food—where people are, food is plentiful. Seeds spilled out of a bag. Scraps of bread fallen from a sandwich. A greenhouse full of fruit and vegetables. The birds know how to eat. People know how to unwittingly feed them.

And so, Miriam walks.

Soon, the rain stops.

In the distance, she can see it—the shape of the buildings. The angled roof of the greenhouse. A few cars and trucks—big trucks now, like tractor trailers pulled in between buildings. Houses and trailers.

She thinks: *This is for Isaiah. This is for David.* But most important: it's to stop what's to come, the death of a courthouse full of people. An event, too, that is surely not the end of the Coming Storm but just the first cannon-boom of thunder.

And Miriam thinks selfishly, *If I stop them, then I save Mary.*

Mary, who is as much a monster as the rest of them. Worse, maybe. Smart and cruel and irretrievably broken. If Miriam's salvation is to come from this woman—and it may not—then she has to stop the bombing.

Miriam looks around her. The birds are starting to gather. Crows in the branches of creosote. Ravens perched on saguaros. Hawks and vultures in the sky: the hawks dipping and diving, the vultures merely gliding. Shrikes and blackbirds and mocking-birds. A red flash from a vermilion flycatcher. The ochre belly of a goldfinch. The flitting shape of a cactus wren. More flying in. Dozens at first, then twice that, then twice *that*. And still some coming as she walks.

Her mind is fractured. Like Miriam's persona is a mirror chipped at the edges—bits of her reflective glass buried in each bird. She is within them all and yet remains in her own body too. She shares in them and maybe, just maybe, the birds share in her, too.

It scares her. Turns her blood to cold piss, turns her piss to blood, turns her stomach into a clutching fist. This isn't human. She knows that. As she walks and the birds follow—as her mind follows with them, peripherally—she tries not to shake. But she does. Wet and cold and scared, she shakes. And yet she doesn't stop.

Bare feet on rock. The soles of her feet are cut up—but scabbed over, callused now, like her body has urged healing beyond what should be possible. The gunshot wound in her chest—stitched with dead grass. Stitched *by* birds, unless that was a hallucination. At this point, who can tell? Her belly, scabbed over. Everything hurts. But even so, she feels light, buoyant.

Like a balloon with some helium left, just drifting along the ground.

Some of her birds have already gone ahead to the camp.

She gets there soon after.

The fence awaits. Tall, chain link, razor wire facing outward like claws ready to cut her apart. But she already knows the fence is warped and weak, and the ground here is shallow and the posts are probably not in as deep as they should be, and so all she has to do is wish for the fence to go away and—

Vultures dip and dive. Big birds, vultures.

Heavy birds.

One by one, they slam into the fence. The chain link rattles like sleigh bells every time they hit—one after the other, each a little feathered wrecking ball, flying up and then back and then swooping forward. Some grow bloody. One's neck breaks and it drops, and Miriam flinches and looks away—a little piece of herself ripped out of it and she feels the pain.

Still, the fence stands.

But soon, the birds adopt a new tactic. They do not hit it one by one, but all of them—vultures, blackbirds, ravens, songbirds—fly to it and cling to the side the way a woodpecker hangs to a tree. They swarm the fence so that she can't even see through it—just a writhing mass of feathers, black punctuated with hits of bright color, and the birds rock and lean and squawk and chirp and scream—

The fence leans forward. One post pops out of the ground, then another.

As it drops, the birds take flight. The chain link hits the ground with a crash and clamor.

Miriam walks over it. The metal cold underneath her feet.

Somewhere, someone laughs, but someone else cries out in

alarm—she can hear them a little bit, not just with her own ears but with the ears of her feathered friends swooping about.

What's with all these birds?

Holy shit, call somebody!

This isn't right. This is payback for what we've done. . . .

Miriam walks through the same greenhouse she ran through when she left this place. Nobody's here. Empty now. The plants have been moved. They're readying for something. To leave, maybe—smart; once they hit the courthouse, people will come. Or maybe they're hunkering down. Sheltering in place. Getting ready for the siege that will come. Waco. Jonestown. Ruby Ridge.

Above, through the Plexiglas roof, the darting shapes of birds. Not just birds. *Her* birds.

In through the greenhouse, then back out again. The camp ahead. A few tractor-trailers parked. Windows being boarded up. Someone's pulling rolls and coils of fence out the back of one truck: so, they're staying, then. Digging in.

Miriam watches for a little while. A woman sets a box of what looks to be canned goods down at her feet and stares up at the birds—birds who are now alighting upon rooftops and windows, on the tops of trucks and fence rolls. A Hitchcockian apocalypse. Two men with black rifles slung over their shoulders watch too. One laughs. The other doesn't look so amused.

A third man—young, white, hair as ginger as a gingerbread cookie—comes out of a nearby trailer, a pistol at his hip and boards under his arm.

He sees Miriam.

She sees him.

It takes a moment for who she is to register on his face. Like he can't quite parse what he's seeing—and oh, my, how bad she looks. She can see herself through the eyes of her birds: she looks like the Devil ate her and shat her back out, through bowels lined with cactus needles. It hits him then. His face unfreezes and his eyes go big as the realization goes supernova in his eyes.

The boards drop with a clatter.

His hand goes to his hip, fumbling with the gun.

He's slow. Way, way too slow.

Miriam merely needs to blink.

A black shape flits in front of him. Just under his chin. There's a feathery flutter followed by a spray of red, and his throat is open. Red like a gash sliced in a blood orange, juice dribbling out.

He lifts the gun but it drops out of his hand.

It happened so fast, so wordless, so quiet, that nobody else has even noticed. And so, as this young ginger lad drops to his knees, Miriam walks over to him. Picks up the gun. Now the woman with the canned goods at her feet sees Miriam. And the shuddering body at her feet, blood pooling.

The woman cries out. Turns to run.

The two men with guns—one Latino guy shorn bald, the other a white guy with a slobby spare tire around his middle and a big red beard—turn, not sure what they'll see, and damn sure not expecting to see Miriam standing there.

They raise their rifles.

Miriam already has her gun trained—the pistol bucks in her hand. She's not a great shot, but it's enough: the bullet clips the man in the arm, staggering him. The rifle pulls from his hands as he cries out.

The other one fires.

Miriam is already moving.

The gun chatters: semiauto. *Pop-pop-pop-pop*. She goes to duck behind the front end of a tractor trailer, bullets pinging into the grill—

But then it stops. The man cries out, a warbling shriek—

Miriam doesn't need to look to know. She can feel the little peregrine falcon tearing into the man's face with ease and delight, the way it might rend another smaller bird—a grackle, perhaps—asunder.

Eyes pop under claws. Nose pushed inward by stabbing beak. A lip ripped off, wetting the scream rising up from his throat.

More yelling now. More people coming out of doors. Out from the backs of trucks. Up from the lot, from the trailers, from the tents.

Good. Let them come.

Deep breath. Eyes closed.

The rainstorm is over. But a new storm is here. It's like squeezing a trigger—simple, gentle, a small action with massive consequence.

The birds descend from the sky. Or fly down from the buildings, the trucks, the power lines ahead. They scream and trill. A cacophony of birds, their individual cries lost to the larger din.

Miriam steps out from the front of the truck. She walks forward, looking for her true prey: Ethan, Karen, Mary, Ofelia. Nearby, a tall man with a sawed-off shotgun swipes at a goldfinch whirling into his face. Miriam lifts the pistol and shoots him. His head jerks. Blood pops. He's down.

Another man on the ground. Two hawks rising and falling against him. Talons down. Beaks biting. Bits of red lifted up. His middle a mess. A loop of bowel lifted high. Miriam kicks his gun away and keeps walking.

Somewhere, glass shattering. People screaming. Gunfire chattering. An older man, cheeks like a cratered moon, teeth like broken rocks, runs at her with a knife—but something hits him in the face, something gray and red and furry. A dead rabbit. Flung by a prairie falcon. The man swats at the dead animal, distracted, as the bird descends upon him.

Other people run from the birds. A raven on the back of one woman's neck, its beak plunging in and out. A crow pinwheeling into a young man's face. A fat fuck on the ground, his knee skinned almost to the bone, turning around and firing a revolver in the air like it'll do any good at all.

Miriam walks through all of it like a tourist.

Ahead, she sees Ethan's house. She goes around back, the terror-stricken cries of men and women lost to the cackling cacophony of angry birds. Miriam thinks to go in through the back patio, but there she finds the patio has been boarded up. Plywood nailed over it. Over some—but not all—of the windows, too.

One of those will do.

She barely has to will it—just a slight mental *twitch* of her psychic trigger finger—and a serpentine trail of dark birds rises up over his house like a lashing whip, a dread tendril. The roller coaster of ravens and crows goes up, twists, and then dives back down behind the house—

They form a singular point and crash in through one of the unprotected windows. A funnel of birds, twisting like a whipping snake. In through that space. Miriam feels them penetrate and invade. Landing on coffee tables, couches, perching on counter-tops, pecking at a loaf of bread left out, wings knocking photos off walls. Flying through the halls and doorways and rooms.

Until: there. Her target. Or one of them? Found.

Miriam climbs in through the window: a trespasser. She creeps in through the swiftly made wreckage of the house. Bird shit streaking the walls. Scratches in the paint and wallpaper from beak and claw.

She wanders down the back hallway. Toward the last bedroom. Ethan sits on the bed. Unarmed. Hands flat against his knees. He's scared. He should be. In this room: forty-two birds. Mostly crows and ravens. A few raptor birds and songbirds. One owl perched on a dresser, tufts like devil horns up over its head as its yellow eyes watch his every move.

Miriam steps in. His legs are shaking.

She says: "You thought the apocalypse was a ways off. But

here it is, Ethan. All around you. Turns out you had your eyes on the wrong revelation. I'm the end of your world. *Me*."

"H . . . how are you alive?"

"Your wife said it. Death doesn't see me. Not yet, and not easily." She shrugs, and chews on her lower lip. "I'm one tough noogie, dude."

He shakes his head. Rubs some grit into his voice. "Why even come back? Why not just leave us alone?"

"You *know* why."

"The boy."

"Not just him. Everything. All that you do and want to do. Him, David, the courthouse, Mary. *Me*. I hate you. I want you *gone*. Gone before you can hurt all those people."

She watches the fear leave him. Like a ghost peeling away from a body gone dead: a fog lifting. His frown turns upside down. The old grin, that smirky twist, opens up and now he's laughing, just laughing like this is the funniest joke he's ever told. Miriam laughs too, because why not? Why not enjoy the absurdity of it all? Before, at the Caldecott estate—and later, on a boat with Ashley Gaynes—she couldn't control what she was or what she could do, but now she can. She's given something up: some dream, some idea of herself, a bit of *humanity* (because being human is overrated, anyway), and now here she stands. Doing what she was meant to do. In a crass menagerie of hungry, mad-eyed birds.

"You don't get it," he says.

"I get it just fine."

"No, you *don't*. You're *too late*."

An icicle in her gut stabs and twists. "What?"

"It's over. The bombs went off an hour ago. Those people are dead."

Her knees almost buckle. The birds shuffle and shudder. Beaks clicking. A low flurry of squawks and warbles rise from the gathered parliament.

Mary's dead.

Quintero.

The woman at the desk. The man at the copier.

Cops, lawyers, officers, criminals, judges, everybody.

"You're lying," she hisses.

"I'm not. You've been gone weeks. We thought you were dead." The smile stays on his face. A cold smile carved into cemetery granite. "And the boy, hoo boy, Miriam. We have Isaiah, too."

"Bullshit. *Bullshit.*"

"A nice stranger dropped him off today. Found him all alone. Your friend abandoned him. The corker is: the boy wanted to come here. We're what he knows. We're his family and he figured that out." Ethan pauses. Sizes her up. "You wanna see him?"

"I want you to die."

A sound behind her. The birds turn, move to fly—already Miriam can see through their eyes what's coming. Karen. *Karen Key.* Hiding in a goddamn closet with Ofelia right behind her. Ofelia with a gun—a small pistol.

Her birds take swift wing. They swarm—Ofelia starts firing the pistol, *bang, bang, bang.*

Miriam's leg jerks, the knee suddenly bent, and she falls hard. Fresh blood down the meat of her thigh.

A red snow shovel slams hard against her back—face against tile—

She tries to stand, ignoring the pain—*death doesn't see you, not yet, not today*—and she takes the pistol, the one she stole from that ginger kid, and points it at Ethan. Ethan, who launches himself at her. His shoulder under her chin: teeth clamp down on her own tongue, mouth filling with blood. He's strong, too strong, and he flings her into the dresser—but then he's whirling about, howling, clutching at his ear as a little wren hangs there, pecking and clawing.

Miriam has one shot. One. Not to save anybody. But for revenge.

She stands. Gun up. Pain throbbing in her leg. Breath gone from her.

Then a wave of something inside her. A feeling. Warm and deep. Pleasure and pain bloom together in a braiding vine of new growth. Her legs buckle. Her mouth goes wet. The gun slides from her grip.

And all the birds stop too. They settle back on their perches. They start to murmur and squawk, one by one taking flight. Heading back out the window, a few feathers floating in the space where they once were.

Miriam rolls over on her side.

Ofelia comes, stands over her. The girl's face is all fucked up. Like she tried to make out with a thorn bush: Scratches bleeding. Her lip torn open. A beak wound just under her eye, pumping little jets of fresh blood. She swallows, says, "Feels good, doesn't it? What can I say? I got a gift."

Then she spits on Miriam.

"Don't have to do this," Miriam says, moaning. Trying to push past the good feeling in her belly, the warmth between her legs. "Please."

"You found your way out of Hell, little bird. So why'd you come back?"

Ofelia kicks her in the side.

The pleasure is gone then: a merciless void.

She tries to pull herself up, but Ethan backhands her, then rushes to his wife—his bleeding, trembling wife. Sitting there in her chair. One ear almost torn off. Scratches and cuts mark her, as they do Ofelia. Bird waste down her chest.

"You're going to pay for this," Ethan says, his voice trembling. He strokes his wife's cheek, his fingers coming away red. "But first, I want you to see that we weren't lying. I want you to see where you failed. Then you'll get your justice."

FIFTY-SEVEN

WAVE OF MUTILATION

Hands bound behind her back with zip ties. Kneeling there in the open air of the camp. Tents fluttering around as the last winds of the storm pass by. Sun is up and out now, emerging from a bank of gray, anvil-struck clouds like it's here to see what's to come of her. It hates her and always has. The sun will enjoy this.

The remnants of the Coming Storm have gathered. Many mutilated by birds—birds who are now gone, who have taken many pounds of flesh before Miriam could no longer control them. Ofelia did that to her. Broke her connection—one power against another, hands snapping her antenna.

Bitch.

Miriam spits in the wet dust. She's surprised it isn't red.

Doesn't matter much. Blood pumps out of the hole in her leg. Maybe the bullet hit an artery. Her head dips and sways. She's woozy. Finding her own thoughts is hard and getting harder: it's like being drunk, like she has to think her way through the fabric of a heavy sweater.

Folks watch her. Many still bleeding. Pressing rags to injuries. Over there: a big-boned hound dog of a woman has a handkerchief pressed over a ruined eye. A skinny weasel dude next to her is trying to staunch the blood pouring from a gash in his head. He's doing a piss-poor job of it and has to keep blinking it away. People limp up. Shift nervously from foot to foot. Feathers blow on the wind.

The crowd parts. Ethan steps up. Ofelia comes behind him, wheeling Karen. Ethan holds out his hand, then snaps his fingers like he's summoning a dog. And Miriam's heart, or what passes for it, shrinks like a grape gone raisin.

Isaiah hurries to catch up. He takes Ethan's hand.

For a time, they just stand there, staring.

Isaiah says, "I'm sorry."

Miriam nods. "I know, kid."

"Don't worry," Ethan says. "We're gonna be good to him. Give the kid whatever he wants. Popsicles. A PlayStation. A helicopter ride through the Grand Canyon. He knows we're family. He's got a soft spot for you, but one day he'll see you for the monster that you are." He sniffs. "Anyway. Here."

He pulls out an emergency radio, the kind you wind up, the kind without batteries. He fiddles with the tuner and it goes through a babble of music and words and static before settling on a news station:

"—are calling an act of domestic terror but others are hoping remains an isolated incident. The incident today at the Pima County courthouse is reminiscent of the Oklahoma City bombing, where Timothy McVeigh and Terry Nichols carried out an attack on the Alfred P. Murrah Federal Building in a perceived retaliation for what happened at Waco and Ruby Ridge—"

It goes on like that for a while. Nobody's tallied the deaths yet, but they're speculating over a hundred dead, with maybe three times that in nonfatal injuries. But they're still pulling folks out of the rubble. They describe the wreckage on the scene. Someone mentions gunmen. An expert comes on, talking about where the bombs were placed—"Looks like they may have been placed in a duct that traveled down the southwest corner—"

No, goddamnit, fuck, fuck, fuck—

She didn't do it. She didn't stop anything.

Ethan grabs the radio, turns it off.

"You've done us a grave disservice," Ethan says to her. "You hurt us. But we persevered. And now it's time." He pulls a black pistol from the small of his back. "Say good-bye to the boy. He seems fond of you."

The boy steps closer.

Miriam looks to Isaiah. "Isaiah. Where'd Gabby go? She was supposed to be watching you. Is she okay?"

He nods and says, "A nice man brought me here."

"But where is she? Why did she leave you?"

"*It was a nice man with one eye.*"

And then Isaiah pulls back and reaches for Ethan's hand.

Ethan points the gun.

And stiffens up. His arm out. Tendons going taut on his neck. Eyes starting to bulge. Miriam thinks: *This is not where he dies, not how he dies,* but then she realizes: Isaiah is like her, he has powers, he can *change* things, and—

Ethan's head snaps back. The veins in his body rise like snakes swimming close to the surface of swamp water: the whites of his eyes go suddenly red. Blood jets from his nose and now Ofelia screams, she's pulling Karen away—

Then comes a growl and a roar, the sound of a beast awakening. The hiss and squeal of some demon. The ground shudders beneath her knees and she thinks, *This is it; this is Hell opening up beneath me,* and she wonders if there are bombs going off and if this is when she really dies or maybe she's already dead out there in the desert, face down, all this a hallucination born of the rip-and-tug of vulture beaks prying her brains from her broken skull.

People scream and run. Ethan's face is a mask of blood. His eyes stare out, dead as train-smashed pennies, and then he collapses.

Isaiah says, "Now you know what I can do. I'm sorry."

He breaks into tears and holds her. Miriam cries too. Then she falls out of his grip and over into her own blood.

It's then she sees what's coming. It's not a beast, not a demon. It isn't Hell itself and it's not bombs going off. It's a truck. Black. Military. Shining from the rain. It barrels forward, a bank of lights on top of it shining bright—men in black fatigues storm out, guns up, and at first she thinks, *Who are they?* But then she knows who they are: the Shadow Wolves. Nez, Octavio, and the others. Guns chatter and bark. Lots of yelling. Miriam does all she can do, which is press her forehead to the ground and scream into the earth.

Someone kneels by her and, with big hands, helps her up. Her bleary eyes see the Trespasser looking down at her—the ghost, the hallucination, the vision summoned from inside her own haunted head.

"Miriam, come on, we have to go."

That voice. That's not him. That's not the Trespasser.

A nice man with one eye.

It's Louis.

PART SEVEN

STORMSWEPT

THE DEVIL'S BEACH

Evelyn Black sits on a blue beach chair, smoking a long Virginia Slim. "Want one?" she asks, offering the mint-green pack with her free hand.

Miriam sits on a beach chair, hers red.

"I don't," she says. To her surprise.

"Eh," her mother answers, then puts the pack away and keeps puffing. The water washes in. The water washes out. The sun is filtered behind gray clouds.

Her mother's all beached up. A Jimmy Buffett Parrothead shirt. Flip-flops. Bare legs showing varicose veins. A few liver spots on her hands. She smells strongly of coconut tanning oil.

"Are you her?" Miriam asks. "Or are you him. Or it. Or whatever the fizzy fuck the Trespasser is."

"Language," her mother says.

Huh. Maybe it *is* her.

Evelyn Black just shrugs. "I don't know. I'm here, though, and you're here. Sun's out. I've got cigarettes." She hums a few bars of "Margaritaville." Which shows Miriam exactly where they are.

"I'm in Hell," she says. "This is it. My final punishment. Me and the maybe-ghost of my mother. She's smoking. I'm not. And I have to listen to her rendition of a Jimmy Buffett song. Satan's favorite song, if I'm not mistaken." She rubs her eyes with the heels of her hands.

"This isn't Hell. You're not dead. I'm not dead either."

"Uh-huh. You're pretty much dead. In my world."

"Well," her mother says after a long drag. "This isn't your world." Then: a long exhale of smoke. *Whoosh*. Miriam smells it. Mysteriously, it just makes her feel queasy. No nic-fit lurks within like a nest of chewing termites.

Maybe Hell's not so bad.

She leans back on the chair. It creaks. A breeze blows. Salt air.

"So, what now?" Evelyn asks.

"I dunno. We sit. Maybe I go for a swim. See how far out I can go before I drown. What happens when a dead person drowns? Hm."

"You're not dead."

"Sure. And liquor's not delicious."

"You aren't dead. You're not really *alive*, though, either. But you will be again, soon. *So*. Same question: what now?"

"Ugh. Fine. I'll play. I don't know what now. I go on being me. I go on doing what I do. Not because I want to but because, like you are oh so fond of saying, it is what it is. Life sucks, so fuck a duck in a bucket."

Evelyn stabs out the cigarette in a little '70s-era ashtray sitting in the sand by her chair. "That's your plan? Do the same thing you've always done? Keep on—what? Stepping in it? Getting other people's crap on your sandals? Saving people who don't deserve saving from certain doom? Poor Penelope, tied to the train tracks? Miriam. *Miriam*. Think about yourself."

"That's all I do. I'm a very selfish person."

"You think that. But maybe you think wrong. Maybe you don't think enough about yourself." Evelyn turns and lowers her sunglasses. "Maybe you can still change yourself. Maybe there's still a way out."

"You know? Whatever. There's isn't. Fuck off."

"You could be nicer to me. You almost got me killed on that boat."

"I basically did get you killed. So, yeah." A regretful sigh. "I could be nicer to you; you're right. Sorry. It's just—" She leans on the arm of the chair, facing her mother. "The woman who *may* have known how I got clear of this curse of mine, she's gone. Blew herself up in a bombing I was powerless to stop."

Mary, dead.

And why?

Miriam knows why. The woman hated herself. Just as Miriam has, at times, hated herself. Just as Miriam once planned to end her own life when the pages of her diary ran out—a suicide scheme interrupted by a killer named Harriet.

She squeezes her eyes shut. "So, what I want? It's now impossible."

"Like the impossible ever stopped you before."

Miriam shrugs. "Point." Then it strikes her: "You're not him. It. The Trespasser. Are you?"

"What do you mean?"

"I mean, the Trespasser wants the opposite of what you're saying. At least—I think. The Trespasser is a part of my curse. He doesn't want to be gone from my head. He wants to stay around. Wants me to keep on keeping on."

"Well, that Trespasser sounds like a"—Evelyn leans even closer and lowers her voice, enunciating each syllable—"a real *ass-hole.*"

Miriam laughs. "True story."

"Anyway. I'm just saying, Miriam. Do what you gotta do. For you, not for them. You did your time. I love you. Time to love yourself."

"My time isn't—"

Up, she's about to say, but Evelyn is gone. All that's left is the water, washing up higher and higher, sucking sand back out to sea. Way out there, past the clouds, past the sun: thunder rumbles and lightning tastes the horizon.

FIFTY-EIGHT

A NICE, ONE-EYED MAN

Beep-beep-beep—light rushes in. Sound. Air. The world a pair of clapping hands, her in the middle. Upright. Hands gripping sheets. Long, keening gasp.

And there he is. Louis. Grabbing one of her hands in both of his own. He's clean-shaven, like he was back there in the compound. He's got *both* eyes there, which doesn't make sense, doesn't work at all, and then she realizes: this is still a dream, still a vision, but that eye doesn't look quite right and she thinks:

It's a fake. He's got a fake eye. Took him long enough.

She lurches up, throws her arms around him.

And she kisses him. An ugly kiss—face smashing against his, teeth against teeth, a kiss without propriety, a kiss without *care*, and she knows she should care about the corpse breath she probably has, and how her lips are as dry as a rough-hewn two-by-four, and how he's got a fiancée named Samantha, but for now, it's a kiss with gravity, straight-up, no-fooling physics.

Someone clears his throat.

She opens her eyes.

There are others in the room. Two doctors. Gabby. Isaiah. Isaiah's smiling a big smile. Gabby is too, but her smile looks sad: mournful in its way.

Miriam pulls away. Louis does too.

"Ah," he says.

"Oh," she answers.

A doctor steps in. Little guy, big forehead. Tufts of white hair sticking off the sides of his head like ruffled ostrich feathers. He adjusts his glasses and says, "Welcome back to the land of the living, Miss Black."

She gulps. "Yeah. Thanks."

A nurse scoots around, hands her a cup of water. She sips it noisily.

Everyone stares. The doctor says, "Let's have a conversation." To the rest of the room: "May we have some privacy?"

They all filter out. Louis gives her one last squeeze. Gabby gives a small wave, the sadness there plain to see.

"I don't . . ." she starts to say. But her voice is scratchy and raw.

"I'm Doctor Flaherty. You're in Tucson, at the University Medical Center. You've been in a medically induced coma for three weeks."

She blinks. "Oh."

Flaherty pulls up a chair. He sits and leans in like they're girl-friends or something. "The reason we did that is because your brain has been injured. And, far as I can tell, *reinjured*. You may have had a series of concussions in the past, by the look of it, and all of that resulted in a TBI, a traumatic brain injury. So, to keep your brain safe—while we also worked on that gunshot wound to your leg, and the one in your chest—we induced a coma with propofol." He laughs, like this is hilarious. And shit, maybe it is. "You're one broken cookie!"

She shrugs. "Yeah. I know."

His face falls. The humor leaves. "I don't know what hap-pened to you out there. But a bullet wound stitched up with . . ." He frowns, as if this is distasteful. "Organic matter. Leaves. Grass. We found a . . . feather inside you." He makes a small sound ("*ah*") and reaches in his white coat. He shows her a large glass vial. A black feather is the only thing inside of it. He shakes it.

"A souvenir, for me? You shouldn't have."

"Well, everyone else got a T-shirt. From now on, Miss Black, you're going to have to be more careful. Particularly with this." He gently pokes his finger into the center of her forehead. Her eyes go crossed watching it. "Your brain won't handle being rattled around in there anymore. Your skull isn't a dice cup."

"You'd be surprised."

"Mm. Still. Keep it protected. Maybe wear a helmet."

Hah. Yeah.

"You've got visitors, but you need rest."

"I want to see them."

"Not now. Later. Tomorrow, maybe."

"Yes, now."

"Pushy patient. Did I save your life?" Before she can answer, he says, "I did, at that. So, trust me when I say: you need to rest. Have a little water. Eat a little generic hospital Jell-O. If you need anything, press the button."

She presses the button.

A nurse pokes her head in.

"Just testing," Miriam says.

Flaherty frowns.

FIFTY-NINE

FEEDING TIME AT THE RAPTOR PADDOCK

She eats like a woman possessed. After three days, she hasn't had a proper meal, not really, because what they bring on those plastic turd-brown trays isn't enough to feed a fat sparrow. But now, *now* they're letting her off the leash, and now she's down in the cafeteria. Which, to her surprise, is a buffet. The plate before her is mounded with breakfast items. All of it terrible.

Miriam doesn't care. If she could shovel these watery eggs and papery bacon pieces and gummy potatoes into her mouth with an *actual* shovel, she would, but right now, she's forced to use her fork and spoon in tandem.

"You still eat like the Miriam I remember," Louis says, sitting across from her. He's just sipping a cup of coffee.

"Want some?" she says, cheeks bulging like a hamster who ate a whole saltine cracker. She slides the plate toward him.

He chuckles. "I think I might lose a finger if I went in for it."

"Your loss." She pulls back. "Actually, not your loss, because basically, this food is awful. But it's the best awful food. I don't care. I have no fucks to give. Just . . ." More food. *"Hungry."*

He watches her the way someone watches a shark eat a goat. Eventually, the plate is clean.

"Now," she says, breathing in through her nose as she wipes her mouth. "Hi! How are you?"

"Just dandy, I guess."

Way he says it, she knows it's not true. Wraiths flit across his face: specters of what happened back at the compound. She knows he probably doesn't want to have the conversation. He's guarded against it—that much is clear. Miriam can't care about that. She has to know.

"I don't get it," she says, wincing as she leans forward. "You. There. At the compound. Saving my ass. It doesn't add up."

A flash as the ghosts behind his eyes stir. "Your friend. Gabby?" Way he says it, she wonders if he knows that they had a thing. "She went a long while without hearing from you. Didn't know who to talk to or how to find you. She reached out to me. Said she took my number from your phone a while back."

"Sneaky."

"And life-saving, as it turns out. For all of us. I went down to see her in Virginia, at her sister's, and while me and Samantha were gone, neighbors said someone broke into our apartment. Messed it up pretty good. Seemed like something bad was happening. So, I wanted to go find you. Kick down the doors of that compound—I even thought, maybe I'll drive my truck straight through the gates. Battering ram, boom. But the boy had another idea."

"The boy. Isaiah."

"Uh-huh. It was his plan for me to bring him there. He said he wanted to go and could handle himself. I didn't know how, exactly." Louis clears his throat. None of this makes him comfortable. All the events of Miriam's life are barbs of rose thorn: run your hand over them and they cut you up. "I made sure they couldn't recognize me too easily. Shaved. Cut my hair shorter. I even went and got a fake eyeball."

"No more sexy eye patch." She makes a pouty face.

"Seems my pirate days are over, matey. Anyway. We went there, and I had no idea what had gone down or what was coming. Gabby had told me some of it, but she didn't know

everything either—and this is your friendly reminder to start
writing all this stuff down and telling everybody everything. No
more secrets from you."

She shrugs.

"At the same time they were blowing king hell out of that
courthouse and killing all those people, me and the kid were
trying to get a sign of you at the compound. Then you showed
up. You and your friends."

Like he can't bring himself to say it. *Those birds*.

"Thanks," she says. "For coming."

"I'll always be there if you really need it."

"No," she says. "You won't. And you shouldn't. You're with
Samantha, right?" He nods. "Stay with her. Get married. Have a
litter of puppies. Go fuck off to somewhere tropical for a while
and be happy."

"She's, ahh. Here."

"Here, here? Like, what, under the table?"

"In town. Tucson. I brought her."

"How much does she know?"

"Some of it. Not all of it. Not the . . ." He clears his throat.
"Weird bits."

"Oh. Well. Yay."

"Maybe you can meet her."

"Sure, sure. No way that can go horribly wrong."

"Well, if you don't want to—"

"Yeah, no, yeah. I, yeah. Of course. I do. It's fine. Bring her
by and she can witness me in all my dilapidated, brain-injured
glory. I look like something the cat threw up, so she can be well-
assured I am not a threat to your relationship."

"Great."

"Super."

"Really great."

Nod and smile, nod and smile.

SIXTY

SNAFU

Night comes and she can't sleep, so she watches TV. The news is still all about the courthouse bombing. Miriam knows she shouldn't watch, but you pass a crash, you rubberneck whether you mean to or not. Her whole life is an act of rubbernecking, and here she knows she's at fault, so she keeps the channel tuned.

They've upped the injured count but knocked down the fatalities. Eighty-nine dead. Three hundred injured, many seriously, some critically. Some are even in this hospital, as it turns out.

They show the wreckage again and again. Disaster porn. Talking heads talk about it. They squeak markers over it like it's a football play—here's where they think the bombs were, here's where the shooters entered.

Then: they put a pair of faces on screen.

Hugo and Jorge. The old security guards, like the two shriveled puppets from the Muppet Show balcony.

They're alive.

That's something, at least.

Then: a knock at her door.

She turns the TV to mute.

Another familiar face enters. Agent Tommy Grosky.

"Another fine predicament," he says, a soft smile connecting his big cheeks. "Hi, Miriam."

"Agent."

He pulls out flowers from behind his back. "A gift."

"You pull those out of your ass?"

He shrugs as if to say *Hey, maybe*. He sets them down—they're already in a small vase—and sits. "How you holding up?"

"I'm not dead. My brain is only a half-deflated kickball. I failed to save the people I wanted to save. Any hope I had of getting rid of this *thing that I have* is gone, blown up with the Pima County courthouse." She turns the TV off. "So: situation normal, all fucked up."

Grosky looks over his shoulder at the now-dark TV. "You watching the news, huh."

"Yep. Good times. I notice nobody is pointing the finger at the Coming Storm yet. You even know about them?"

"We do. But what happened there isn't something we can really explain yet. When we figure out a story, we'll go public."

"We?"

"The Agency. We're calling it Federal jurisdiction. Cops don't mind because this isn't a football they wanted to catch."

"Oh. Good luck."

"You mind if I ask you what happened?"

"This in an official capacity?"

"Somewhat. I'm doing a favor for friends out here. And a favor to you, too. They won't understand you. But I think I'm starting to."

She sighs. "Now?"

"Please."

"Ask away, big guy."

He does. Little notepad in which he writes not much at all. He asks her what happened and she lies. Says mostly she doesn't remember. Says she got kidnapped, doesn't know why, then: freaky shit happened. Storm came, birds came, she barely escaped, got shot.

"You don't remember much of it at all?" he asks, dubious.

"Brain injury. Check the charts. My thinker done got boo-booed."

"So, you don't know anything about the birds."

She shrugs. "Nature's weird, hoss. Storms make animals do goofy shit."

"You were trying to stop the courthouse bombing."

Another shrug.

He says, "And you didn't manage it."

Another shrug. This one born of ill-contained anger, like she's a stoppered bottle about to pop. "Who knows."

"You think you accomplished nothing," he says.

"It feels like that."

"They were gonna do more, you know."

"What?"

"Bombings. Pima County was just the first. Miriam, they found a basement underneath Ethan and Karen Key's 'house.' It was loaded for bear with bomb-making material, ammunition, Semtex, guns, knives. And *plans*. They were going to hit more courthouses. More government buildings. Kill politicians." That means Mary helped them plan not just for this but beyond. It wasn't just a suicide. It was a message: People are poison, people are weak, and in one big fire sale, everyone has to go. Grosky goes on: "Hell, going by some of their emails we found, I think they might've gone after the president one day. Probably would've never gotten close. But you never know. They were trying to start something. Something big. Already other groups in-state have started acting up—but there hasn't been a tipping point. No other attacks. Those other whack-jobs will back the fuck down now. But if the Coming Storm managed more attacks, all bets are off. Can't put those snakes back in a can."

"I . . . I don't—"

"You did do some good here. Just not the good you thought."

"Oh." She swallows. "Cool."

"Yeah. Cool. Anyway." He stands up with a groan. "Enjoy the flowers. Hope you're not allergic? As always, if ever you wanna work together—"

"You really need my help, just call," she says.

His eyes go wide. Ooh-la-la.

"I don't know your number."

"I don't either. But I'm sure we'll figure it out."

SIXTY-ONE

ALL THAT'S LEFT IS THE WATER

Morning comes. Time to go home. Not that home is a place for her, but they're kicking her ass out of the hospital. She's packing up what little she has—someone had to actually gift her a pair of shoes (which the nurse whispered conspiratorially, *These came from a dead woman, shhhh*) because they picked her up barefoot. She's wearing a University of Arizona T-shirt and jeans too clean and too nice to be her own. These, too, gifts from the hospital.

As she's about to head out, the phone rings.

She answers it.

She listens.

She says, "Oh. Okay. Thanks."

Blink, blink. The water in. The water out. Thunder. Lightning. She blinks back tears as she takes the receiver and eases it back into its cradle.

Like a zombie, she stalks the halls and, by some miracle, finds her way out.

SIXTY-TWO

OF COURSE

They wheel her ass out. Hospital policy, they tell her. She tells them they can stick the entire wheelchair up their no-no holes, but they *insist*, or they won't discharge her. They say it's for insurance, and she explains she doesn't *have* insurance, but blah blah blah, she ends up in the chair.

She thinks then about Karen. Shot in the head but still not dead. What about now? What happened to *her*? And Ofelia? Should've asked Grosky. Fuck.

Sliding doors. Outside. The god-awful Arizona sun is in full effect, staring its horrible, punishing eye right at her through the trees and across the parking lot. She gets up out of the chair. Wincing. Pain in her leg. Pain in her chest. Her head still feels like it's stuffed with tar-soaked cotton.

Limps a few steps forward and then—what?

As if on cue:

A van pulls up.

A motherfucking no-longer-a-wizard van.

The motherfucking no-longer-a-wizard van.

Miriam whistles as Gabby gets out. Isaiah, too, hops down out of the back—this time, he's wearing a Wonder Woman shirt. Gabby takes his hand and idly, quietly, Miriam thinks: *If you knew what that kid could do, you might not touch him.* No wonder Ethan wanted the boy. A single touch and he could pop you from the inside like a microwaved sausage.

"Hey-o," Miriam says, trying to sound chipper. Failing.

Gabby comes up. Gives her a kiss on the cheek. "I got you a present." She thumbs toward the no-longer-a-wizard van.

"You shouldn't have. Also, you know it's stolen, right?"

"I do. And it's also not really my present. It's a gift from an FBI agent. He said he wanted to do something nice for you. So, he pulled this out of impound and fudged some paperwork."

Grosky. What a sweetheart.

"Hey, kid," Miriam says to Isaiah.

"Hey, lady," Isaiah says back.

Gabby: "The van's all fueled up."

"Cool. Let's rock. We can go . . . anywhere. Like, say, maybe . . . Florida."

"We can't," Gabby says.

"Huh?"

"I'm not . . ." She stiffens, wincing, hands into little fists. This is hard for her, and that means Miriam knows what's coming. Still: she lets her get to it on her own time. In part, a kindness. In another way, a cruelty. "I can't follow you anymore. I'm going to try to adopt Isaiah. I've already convinced my sister and her husband to act as foster parents to him and—I know. *I know.* I see that look. I feel like shit about this. But you lead a life that I don't understand, and he's a special kid and . . . we've all been through a lot."

"No doubt." Anger shoots through her. Irrational and hot, like a safety pin cooked over a lighter flame. *I'm the one who's been through the most. I deserve you. I deserve a chance. I deserve to send you away, not the reverse.* All stupid, horrible thoughts that she has to stuff in a bag and toss in a river. "I get it."

And she does. It's not a lie.

"You take the van. Florida or wherever. We've got a return ticket for Greyhound."

"Go. It's cool. Just . . . go."

Gabby leans in for a kiss. Miriam gives her the cheek.

Miriam goes to Isaiah. Kneels down. "You heard the lady. You're a special kid." *A kid who can kill people just by touching them.*

"Yeah, I guess."

"Hey. Listen. What you can do? It isn't who you are."

He blinks. Considers it. "Are you sure?"

"I am sure."

"Then that's true for you, too, huh?" he asks.

She shrugs. Because she doesn't believe it. *Do as I say, not as I do.*

A quick kiss on his forehead. A swat on his ass. "Thanks for saving my bacon," she says. "Now go on. Scoot. Shoo." *Fuck off, you're free to go.* Miriam asks Gabby, "You need a ride to the bus station?"

"It's walkable, actually."

"Well." Seconds pass. Stretched to minutes. Stretched to hours, to days, to weeks, to an infinity times an infinity. "See you."

She hops in the wizard van and drives to Florida.

SIXTY-THREE

AND THEN TO PENNSYLVANIA

Your mother passed away in the night.

That, the phone call she received. From one hospital to another. It happened days before. Took them a while to track her down. But they did. And now she's here. At a funeral she planned, at a funeral home near her old house in Pennsylvania, not far from the Susquehanna River. A wet spring day. Cool and spry. Spritzing rain. *Better than having the funeral in Florida,* she thought. Because funerals, she read once, shouldn't happen on a sunny day.

It's the classic scene. Black umbrellas. A few punctuations of red. They go to lower the casket into the ground. Miriam sees a bird nearby: a fat-bellied crow hanging out on a low-hanging branch of an evergreen.

For a time, she joins with the bird. They fly. Rain beading on black feathers. Circling higher and higher. A few more crows nearby, cawing and calling. And then she's back and it's over. All the funeral attendees have gone and she's left alone, standing there, staring at the hole underneath a small tent.

Someone fires up a nearby backhoe. To move dirt in.

Odd, maybe, that she's been to alarmingly few funerals. Lots of death, but not much of what comes after. Not much of the bodies in the ground.

She says good-bye to her mother.

Then she goes to a nearby bar and gets drunk, really drunk, and cries.

SIXTY-FOUR

SHOEBOX ESTATE

Her mother's house in Florida is just as it was left. Miriam thinks to rent it out, and maybe later to sell it, but somehow she ends up staying there for one night, then one week, and then a month. Her Uncle Jack—who was at the funeral, and who ended up at the bar later that night—tried to act all sad, but then she told him that the house he was squatting in, Mom's old house, was hers now. He called bullshit, said, "She sold that to me for a dollar." And Miriam explained that's not what the lawyers told her. They don't have a record of it even if it was true. She said in slurred words, "You wanna lawyer up, you slack-jawed cock-warbler, you go right the fuck ahead." He said, "Nice job, *killer,*" because he knows that bothers her, and it took every ounce of willpower she could muster not to punch him in the throat. She hasn't heard from him since.

Comes a time when someone knocks at the door, and Miriam thinks it's one of the neighbors—they're old here, and nice, irritatingly nice, always bringing by casseroles and soups and salads. But the man at the door says he's a lawyer.

Oh, shit.

She starts to say, "My Uncle Jack is a fucking half-wit—you can't trust a word that comes dribbling out of his spit-cup—"

But the lawyer explains that he's a lawyer for a woman named Mary Stitch.

So, Miriam invites him in.

The lawyer is a man too loose in his suit. Like he's hot. And he should be, because Florida is basically Satan's dick. The lawyer looks sweaty and ill, and he dabs at his slick brow with a once-white, now-yellow kerchief.

He explains that Mary Stitch changed her will recently, and was confirmed dead in the Pima County bombing.

Miriam was in the will.

"Whuh," she says. Because that sounds like nonsense.

He says it isn't nonsense, and she left to Miriam a shoe-box. And in that shoebox, Miriam finds a bottle of mescal, two glasses, and a small, rolled-up piece of paper. When the lawyer leaves, Miriam undoes the rubber band around the paper and unrolls it. It's a note.

> *You're a better woman than me. If you're still alive,*
> *and I bet you are, here's a favor: you want to get rid*
> *of your curse, I know how it happens. You have to*
> *reverse what happened. Undo what was done. The*
> *thing that made you who you are. You want to get rid*
> *of it? Then you, dear Miriam, have to get pregnant.*
>
> *Good luck, honey.*
> *—Mary*

Miriam holds that for a while.

Then she drinks a lot of mescal and burns the note with a lighter. She finds something else in there too, underneath the glasses.

A playing card. With a spider on it.

No idea what that means. But she burns that, too. Just in case.

SIXTY-FIVE

RINGY-DINGY

The phone call that comes later, months later, goes like this:

Him: You skipped on out me.

Her: No duh.

Him: You didn't want to meet Samantha?

Her: No duh, part two, revenge of the duh.

Him: Well, we're coming to town.

Her: Pssh. You don't even know what town I'm in. I could be in Nome, Alaska. Or Eat Butt, Montana. Maybe I'm on the moon.

Him: You're not far from Fort Lauderdale.

Her: Wait, are you the psychic now?

Him: Gabby told me where you were. Gave me this number. (Gabby. Of course those two are talking. Well, shit.)

Her: So, you're saying I have to meet Samantha.

Him: I did save your life.

Her: And I saved yours some time ago.

Him: I saved yours twice.

You maybe saved it more than that, she thinks, and she maybe saved his more, too, but at this point, who's counting?

She tells him yeah, yes, fine.

She'll meet Samantha.

SIXTY-SIX

EVEN AWFUL THINGS ARE MADE BETTER BY BREAKFAST

There's this breakfast joint in Fort Lauderdale, near the Stranahan House by the river. Dinky joint called the El Presidente. She waits outside. Wants to smoke less because of any nic-fit and more because she's bored and this would occupy her. Now, as it stands, her hands feel empty, restless, like birds in cages.

Eventually, Louis pulls up—a pickup truck, new, shiny red. A woman gets out. She's pretty. Miriam's seen the photos. Pretty, but not so pretty she's a wowie-kazowie kind of looker. Maybe just pretty enough to be boring.

Samantha marches right up to her. Nervous, obviously. Miriam's hair now is the reverse of what it was months ago—it's now almost all pink with just a few bands dyed black, and she's in a torn black shirt and fucked-up jeans, so she knows she's quite the sight. But Samantha takes it right on the chin and thrusts out her hand.

Which means she probably doesn't know what Miriam does or who Miriam is. Louis, for his part, sees what's happening and tries not to look nervous, but of course he looks nervous and, oh, piss on it. Miriam likes that he's freaked out. Fine, then. Let's get it over with.

Miriam reaches out and—

SIXTY-SEVEN

NICE JOB, KILLER

Nine months. Samantha's bridal veil floats around her. Bubbles escape from their trap behind her lips as the hands around her neck choke her so hard, her mouth can't help but open. The hands throttle her. She tries to get out. Hands out of the bathtub water, sliding along the porcelain edge, trying to pull herself up and out, but no grip, can't manage, back into the drink—

Choking. Drowning. *Glub, glub, glub.*

Another try. Hands up. Both of them together. Concerted effort. They find the arm of her killer. Use that like a kid climbing a rope in gym glass.

Pull. Pull! She yanks hard—

Up, out. Long gasp. Water out of her eyes. Hair slick across them.

The hands slam her against the wall.

Louis leers at her. Teeth bared.

He dunks her back under the water, and this time, her hands find no purchase. Water rushes in as she gasps. Fills her lungs. Death settles in.

SIXTY-EIGHT

OH, SHIT

—shakes Samantha's hand.

Samantha has a good grip. She pumps Miriam's arm, eager, too eager.

"Nice to meet you," Samantha says. Smile. Big smile. Forced smile.

"Nice to meet you, too," Miriam says, forcing her own smile right back.

A grim rictus reaper smile.

"Shall we?" Louis asks.

ACKNOWLEDGMENTS

None other deserves an acknowledgment here as much as my agent, Stacia Decker—not only did she help bring Miriam to the bookshelf when nobody else wanted to, she also helped bring her back to the bookshelf when we weren't sure that was even possible. And to that, thanks too to Joe Monti, for being there and ready to take her on, even when Miriam was at her spittiest, cussiest worst.

Thanks to Michelle, my wife, who is my own brand of Miriam, and who is the first and ideal reader for these books. (I will tell you a brief story here: we came back from our beach vacation with a series of seashells, which we put in our bathroom sink. My wife went into that bathroom and emerged after discovering that the seashells had left behind a distinct, dead-ocean scent. Her comment: "It smells like Aquaman's taint in here.")

Thanks to Kevin Hearne, who said very nice things about these books before I ever knew him, and who continues to be so nice a human being that one must suspect he has a variety of bodies hidden in his basement to compensate. Which is okay. I won't judge him on this.

Thanks to David Knoller and John Shiban for (almost) getting Miriam on TV.

Finally, thanks to the readers—really, without the fans and readers of these books, I don't get to do what I do, and this book wouldn't be here.